A SILENT LIFE

A SILENT LIFE

RYHAAN SHAH

PEEPAL TREE

First published in Great Britain in 2005
Peepal Tree Press Ltd
17 King's Avenue
Leeds LS6 1QS
England

ISBN 1 84523 002 7

 Peepal Tree gratefully acknowledges Arts Council support

This world's hope is a blade of fury
and we who are sweepers of an ancient sky
discoverers of new planets, sudden stars
we are the world's hope.
And so therefore I rise again I rise again

Martin Carter 'The Knife of Dawn'

Life is a future and well-travelled track.
Nothing dismisses us. Nothing leaves.

Jorge Luis Borges, 'For a Version of *I Ching*'

CHAPTER ONE

I laughed a lot then, snug in my grandmother's lap. That was when I caught dreams that ran free above the treetops and told Nani how I would discover whole new worlds, dance barefoot across the sky, a huge canvas that needed me to make my mark on it to save it from emptiness.

"Where does it end?" I asked her.

"In God."

"And where does He end?"

"Where dreams end."

She offered this with finality like the ameens in her prayers and hummed something keening in Arabic. She did this a lot, hum Muslim prayers. Even at ten, I sensed that her eyelids closed over deep wells of sadness that went clear to the centre of the universe. Nani was clinging to the edges of those wells and I sensed that if she ever let go she would fall and fall. The humming kept her safe, I believed, anchored her to this side of the world. It was a thin edge of sound, a rustle that barely stirred the air but it marked her presence among us. If the humming ever stopped, Nani would disappear. I was so certain of this I'd let her hum a while before I plucked another dream from the sky and shared its secret with her. She would rest her head against mine and our twinned faces would glow in the brilliance of another dream unfolded. This made her my best friend throughout childhood and I heaped my dreams high on her lap, knowing that they would be safe from harm. She never questioned their possibility no matter how fantastic they were, though when I asked her once if dreams always came true, she answered, "If you don't break them."

"How could I break them?"

"By holding them too tight."

I wanted to ask what she meant, but she started to hum a prayer so I let it go. But I knew that I was right about Nani's sadness. To make up for it, I scooped brilliant fancies out of the air and shared them with her. She heard how I would toe-tap my way across the sky, float serenely as a cloud, and wear sunshine like diamonds on my skin. I teased up wonders that made Nani laugh, but her laughter always stopped short of her eyes. Her mouth would curve its smile, her dimpled cheeks would lift, but her eyes never joined in the laughter. They always looked walled up, as if they never looked outside of herself. And what she saw inside made her eyes dead.

All day she would sit in her rocking chair with her hands prayer-folded and keep company with silence. I and silence were her only companions. When my younger brother and sister were very small they would run screaming if she tried to hug them. They would hang on to Ma's skirts until she calmed their fears. Now, a little older, they stepped around Nani as they would a piece of awkwardly placed furniture. They made up stories about her, filling her silence with tales of jumbies that crept about on dark nights and stole the tongues of those who were thereafter banished to a soundless place. For them, Nani was a curiosity around whom they spun fantastic tales that made them heroes among their friends. They constructed them in whispery breaths in empty rooms and whenever I picked up the echoes of another story, I would follow the trail of sound and shush their mouths. They would simply laugh and scamper off to find another spot to hide and spin their stories. Ma paid them no mind, and paid me no mind when I complained. She shrugged. They were just children stretching out their heads. She was grateful that I spent time with Nani.

"Her quiet is full of noise for me," she said. "I don't want to hear that confusion in my ears again." She saw my question coming and cut it down sharp. "She alone holds the roar in her head; her tongue has long now done with talking. It's clapped down hard on her words."

"What words, Ma?"

"I was too small to understand."

"Did she tell stories?"

"Oh, she told stories alright."

"What kind of stories?"

"Big-people stories full of words from foreign places."

"Did you like them?"

"I told you I was too small to understand. But I know that even Pa didn't understand them."

"How come? He was big."

"Yes, but they killed him."

"How?"

She had said too much and hauled back her words and shut up her face against any more questions. "Enough questions, Aleyah. Come, help me pick this rice." She shoved a bowl of brown rice into my hands to hush up my mouth. I hushed up all right: stories heavy enough to kill a man would crush a child easily. After that I listened to Nani carefully, but heard no words drop stone-heavy from her lips. Those must be the ones clapped down tight under her tongue. If they escaped they would shape stories again and someone else would get crushed. That was why Nani hummed: it was to guard her tongue from talking.

But her words were remembered in the small country town in Guyana where we lived, and it was not long after that I first heard of *the hanging*. These were heavy words. I knew it immediately because they were said in voices so weighted down by seriousness that they barely rose above a whisper. They came from the family women who had come to help cook sweetmeats for the Eid festivities. After going upstairs to cast long eyes over Nani, who was sitting and prayer-humming as usual, they bustled back to the kitchen and talked to each other from between cupped hands, their fingers closing around the words poured into each other's ears as if to prevent the wind from taking them and scattering them about the countryside.

"You see how her eyes turn in to look at herself?"

"Prayers can't help much with what she must see there."

"She's finding out that a lil piece of rope can stretch all the way to Hell."

"And that there is a hanging at both ends."

9

"True."

"She was swinging with him that day."

"She's just waiting for the burial, now."

"The body is already still."

"Home for a dead spirit."

"Well, Allah gives peace."

"Alhamdulillah."

"But Pa Nazeer took a rope and shaped it like the world and put it round his neck. He made his own peace."

"Ameen."

Pa Nazeer. I had not heard him called that name before. I thought it handsome. It was the kind of name that would have mantled its owner with dignity, given him proud shoulders and straight-backed confidence. He would have been vain with a name like that. Then I saw him there with a slim waist and neat moustache that he trimmed fastidiously, one hair at a time. He was humming a song as he used a pair of dainty clippers at the washstand. He was washed in sunlight, looking almost ghostly.

"Baby, get my trousers for me, the pin-striped ones. I tell you, girl, today is the day. Yes, sir, today I'm bringing home that new car." He did little jigs between the snip-snip of the clippers. "Yes, girl, I told you that one day Nazeer Mohammed Raheem will make them sit up and take notice and that day has come. They laugh at how I just talk talk all the time and could never make something of anything, but this deal I sign up today will mean, first, the Ford motorcar. Girl, you should see how it shines, how it stretches itself out like a long, silver cat. And wait 'til you hear how it purrs! And now that things are rolling, the house will come next, two storeys, and we will throw a big verandah in the front and have big steps leading up to the front door. The neighbours' mouths will hang open and catch flies when they see that! Baby, I tell you, it's going to happen, just believe in me, girl, believe in me."

A woman entered the room and he took her arms and spun her round and round. The air was silent but their ears heard music. I could tell by their fluid movements that they had heard this music many times before; they had mastered this dance of silence. The morning sun streamed through the open windows and cast spotlights on the floor, and Baby followed Nazeer's steps

10

from light to dark, dark to light, over and over, her steps going wherever he led, at whatever pace he chose. He held her close then spun her round again and her dress flowed out in a swirl of colour. They were pretty to watch as they flitted in and out of the morning light. He was a prince and she his newfound princess.

It was only her smile that gave her away as my grandmother. Nothing else was familiar, not the diamond-lit eyes, the bright, black hair that flowed to her waist, nor the slim wrists ringed with gold bangles. Now, age had smudged the fine lines and erased much of the brightness. But her dimpled smile had stayed like a keepsake of a sweeter time. She had been a beauty, my grandmother, and had found her handsome prince. I sighed, dreamt open-eyed of palaces and beaded gowns and rainbow-coloured gems that trapped light and glittered in the belly of the earth. I imagined myself grown beautiful, too, and living such a dream.

Then the silent music that filled the air slowed and Nazeer and Baby were barely moving. The sun withdrew, and the room grew smaller, forcing the dancers to make smaller and smaller steps. I held my breath. I felt that any movement would explode the loud silence. I held my breath for an eternity and when I exhaled, the room exploded with light, and the walls drew back to their farthest corners.

Baby was weeping. "I'm so tired, so tired of this. You create emptiness. Over and over you bring me a heap full of nothing. My arms ache from holding it up, from trying to make a life for us from all this nothing. I can't live with this emptiness."

Nazeer stood silent. The moustache that he had clipped so carefully was out of place, a vanity that did not sit well with tears. Baby stood before him, piling stone upon accusing stone. With each stone, Nazeer's shoulders slumped and his backbone grew shorter and shorter until he was not there any more.

They were gone, pulled through the wide-open windows of my room, and when I ran and peered outside there was only the hot sunlight glittering everywhere. I wanted to see the prince and princess dance again, but there was only the trees swaying in a slight wind. I sighed and turned back to my empty room but I knew that I would see them again because they were a part of me and could never leave.

11

Later that day, I edged up to the words "the hanging" with my mother in the kitchen. She clapped a big thunder of pot lids to scare away the words.

"You stop listening to what kitchen corners tell you, you hear? A lil piece of rope is not going to stretch down through all these years to tangle up your life. I'll make sure of that, so you leave it alone. The past is dead and buried and done with."

I wanted to tell her that this was not true, that the past was always there, that I'd seen the old world whole and living right in front of me. I thought everyone's eyes could do this, that it stood to reason that nothing that lived could ever be laid aside and forgotten. To my child's mind this made perfect sense, that we carried around inside us the voices, the stories, all the history that lay behind us and that without these we would be ghosts without form or substance, nothing but transparent shapes inhabiting the moonlight.

"Don't you see, Ma, don't you see?" I wanted to insist, but my mother's words had been so final, like a door slammed shut, that all I did was ask if someone who lived in the past was dead.

"Yes," she replied, thinking to end my questions.

"Like Nani?"

Her answer was slow in coming. It was dragged up from a deep place. Ma pitched her eyes way off to the horizon as if to try and disown the words that her tongue shaped.

"Your Nani's spirit flew away one day but her body goes on breathing. That happens when the spirit gets frightened; it breaks away because its eyes look on a deep, dark hell."

"What did her spirit see to make it run so?" My question was barely a breath in the air but my mother heard.

She turned her eyes away from the horizon and looked at me and said, "The unforgivable."

She went back to her pots. She was done with talking for now so I crept upstairs to look at Nani. She sat as she always did with the hum of a prayer buzzing around her. I had not noticed before that she was a skeleton really, bones draped with wrinkled skin, eyes sunk deep into dark sockets. But I was not afraid to rest my head on her lap, as I had always done, then wait to feel her hands stroke my hair ever so gently, a whisper of a touch. Still and silent,

I could feel the faint rise and fall of her belly as she breathed in and out, in and out, slowly, as if willing the next breath to stay undrawn. But the breath would come. A thousand questions pressed up against my tongue, but I knew that Nani would not answer them because that would mean dragging out the words she guarded so carefully, those heavy words. And she was so slight and frail that I was afraid that the effort would break her.

Nani's sister, though, might give some answers, if I listened closely to her rambling talk. Great Aunt Khadijah talked about everything, and at length, whenever she visited. She lived a fat, contented life among her eleven children, travelling from one household to the next now that her rice-farmer husband had died and left her everything: fields, tractors, combines, the rice mill and their six-bedroom home. Four sons and an unmarried daughter worked the fields, each hoping to gain the fattest share in her will. Fights would erupt every so often among her children and then she would come and visit us, bustling in with her busy mouth that ran with stories so joined up tail to head and head to tail that it made your breath race just listening to her.

"Her mouth has no cover," my mother would say under her breath, as her aunt would get up from the kitchen table to take her talk away to her baby sister.

"My husband, Aziz Sankar, Allah rest his soul, left the property to me, Baby, and now they're all scrambling at each other's throats to get everything for themselves. It's better if we were poor like Ma and Daddy. How they worked, eh? Weeding in the backdam, cutting cane, loading punts, getting up long before the sun showed its face, saving for their future in the two cents they tied up in the corner of their handkerchief every week. That was for a house so that we could move out of that trench-top logie. You remember that logie, that barrack house they built for slaves, Baby, and how it hung its backside – excuse my language, lil sister – over the trench water? No, you were the baby. By the time you were born we had a lil mud hut that Ma daubed every day with fresh mud and cow dung to make it shine like marble. We all used to look at it with her eyes and see a grand palace."

Great Aunt Khadijah would hold her sister's hand and sigh. "What to do, Baby, what to do?" Her stories varied little on these visits. She would go into great detail about all kinds of legal matters, property values and transfers and who would get what when she died. All this she discussed regularly with her city lawyer, Ramdass Gossai. She called him easily by his first name, telling her sister how Ramdass this and Ramdass that, puffing herself up with the importance of her association with the great man whose name appeared regularly in the newspaper. To have him represent you in court: that alone made your case celebrated.

My great aunt brought her worries to wash around her baby sister because of her silence. Here she would get neither advice nor criticism so she poured her stories over Baby's head.

"I should be like Shamroon and not have any children, then I wouldn't have all these worries on my head," she said during one visit, but as soon as she said this, her hands flew quick as a bird to stop-up her mouth. "No, no, not that."

Shamroon was their sister-in-law. Every street corner knew her story. Twenty years of retelling had made it stale and ordinary so she was allowed to go about her business without trails of whispery gossip following her about. Their brother, Rayman, said he had married a mule and had flung himself out of the house after just two years of marriage. He had taken to the rum bottle and another woman whom he called a barren-belly whore before leaving her too. Shamroon had taken him back and watched as he poisoned himself with rum. Her kitchen garden provided just enough money for cheap white rum for him, and food for herself. Their small wooden house shook with kicks and curses on the days when she did not have enough for his rum

The neighbours would hear Rayman's voice fly above the rafters and out through the zinc roof. Its fury bruised the air. "You're a real good-for-nothing who can't even make a few cents to give your husband. You bring your mule belly here and expect me to mind you? Why? There's nothing here to make you and me one. You hear any baby hollering for its daddy? No. So, what if I make you holler instead? You think that is not fair?"

That's how it would start. The curses would follow. It always ended with Shamroon being thrown out of the door that was slammed in her face. "You go wash out your belly in the dust. That's all it bears, dust and ashes like the dead."

At first, the neighbouring women would rush over, pick her up and urge my great aunt to leave her husband.

"It's not your fault, you know."

"He couldn't make a baby with the other woman either. Something is wrong with him, not you."

"Take him to a doctor."

"He won't go," Shamroon said.

"Pride."

"Foolishness."

"Then save yourself, daughter."

"But where would I go? What would I do?"

"Go back home, to your parents."

"No, no, I'm married now. My home is with my husband."

"But, child, what kind of home is that?"

"It shakes with devil curses."

"It beats you black and blue."

"It's all I have. I have my duty," my great aunt said. The circle of women parted to let her go but their eyes followed her. A few looked back to the spot where she had been thrown and knew the horror of it. They looked up and caught themselves in each other's eyes and hurried away to homes built of silent walls. These women were the most cruel with their taunts in the early days of Rayman's and Shamroon's commotion, as if throwing it all at Shamroon relieved them of a burden.

"He beat you today, girl?"

"She likes it."

"And she with no children to mind!"

"She could just get up and go, easy-easy."

"She likes it."

"They say if he beats you, he loves you, eh Shamroon?"

"It's her duty."

"It's her fate."

"To be beaten."

"Cursed."

"And kicked like a dog out the door."

"That woman is too stubborn," Great Aunt Khadijah said to her sister. "Rayman is right that she's like a mule, she's mule-headed. I told her so many times to leave him and come and stay with me, but she won't give up. 'He's my husband,' she says, turning up her nose at my offer, like she alone in the whole world got a husband.

"I tell her it's not charity I'm offering, that she will work and earn her keep, but no, she has her duty, she says. Duty, my foot! There's no duty in being abused so. But Shamroon chose her bed and she lies in it without complaining, I give her that. She takes care of Rayman, now that his liver's sick and dying, as if he's the most wonderful husband on God's earth.

"You think she just loves him, loves our brother with the kind of heart that only sees what it wishes? It must be a nice blindness. What if we all did that, eh Baby, just make everybody over to fit our eye? It would make our hearts lie down easy, eh?"

Great Aunt Khadijah stopped abruptly and her hand flew up again to stop-up her words, but it was too late. In that moment, her sister's quiet ended. My grandmother's rocking chair started to pitch back and forth with a hard violence. It was as if the floor had storm waves under it. Nani was humming loudly and staring at her sister.

My mother rushed in and shook her aunt by the shoulders. "You and your busy mouth! You've gone and upset her."

"But what did I say?" Great Aunt Khadijah asked. "I only asked her what if we can make people over… Ohmegod, ohmegod, ohmegod."

My mother circled Nani in her arms and held onto her as if she were holding a wild horse at the end of a rope, waiting for it to tire. Her baby-shushing sounds were a soft refrain to the fury of my grandmother's rocking and humming. Great Aunt Khadijah watched, holding her head in her hands, wailing "Ohmegod-ohmegodohmegod," over and over. "Why I had to go and say something like that?"

A confusion of sound rose to the rafters that afternoon; it crashed about among the beams and cobwebbed corners before breaking into splinters and floating out to fall onto the town's ears. Neighbours locked their doors and windows against the shrieks. They brought their children in and took out beads and talismans and prayed as against a plague. That day, it was easy to imagine that the small bit of heaven above our town was filled

16

with the assembled gods of all the world, hearkening to their believers' prayers.

From a dark doorway I kept watch and saw the scene before us quiver and shake with earth-rumbling fury. The rocker was a live thing that crashed back and forth. But for my mother's arms holding Nani tight, it would have keeled over and taken them both down.

Then I saw the wild rocking become gentler, as if softened by the slanting afternoon light and a whispery breeze. There on a rug, where the rocker had stood, was a little cradle that Baby was rocking gently. She was smiling. She picked up the baby and called to her softly. "Shabhan. Shabhan. My first-born."

Nazeer came up behind her and took them both in his arms. "She has your eyes."

"Your smile."

"Your lips."

"She'll be a dancer like you."

"A beauty like you."

Nazeer went out. Baby stayed and rocked the cradle. The room was quiet. Nothing stirred, not even the curtains at the open window. The light froze, the colours faded and the scene withdrew from my eyes, greying like a photograph on a sun-kissed wall.

"Shabhan, Shabhan," I heard again, but it was my father's voice. "Let go now. Let me take her." His voice was sharp and urgent. He wrested my mother's arms from around Nani and carried my grandmother, now exhausted and quiet, into her bedroom. I heard the hard breathing of my brother and sister beside me. I did not know how long they had been there and how much they had seen. Fright made them round-eyed. I took them downstairs to the kitchen where Great Aunt Shamroon had arrived and was trying to console her sister-in-law.

"Ohmegodohmegodohmegod," Great Aunt Khadijah was still saying.

"When I heard the screaming come flying through my window I said a quick prayer and ran over here," Great Aunt Shamroon said.

"I clean forgot myself to go and say a thing like that."

"What you said to her, sis?"

When she told her, Great Aunt Shamroon put a hand to her mouth. "But how you could go and say a thing like that? You know how she was shaping him over to fit her eye."

"I wasn't thinking, Sham. The words came out of my mouth just so."

"Well, it's done now. The past is with us again and the rememberings will fly about her head for a while."

My great aunts kept silence in the kitchen and we children sat at the edge of their wide skirts and kept our tongues quiet and our ears open. Who had she shaped to fit her eye? The question hung before me and I waited to see if my great aunts would pick it up and answer, since with the past now raised up among us, it would want to tell its stories. The kitchen stayed quiet for a long while until Great Aunt Khadijah picked up a tiny bit of story, a small scrap no bigger than a thread, but she pulled at it and, in doing so, began to unravel a tale.

"A firecracker, she was a firecracker," she said.

"A fireball," Great Aunt Shamroon added.

"A pepper mouth."

"A hot sauce."

"You remember, Sham, when she decided that Nazeer was going to run for mayor? Him! This lil, no-education boy with nothing but a dancing waist and a head full of curls to his credit? She was going to make him mayor of the town!"

"How she pushed him! Filled him up with her ideas of what, what was it, Sister Khadijah?"

"Oh, I don't remember now, but something about the people, no, no, the masses, and how they must cooperate and make a better life for the poor. Oh, the ideas she had, that one! It was socialism this and socialism that, as if anybody round here could understand any of that, or cared! She would pull up herself so high, you remember, Sham, and mouth off these important-sounding words."

"And all Nazeer ever wanted to do was dance, poor boy."

"But she was a fire that burned bright even when she was a little girl. I tell you, Sham, it was that very spark that caught Nazeer's eye. I was there that day at the fair. Baby was no more than sixteen

18

and she was like a jewel; she had Ma's fine bones and Pa's heavy black hair. Nazeer was there, on stage, dancing, his feet twinkling like diamonds to the music and setting all the little bells around his ankles jingling. I can still hear that silver sound rising up to the sky that night. It was a moonlit night. The Farmers' Fair was always held on a full-moon night."

I heard the silver sound, the jingling bells. It curled itself into my ear, swirled around inside my head and put Nazeer, my grandfather, on a stage. His chest was bare and he wore billowing pyjamas held by sequined braids at his waist and ankles. His feet were bare and painted with bright reds and ochres. He wore rings in his ears and on his fingers. He looked like a movie star and he used all the sinuous movements of neck and eyes and fingers that were part of the poetry of the dances we saw in Indian movies. He had an easy grace and the audience loved him. Then I saw it, just as Great Aunt Khadijah had done. As he was lifting his head from a deep bow, he froze for no more than a second. In that second he saw Baby standing in the front row, cheering and smiling at him.

I saw how he looked at her. He saw the full moon rising in her eyes, and saw himself reflected there. He saw that he was tall and straight with muscled arms that brandished jewelled swords. He saw that he could run on winged feet, swim all the seas of the world and slay mighty demons with a single blow. He saw all this in a single moment. His world, which before had been made of disparate parts, fell into place and, for the first time, made sense. When she felt his eyes fall soft on her skin, Baby blushed and knew that he was hers. I heard Great Aunt Khadijah laugh. She was standing right next to Baby and was looking from one to the other. She laughed again and the rich tones carried far, reaching from that distant time back into our kitchen.

"From that time on, there was no separating them," my great aunt was saying. "Ma and Daddy liked him. He had an easy way about him that made people take to him, and he entertained us with his dancing. He even showed Baby a few steps – though she was always more serious-minded and reading all kinds of books that she got from god knows where. Daddy said it was no use her killing herself so over those books since they wouldn't help her mind a home and family, but she just kept on reading and reading.

Only Nazeer's footsteps in the yard would make her put them away.

"We had a double wedding, you know. Baby, she was just seventeen and I was twenty-one. Rayman was not to marry you, Sham, 'til years later. What a time we had! On our wedding day we put on new dresses and new lives and our hearts were sure of a fairy-story ending. But life carries you off on its own twists and turns. One day it burns bright and the next day it's raining down ashes."

The mood of my great aunts turned solemn. The house was quiet. No one stirred upstairs. We heard no footsteps, no voices. The sun was sinking into the night and in the darkening kitchen we looked at our feet and kept our words to ourselves until Great Aunt Shamroon spoke. "But a woman to blaze so bright on a stage? She should've known her place." She said the words as if continuing a conversation that had begun somewhere else, sometime before. "She must have known that a thing like that could only bring sorrow on your head. What made her think she could push herself up so and turn the whole world around?"

Aunt Khadijah's reply came quickly, right on the heels of the question. "She couldn't help herself, you know, Sham. She did try to stay back and let Nazeer do the stage work, remember?"

"But all he could do on a stage was dance."

"Not talk."

"And such talk!"

"Talk that tangled up his tongue, it was so heavy."

"And how they laughed, how the people laughed."

"Yes, it followed him about for years."

"What else could he do but choke it off 'til it died?"

"Yes. What else?"

CHAPTER TWO

When I was a child, a mere child, a little girl with two plaits tied up with ribbons, I had such silly ideas about the world. I created sugar-spun stories of kings in crystal palaces and saw myself dance in candy-coloured gowns under chandeliers of pure starlight. How frivolous, I think, now I am fifteen. My dreams do not run wild above the treetops any more. Now, they are shaped to fit a world that blooms with the sun but which runs with mud on rainy days and has room, enormous room, for argument, illness and death. I had seen such things before, but had not believed they had anything to do with me. Even the mysteries of my grandmother's life had been little more than a story that hung about our home and came out of dark corners to haunt the memories of those who knew. It had made me quiver with a child's curiosity. Now, however, when I look into the mirror and see my breasts and hips rounding into womanhood, I am aware of the past looking with me. It is more than just a curious tale now; it is the world from where my journey began. And I have such ideas for that journey.

"People here are so poor, Nani. When I grow up, I'm going to change all that." I say this one morning, sitting at her knee, spinning out my words lazily, building bright imaginings on the flat fields of the countryside, transforming them into rich acres of land where people work happily and reap hills of golden paddy much taller than themselves. I sometimes write these imaginings into reports for my Economics class and the teacher, Mr. Moriah, jokes that my ideas are better than the prime minister's.

"I like his class best, Nani. He makes us look at our own homes and how we live and work and spend our money and so on. He makes the textbooks live with real people. I like that you can make whole, big plans, that you can set things up so that everyone can have a better life. Isn't that good, Nani? I like to think up ways to do this."

I stop and giggle and look up at my grandmother. "Mr. Moriah says he has to keep reading and studying all the time just to keep up with me and all my ideas. He likes it that I have so many questions and that I think of all kinds of ways to change things so that …" My words fall away abruptly when Nani's rocking chair comes to a sudden stop. Her humming also stops and I am afraid of the silence. My mother puts her head through a doorway and listens to the quiet and when she comes over, we watch Nani, bracing ourselves for we know not what.

"What were you talking about?" my mother whispers and when I tell her she stares at me hard and throws up her hands.

But my grandmother is smiling. The smile softens her face for a moment, but is gone as quickly as it came. She goes back to her rocking and humming and when her face shuts itself up once more, my mother takes me by the arm and hurries me downstairs to the kitchen where she gives me a bowl of onions to chop. She is gathering her thoughts, so for a while the kitchen carries on with its busy sounds of simmering pots and chopping knives until my mother says, "That was the trouble, you know."

"What trouble?"

"The trouble with Ma, your Nani. She wanted to change the world, well, change this little corner of it. She wanted to save everybody from illness and poorness, even death if she could."

"Isn't that good?"

"Where's the good in saving the world and losing your own soul?"

"You told me one time that her spirit fled."

"And her soul has been dying ever since."

"What happened, Ma?" My question is bold with my new, grown-up confidence. "Tell me."

"Oh, your grandmother was one for reading and talking all day and all night, or that's what it looked like. She used to write letters, and packages of books and leaflets used to come with strange stamps from foreign places. I used to rip the stamps off and keep them in a box and look at them with wonder."

My mother's words fall softly into the warm air of the kitchen. She is a little girl again looking out from behind her mother's skirts at the people who came and filled up the small kitchen that looked out on a patch of garden where her mother grew tomatoes and peppers that she sold at the town market, all spread out in shades of red on a hemp bag. That is the picture she paints. "She used to sell what she did not give away," my mother says, smiling to herself. Her father mostly busied himself with buying and selling things, anything, she says.

"'The quick turnover is the trick,' Pa used to say to me, before he would hurry away to look over another used car or a bit of scrap iron, one time even old paddy bags. That was his thing, and he was good at talking people into buying up his bargains. But it was a sometime living. If no one had anything to throw out, he had nothing to sell. He still used to dance at fairs and concerts and weddings, but that was for fun more than anything else. I remember how he used to sweep me high into the air and spin me round and round to all kinds of music, with silver bells tinkling round his ankles like fairy laughter. That's what I thought fairies sounded like, like silver bells jingling happily when my father danced."

The memory sweetens my mother's face, then abruptly her tone and look take on a serious edge. "Ma was the one that made sure I did my school work. It was books and study all the time with her. 'Shabhan, you mind your school work now. You need a good education if you're going to do any good in the world.' That's what she used to say to me every god day. Until the trouble."

She pauses, then takes a deep breath before she continues. "They used to come and stand around in our kitchen every day. They came from the sugar plantations and the rice fields: poor women with sunk-in eyes and rickety children, and men with rum bellies and swear words that Ma used to hush up quick-time. They used to bring her their troubles. They had trouble with their bosses, their wages, and the way they had to work. They worked worse than mules, they said. They were poor, all right. We weren't much better off than them, but they came because my mother fed them hope. They were hungry for it. She fed them hope from torn-up leaflets that had words like 'power' and 'ownership', and how the workers must come together and manage the land and the tools of their labour. Things like that. They were written in important-looking type on bits of coloured paper." My mother laughs. "What did they know about things like that, eh? Most of them couldn't even read. But the people used to stand up quiet-quiet and wait 'til Ma finish talking, then they would ask her to help them get one more cent for each bag of paddy that they were selling to the big rice millers." She laughs, but this time her laughter is bitter.

"Did she help them?" I ask.

"Oh, yes. She helped them arrange strikes and marches and Pa was out there at the head, marching with the leaders."

"You mean grandfather? Pa Nazeer? He led strike marches?"

My mother does not answer directly. We sit in the quickly darkening kitchen. Shadows fall on her face and make it gaunt. "It was man's work. The managers dealt with men. It was fun for him at first. He liked the crowds; he thought it was all a stage, a real-life dance to the chants of the workers. He really enjoyed himself. But then the questions would come. People expected him to know about all the things that Ma knew. When they found out he didn't, they'd watch Pa stumble and mumble and try to duck away from the questions they threw at his head, and then they stopped clapping back their laughter into their bellies." She pauses and adds, "I was just a little girl then, but I think one day the confusion tore up his head and …"

I wait for my mother to continue. By now I can barely see her in the dark. I just hear her voice and her breathing. "And then? What happened?"

"Ma took me out of school. She said it was no good for girl children to learn anything. I was ten years old and I liked school and books and my friends and all the games we played. I cried so hard, and Pa went and locked himself up in their bedroom. He didn't dance any more and one day his hair turned white all over. My father had hair so black, with waves so high they could have sunk the Titanic self, but one day he woke up with white-white hair; and his shoulders that used to stretch out so wide when he

24

danced were all shrunk down, and he looked about ready to curl up and die. In one night, my father turned into an old man. That's when everybody started calling him Pa Nazeer."

"But what happened, Ma?" This time my question is insistent.

"Something broke." That's all she says before she gets up and switches on the lights. I remember thinking something like that when I was a little girl, when I had sensed my grandmother's sadness – that something had broken, a dream, an idea, something she had held close to her heart. The electric glare of the lights hurts my eyes, which had grown accustomed to the dark, so I step out into the back yard and, sitting under a tree, I turn my mother's memories, over and over again, in my head.

The night air is warm and barely stirs the leaves of the trees and I must have dozed off for a while because when I open my eyes and look down the red-brick dam, I see that a crowd has gathered in the market square. It is a public meeting and a slim man with an elegant moustache is talking into the microphone and punching the air around him. My eyes open wide: it is my grandfather, Pa Nazeer. His hair flows in black waves, high from his forehead, just as my mother remembers. I creep up closer to the stage and hear him talk about the people, the workers, and about creating a just economic order.

"We must own the tools of our trade. We must share the fruits of our labour. Then we will all live in a just and safe world." His voice is clear but he speaks hesitantly and the gaps between his words break his sentences into awkward phrases. No one cheers.

From the back of the crowd, a voice asks, "Hey, Nazeer, boy, tell us how we're going to make this happen?"

"Yes, man," another voice joins in. "What's all this dialectic whatsit you talking about?"

"Dialectic materialism," a deep, school-masterly voice adds.

"Yes, that. Tell us what that means, man."

"Yes, Nazeer, tell us. And what is this sharing you talking about? Why I must give anybody anything that I break my back to work for, eh? You've got to explain to me better about this socialism thing."

"And talk up, man."

"Yes, talk like a man, man."

25

On stage, my grandfather has lost his colour, has gone pale. He starts to stumble and stutter. The crowd laughs. A man calls, "Look. He needs his wife to come and help him out now. Let Baby come help you, boy."

Almost as soon as he says it, she comes out from the darkness at the back of the stage, my grandmother, Baby. She whips the microphone from her husband's hands and breathes fire into it. She takes the same words that Nazeer had mouthed and lifts them high into the night sky where they burn with a hard brilliance. The crowd is dazzled and they cheer.

"You think you're poor," she tells them, "but you're not! They, the plantation owners, are the poor ones. Without you, they're nothing and that is the power that you have in your own two hands. Let me see those hands, let me see you lift them high in the air!"

The people raise their hands and cheer and stamp and shout. When the noise dies down, a woman's voice carries from the back of the crowd: "But how she can show up her husband so in front of all these people?"

"How she can make him look so small?" another asks.

"She's forgetting her place."

"Baby's gone too far now."

"Trouble is here. See, even the moon hides its face from the night."

"Yes, the darkness is heavy tonight."

The crowd is so taken now with what Baby is saying that no one sees my grandfather walk away and become one with the darkness. Even his starched white shirt disappears in the black shadows. He walks on the brick dam, going deeper and deeper into the back of the town where the houses lean up against each other and the bushes grow big and wild over every wall and fence. I follow him, walking faster and faster to keep up. He leans forward from his waist, cutting his way into the night like a ship's prow. His feet hurry, almost running now, then he slips and falls, and I fall with him over a grassy bank into a dry punt trench.

He lies on the cracked earth with his arms extended, a man crucified. He swallows air in big gasps and his chest pumps up and down, quickly at first, then falls into a smooth, steady rhythm. He

26

sleeps but it is a troubled sleep, twitching and thrashing around on the hard, cracked earth. I want to stay awake, watch over him, but I must have slept, too, because when my eyes open again, I see a glint of white near his head that had not been there before. I crouch down to take a closer look and what I see there makes my heart stop and close up into a fist. My mouth hangs open and swallows up the night. I am watching my grandfather's hair go white! It starts at the roots and creeps slowly upwards, up each shaft of his thick hair until the whiteness reaches the very tips and flies off into the night. For the briefest moment, his head is ablaze with light, then it lies there, still, with its new whiteness glinting in the dark.

I have no idea whether the transformation took hours or seconds. With no moon in the sky there is no movement on earth to measure time by. I sit and watch my grandfather closely, fear making my back rigid. Anything can happen in that blackness and I feel that, if I even blink, he will, in that split moment, sink down into the punt trench and be swallowed up by the earth. So, I keep my eyes wide open and watchful until first light. When morning comes, my grandfather's hair is long and white and as new-washed as the day. It lies softly on the parched earth, downy as baby feathers, silken as new-spun thread. I reach out and stroke it, over and over, letting its softness slip through my fingers, and when the first cock crows, I touch his forehead. He awakes at once and is up in one smooth movement. He hurries home and when he arrives, Baby is waiting.

Fear makes her eyes big. They are fat with weeping. She screams and screams when she sees him but Nazeer pushes past her without a word, without even looking at her. He goes into the bedroom and shuts the door, leaving her standing outside.

Baby pounds on the door, calling his name over and over, but the door stays shut. "Nazeer, Nazeer, I'm going to stop all this now. All the books and leaflets – look, I am tearing them up. They're dead. I'll burn them. I'll bury them. I'll be a wife to you and a mother to Shabhan, that's what I'll be from now on. I'll chase everybody from my kitchen the next time they come here. I'll never go near a platform again. I just want to see you dance on a stage now. You'll dance again for me, Nazeer.

"And I'll make that other baby you've always wanted. I know you want a sister or brother for Shabhan, but I've always been so busy carrying on with all these people that I clean forgot myself, forgot who I was. Nazeer, Nazeer, I'm sorry, so sorry. I won't talk to anyone but you from now on. I'll stop-up my mouth, I'll throw away the words, I'll put them all on a fire today and burn every last one of them."

The sobbing that punctuates Baby's sentences makes them awkward, and her words tumble around wildly in the early morning stillness. But Nazeer must have understood enough of what she is saying for he flings open the door and stands in the doorway, the light from the window behind him settling on his head like a halo. He takes another step and she sees his hair clearly. It is wild and white on his head like sea froth. Baby cries. She reaches out to her husband but he pulls away.

"No, Baby," he says. "If you ever stop-up your words they'll choke you. You aren't like the other women round here who just keep to their skirts and their kitchens. I like the fire in you, it's true, but I can't be who you want. You want to change the world. Me, I just want to enjoy it. You push me how you want to go and I try to speak your words and fight your fights. Now I'm 'Baby's boy'. That's what the men call me. That and worse. All they know is that their women know their place and don't look to make themselves headmen. They understand it to be so from the gods. In the Bible and the Koran and the Gita, it's the men who preach and do battle and the women – they keep to their own things. So it's been, so it's always been, but you, Baby, you want to turn everything on its head.

"I try to hustle a living for you and Shabhan. I catch my hand at everything to make a nice home, but that's not enough for you. You want to breathe out words that shake up the world and burn a hole in the sky. Worse, I made a hole in myself for you to fill up, but the hole's gone empty now, Baby. Empty, empty."

"Oh, Nazeer, don't say that. Come, sit down and let me put some coconut oil on your head. Come, Nazeer, let me rub your head with some warm oil. The hair'll turn black again in no time."

"No. Shame's gone deep to the roots. No oil can rub that out, Baby."

28

He is mumbling to himself and Baby reaches out to touch him but he flinches before her hand can get near him. When he turns back into the room, I see his shoulders droop, hear his feet shuffling on the floor. At thirty-six, my grandfather has become an old man.

Baby collapses outside the door and dissolves into tears. I reach down to touch her shoulder but feel a hand on mine instead. "Aleyah, Aleyah." It is my brother, shaking me awake. "Ma says to come inside now. Oooh, it's so dark, there must be jumbies out here." He scampers off, shouting, "Aleyah's playing with the night jumbies, Ma."

He is ten now, and my sister, nine. They're so close in age, they are like twins. They still weave stories around Nani and whenever the secrets of the past drop in their ears they tack them onto their tales of monsters and witches. They still step around Nani as she sits in the drawing room in her rocking chair, but they are bolder now and get up close and peer at her as if examining a rare specimen. I shoo them away if I catch them dancing around her, imitating her prayer-humming, even though she gives them and their antics the same blind look that she has for everyone.

I catch them at it again one morning but when I complain to Ma, she just tut-tuts and shakes her head. She is browning vermicelli noodles in a saucepan to make a vermicelli cake and she tells me again that my brother and sister are just children and that Nani knows that their play is harmless. She tips the browned noodles into a pot of boiling milk and continues, "But you, Aleyah, you were her first grandchild; you were special. You are her hope."

She sees the question in my eyes and gathers her memories around her, as I hand her the sugar, cloves and cinnamon sticks to sweeten and flavour the noodles.

"Your grandmother gave up on the world back then and put me in the kitchen and taught me to cook rice and scrub pots and make beds. I used to cry so much. Pa just locked himself up in his room and said nothing to anybody any more. She told me it was no use for any girl child to learn to read books or have ideas more big than their bellies, because all you'd ever need to know was how to make children and look after your husband and do housework. She chased away from her kitchen all the people that came from the plantations and rice fields; they looked like lost children.

"At first they came to the house to ask if they could see Pa. They'd heard that he had turned into an old man and they used to ask how he was doing, and if he was feeling better. They used to invite him to dance at weddings and fairs but Pa never danced again. He hung up his silver ankle bells on a nail in his room. On breezy mornings I would hear them tinkle. They were so sad. They didn't laugh like fairies any more. The whole house was sad. People said the walls wept. And it was true, the wood was always damp when you touched it, and on rainy days it was like the rain was falling inside the house. The house got quiet as a grave.

"And so we lived. For four years, we lived so with only Ma's busyness in the kitchen and my crying to keep each other company. She became so hard, Ma. Pa kept himself like a prisoner in his room. He was locked away for life, and if he walked through the house he was like a jumbie; his feet made no sound and his eyes saw nobody, not even me."

"Then what happened, Ma?" I ask.

"What happened? One day he picked up a piece of rope and made a knot in it. I was at the market that morning and before I left I could hear the silver bells tinkling in the morning breeze. When I came back, they were silent, even though the breeze was still blowing. The knot choked off their sound as well. By that afternoon, we buried him in a simple box. We wrapped him up in yards and yards of cotton, the cotton as white as his hair.

"Ma and I stood up at the back of the yard with the other family women and listened to the men sing the prayers for the dead. People felt so sorry for us. A dead that got carried off with a rope round his neck is not supposed to get prayers said for him, but the moulvi came. He felt so sorry for us, and said the prayers asking Allah's pardon and said how Pa was created from earth, and was now returned to earth, and how on the Day of Judgment he will be brought forth from the earth again. Prayers can sound so pretty, and when you hear them singing in the old Arabic way it makes you remember that you belong to a long line of family that goes all the way back to the time when the world had just started spinning round.

"I felt that the old family were all there that day to carry my father away. I could feel them in the prayers. But it was a small funeral because people felt that evil spirits would come to carry off a dead like that."

Hundreds of questions about my grandfather's death race through my head but I hold them back. If I interrupt, my mother might push away the past again and let the story die, so I stay still and let her continue. "By the time you came, your grandmother had taken to her rocking chair. As soon as I married it was like she just collapsed inside herself, and she's stayed there ever since. But the day you were born, she smiled and smiled and you could see the hope come fresh to her eyes. 'Aleyah, Aleyah,' she said over and over. It was she who named you, even before you were born."

"How did she know that I would be a …?"

"She knew."

"What does she want?"

"Maybe she feels that the world has turned around on itself so many times that all the changing round will make the moon rise from your hands. She tried to stretch her own hands but she got nothing but pulled down for her troubles. Now she sits with her hands in her lap, like they're two dried-up, dead leaves."

My mother turns off the fire under the simmering vermicelli and tips the noodles into a dish to cool, then takes the pot to the sink where she douses it in water. The pot sizzles and she busies herself at the sink. She has turned herself away from the story so I go upstairs and sit with Nani. Her humming is barely a rustle in the afternoon breeze. What does Aleyah mean? My question is just a thought in my head, but I hear my grandmother say, "Aleyah is 'the exalted'." I see her lean into a cradle and pick me up. My mother and father look on, smiling, as she rocks me in her arms, singing my name over and over.

"See her eyes," my grandmother says. "See how they're so black and bright. They're like gems. My own-own grandbabydaughter. When you look into her eyes you can see the whole world turning round in it. Look, Shabhan. Look, Saeed." My mother and father smile and my mother takes me from my grandmother's arms and places me back into the cradle. I am being rocked gently. The motion is soothing and my eyes close for a while. When I reopen them, I look into the bright afternoon light and my head is moving back and forth gently as Nani rocks in her chair.

"I can go away to study, Nani," I say. "Mr. Moriah says I could get a scholarship to study in England after I sit my A-Levels. He and the headmaster have talked to Ma and Pa about it already."

Nani's rocking stops abruptly. I look up at her and add, "I want to go. Will they let me go, Nani? When I come back, I will help to change so many … " I hold on to her arm, shaking it, insisting on each word. Nani starts to laugh. She makes fists of her hands and presses them to her chest, and laughs. It starts out as a whispery scrape in her throat, but when her laughter spreads out into the afternoon air it is a strong, clear sound. I am afraid that it will lose its way and tear away into a scream so I hang on to her hands, making shushing sounds, until they fall back on her lap and lie still.

"What did you do, Aleyah?" It is my father and he is stern.

"I told her about the scholarship, Pa, and she started to laugh."

"Yes, she would."

"Why?"

"Because she thinks you're here to continue what she started. You're her future, her promise coming true. That's what she thinks."

"Do you think so, Pa?"

"No. I think you must live for yourself. Your grandmother made her choices and you must make your own. Your teachers think you should go away to university. Mr. Moriah says your work is very good, that you have real potential and so on, that it would be a shame to hold you back so they want to get you ready to win a scholarship. You want to do that, right?"

"Oh, Pa, Pa."

"Hmmm. Well, they say that you would have to study hard and get top marks at your exams and impress the scholarship commit-tee and so on. You think you can manage all that?"

When he looks at me, I know that the afternoon light is bright in my eyes. "We'll see," he continues. "It's a couple years yet, but your mother is already worrying her head that you'll have to go away so far, to England. The headmaster says there is a scholar-ship you could get to go to England. He says that you're definitely university material. He told me and your mother that we should be proud of you." My father puts his arm around me and says, "But come now, come help me in the shop before you make any more trouble up here."

He pulls me up as Nani closes her eyes. I follow him downstairs, his voice trailing in front of me. "Yes, you study hard and you make your own life. You don't worry your head about all that went on here, you hear? You leave all that alone."

My father is a sensible man and he looks it. He is short and square with square hands, and feet that are planted solidly on the ground. There is no nonsense about him. He runs a small, thriving grocery shop that fronts the kitchen downstairs. A door at the back of the shop leads straight into the kitchen, so all day my mother and father move from one to the other, she going to help him when the shop gets busy, he coming into the kitchen for a long, cold drink whenever he has a spare moment.

As long as we are at home, the shop never closes. On Sundays, people just come to the back door and buy salt, sugar, matches – whatever they run out of. "Saeed, come help me out," they plead, "I need a pound of potatoes for my Sunday curry." My father pretends a fuss but he always obliges. He is a kind man. It was his kindness that made him look at my mother when he first saw her. She was fourteen and he was twenty. He tells me about it one day when I am helping him bag sugar into two-pound parcels to stock up the shelves of the shop. The telling takes on the rhythm of his dipping into the bag of sugar and pouring the honey-coloured crystals onto the scales.

It was at her father's funeral that he first saw her, he says. He had come like so many others to gawk and stare, as if a hanged man's body laid out in a plain coffin was a spectacle of horror. He confesses that he was ashamed of his curiosity. "But then I would never have seen your mother," he adds, smiling. He recalls that she stood by her mother's side with big, weeping eyes. "I felt so sorry for her. That was what made me look at her first: pity. But then I saw how pretty she was. Ah, Aleyah, she had skin like honey, and a face as sweet and round and shining as a gulab jamoon. She held her head up like a swan, and it was covered with the most beautiful lace orni I had ever seen. I was looking at a real-life girl and she was turning into a dream before my eyes."

33

"It's love, Pa." I am giggling and teasing.

"Ah, Aleyah, you're so knowing. Yes, I knew right there and then that she was going to be my bride, and before I left that day, after most of the people had gone away, I picked a flower, a hibiscus, and I gave it to her. She was so surprised. She said nothing, just took it and looked at me all serious, and I just pushed my bicycle and rode off. But the next time I saw her standing by her gate, I knew that she was waiting for me.

"I was so shy I could hardly get a word out. I don't know how she ever understood anything I said. Until then, I thought I was such a big man, you know! She would stand just inside the gate and smile at me, and I used to look down at my feet a lot. Until then, I never knew they were so wide and so square. I remembered thinking that no girl could love a man with feet like that!" My father laughs. "Well, your grandmother used to call her back inside the house every time. She and I both knew the trouble I would have with my family when I told them I wanted to marry Pa Nazeer's daughter. Your grandmother thought she was trying to save me from the trouble I was bringing on my head.

"And, oh, the quarrel and the confusion. My parents rushed off quick-time to another family and matched me up with one of the daughters, set up an engagement day and everything. 'That one you say you love so, that hangman daughter, will make you hang from a rope one day too, you wait and see. I won't stand by and let my own son go off and go hang himself so.' All that they put on my head and more. 'She looks quiet now, but she will turn into a fireball just like her mother and then what will you do? Yes, she's got a pretty face, but a pretty face can turn a man's life into hell.'

"Well, Aleyah, you and I are here today because I straightened up all five-foot-eight of myself – it was two years to the day since I first saw your mother – and I said to my family, 'I'm going to marry Shabhan on Sunday. I've gone to the moulvi and talked to him and he's coming to her house to do the marriage. You are all invited to come.' They never came and up to this day they don't speak to me. They're still waiting for me to hang myself."

My father laughs but his laughter stays low in his throat. It is a heavy blanket that covers up pain. By now, after some seventeen years of marriage, the blanket is well worn, even comfortable. But on their wedding day, the hurt sat heavily on his and his bride's faces. Their only wedding photograph hangs in the middle of the drawing room wall. It is the wall's only adornment, this grey and white picture on the wide cream-coloured wall. In it, they stand unsmiling, side by side, my father too shy to take his bride's hand, too hurt himself to offer her any comfort. The photograph was taken in a studio and their gaze is fixed firmly at the camera lens. They had not dared to blink or breathe until the flashbulb had popped its white light to capture them forever against a backdrop of fine drapery and a chaise longue covered in paisley brocade, our small-town idea of sophisticated living. They look so innocent, so young, with wide eyes and a steady gaze that already seems to accept all that is before them.

It was on his wedding day that my father moved into his bride's home. My grandmother let him, he tells me, after listening to his plans to start a little business once he had enough money together from his work at a rice mill.

"'Saeed, you're a strong boy to take all that happened in this house on your head, but I promise you that Shabhan will make you the best wife.' That's what she said to me. I told her that we would make such a brightness in the house that there'd be no space for dark corners any more. Not long after that, she took to her rocking chair and turned herself into an old woman, killing herself with her memories. We tried all kinds of things to make her get up and live but she just sank deeper and deeper into what she sees inside herself."

"What does she see there, Pa?"

"A long piece of rope."

"Tell me about it."

"I wasn't there but I heard that when she found him hanging from the crossbeam in their bedroom that she just went and sat down quiet-quiet in a corner, all doubled up with her head between her knees. It was your mother who screamed the place down that morning. Then people came and cut him down. All that time, your grandmother just sat in a corner with dry eyes, rocking herself, rocking herself and humming prayers to God."

"Why did he do it, Pa?"

"Only your grandmother knows what happened that morning. People say that the devil came down and put the rope in Pa Nazeer's hands. But other people say that the devil put the rope in your Nani's hands, and that she handed it to Pa Nazeer and watched him throw it up over the beam and wrap it round his throat."

My father sees the horror in my eyes. "They are wicked people who say such things, Aleyah. You're a big girl now and they'll start to throw it at your back, too. Just remember that they won't say it to your face because the words are coming from sour mouths. And the sourness, Aleyah, comes from people who know the rope could dangle from their own-own roof one day. Fear is what makes their talk sour."

CHAPTER THREE

I walk around on quiet footsteps, afraid that any sound will trouble the earth and tumble it into chaos. I am afraid to laugh, thinking it will tempt Fate, and I stay away from my friends but learn that they are all busy anyway, settling into their first jobs, and that Pammie and May are getting engaged to their high-school sweethearts as we always knew they would. Everyone is moving ahead. But, for me, the months drag by on heavy feet and I keep playing over and over in my head the grand theories I had propounded – and with what fervour! – to the judging panel of the scholarship programme, men and women of distinction who had nodded at me kindly, then smiled to one another. I had walked out of the room on numb legs, exhausted and drained of all feeling. Back home, I recounted to Nani all the ideas I had put forward. On retelling, I found them hollow and fantastical, with no grounding in reality.

Sitting at her knee, I had come up with a brilliant discourse, shaped from textbook theories, which would have left the judges astounded at the magic of my vision. Had the panel heard it, they would have arisen from their seats as one and cheered and announced me the winner immediately and sent me home draped in honour and glory. Instead, I had come home to fret at Nani's knee, turning and twisting restlessly until she reached out a calming hand and shushed me like a baby.

"Ssshhh, Aleyah, it'll be alright."

"No!" I said with some petulance. "I just talk words, but you, Nani, you lived them!"

"No, I never did."

"You helped people, you changed …"

"I helped nobody, I changed nothing. When you turn your back on even one person, daughter, all becomes dust."

Her voice was barely a whisper but my questions were demanding, loud. "Who, Nani? What happened? Tell me! I want to know."

"Ssshhh, my child, sssh."

Nani had closed the lids over her unseeing eyes and leaned back into her rocking chair. She would say nothing more and I had listened to her breathing – the long intervals between the indrawn breath and the breath exhaled like a weary sigh – before I left her to go swinging in the hammock in the back yard. Slung between the mango tree and a coconut palm, I had swept upward to the sky, then watched it disappear under the trees' spread of leaves and branches. Back and forth I had swung – sky, trees, sky, trees – for an hour or more. Was it Pa Nazeer she meant or someone else? Pa Nazeer or who? I threw the question to the sky but it remained a blank, staring blue that gave me no clues.

But even this mystery is a minor distraction in the days that follow. The waiting is an eternity and I am so tightly coiled, my nerves so on edge that I jump at the slightest change in the sounds around me. When the steady tick-tick-tick of the postman's bicycle stops before our gate, I am startled by the sudden silence and get up from the kitchen table as I watch my father move towards me with a letter in his hand. I signal to him by a shake of my head that I want him to open it, and my mother and I stand in the middle of the kitchen and watch him tear open the envelope. She appears calm, ready to accept anything. I am cold and my heart is still, then I'm hot, my heart beating furiously. I hear a roar in my ears and then silence. I want to shut my eyes tight but I also want to witness every movement, every change on my father's face as he reads the letter. I see him gasp, see tears in his eyes, then feel his arms around me. I stiffen and start to break away, refusing to be comforted, when he says, "Oh, my little girl, it's you! You won, you won."

I am still stiff with the sweet shock of it as my parents sweep me up in big embraces. They are both laughing, but with tears in their eyes as they kiss me on my forehead and cheeks, over and over.

"Aleyah, Aleyah, oh my girl, oh my girl," is all my father can say as I read the letter for myself to make sure he has not misread the words. It is only then that I let go of the fear and anxiety of the past months. I have won and I rush up the stairs to read the letter all over again, this time to Nani. The words are dry, matter-of-fact, nothing more than an official notice saying I have won the scholarship and that I am to attend a meeting next week to work out the details of my studies and travel. Dry as the words are, I think I see Nani smile, but the spark of light that winks in her eyes is gone before I can be sure, and her response is the same when my father reads her the newspaper report the next day.

He rushes up the stairs waving the *Daily Graphic* over his head and shouting, "Ma, Ma, Aleyah is going to England and she'll blaze like a star just like you always knew she would. Remember how you said you saw the world turning round in her eyes when she was born? Well, it's coming true, Ma."

He pauses. I have run up the stairs behind him and we both look at Nani, whose face wears its usual closed look. If her mouth does curve and lift her cheeks upward and bring a glint to her eyes, it might have been a play of light, no more. My father looks at me and shrugs.

"Hear what it says in the newspaper, Ma, 'Miss Aleyah Hassan, aged 18, has won a scholarship to study Economics at the University of London, England. The four-year scholarship is being made available through grants by the Government of Guyana and the British Overseas Development Office. Miss Hassan is a former student of the West Demerara Secondary School, and won the scholarship from a field of six contenders from schools around the country. In announcing her win, the judging panel stated that, in her interview, Miss Hassan brought an intelligence and enthusiasm to her subject and displayed genuine concern for the development of her country, and the future of the world.'"

My father reads the last phrase with a flourish – he is so proud – but I draw in my breath at the grandiosity of it.

"It's like a dream coming true," I whisper to Nani. "Remember how I was going to dance across the sky?" I giggle into my hands, a little girl again, but Nani's face stays shut behind its stony silence and she rocks back and forth as if she has heard nothing.

My father shrugs again and runs down the stairs with the newspaper. His excitement is not dampened. The patter of his feet on the stairs is like dancing drums. I stay with Nani and take her hand and look long and deeply into her eyes. There are days when she sits as if carved of stout timber: eyes blank, lips taut, limbs set rigid, as if she has lost the will to lift even her little finger, to summon up even the slightest movement. She turns herself into a statue that cares little who stops to look, to comment, to even touch its surface. I put her hand back on her lap but not without some disappointment at her silence, and follow my father into the shop where he is reading the newspaper article to every customer that comes in.

He puts drama into it, even punching the air about him. He rolls his tongue around the names of the judges, all top officials at the Education Ministry and the British High Commission. He reads the final line that I am to leave in two months to take up the scholarship with a voice that falls away into a hush, as if it senses a curtain falling somewhere. This is a new side to my father and I blush at his pride in me even as I want to laugh at his theatrics. He gets some light applause for his efforts on a couple of occasions and, for an encore, he turns the newspaper with a flourish so that everyone can see my photograph with my name printed at the bottom.

When the newspaper sent a photographer to take the picture, I had stood alone, pinned to a spot against a flowering bougainvillea, with, it seemed the whole town looking on. They teased me to make me smile and when I look at the photograph I can see a shy-faced blush trembling at the corners of my mouth. I look so young, still plump-cheeked and round-eyed like a baby – and to be talking about the future of the world!

I expect everyone to challenge me, but they accept my claim, as if it is a matter of course, that a schoolgirl from their town should set about to save the world. I can only suppose that the full import has escaped them. Their world is defined by the boundaries of this small country town and the nearby rice fields and sugar plantations. They accept everything that comes their way with a minimum of fuss: births, deaths, newcomers, new laws, higher taxes. Everything is tacked on, accommodated, absorbed. The occasional unrest of the sugar workers on the neighbouring estates is seen as something foreign; they never care to participate in protests or strikes. It is not their way. All that happens is God's will and they thank the heavens for life and everything that goes with it. My scholarship is now listed in their prayers and many raise their eyes to the shop's ceiling in praise of His blessings.

"Oh, Mr. Saeed, you and your wife must be so proud. To God above we give all thanks and praise," one of the customers says.

"Amen. And Aleyah looks so pretty-pretty in the papers. To think a little girl from our town making such big news, eh?" another adds, her eyebrows raised above a smile.

"And to go away to England, to see the world."

"We're too, too, proud!"

"She'll come back a star."

"I say it's about time this house get a light so big that it just chases out the darkness for good and all."

There are general nods and sounds of "yes, yes" to this comment, and my father does not seem to mind. Maybe he feels the same. He has added rooms to the house, repainted it many times, repaired the roof, rebuilt the front steps, but always knowing that he is stepping around something that sits still and silent and heavy at its centre. He does not do repairs or make changes with any intention of chasing it away. He knows that whatever it is, it has a place there, under the roof, and he has no quarrel with it. It is the same thing that sleeps in his mother-in-law's head and awakens whenever she screams. This does not happen too often now and, as the house grows older, she becomes quieter. Age makes them easier companions.

That afternoon, I put my head on her lap as I have done since I was a child. Now I am to go away and leave this quiet comfort behind. I believe, however, that I will always be able to gather it around me whenever I need it by humming one of Nani's prayers. I know the different tunes, all the rhythms, and I start to hum one of them, then hear Nani join in with the words.

"La-illah-ha-illah-la …" she sings, her voice losing its quaver as the keening verses pitch high into the air. I turn to look at her with a smile. Each note, each phrase follows the one before in quick succession and before long they gather up and rearrange themselves, until the whole drawing room is filled with a song of bright notes. The music swirls. Tabla drums join in and tap out a quickening rhythm. I laugh and clap my hands as the prayerful tune picks up pace and changes into merry music. Then I hear silver bells. My grandfather is there in richly embroidered clothes with sequins twinkling like stars and a red sash flowing from his waist. His hands twirl and his feet stamp to the rhythm of the drums. He spins round and round and his hands reach out and there is Baby, in a splendid red sari shot through with golden threads. They dance. It is no measured European waltz of civilized bows and curtsies, but a dance of fire and spirit that thrills their bodies to swing and leap in rapture. Each step, each look, holds intense drama – they speak of love, joy, and hearts gone wild. The dancers spin around each other, they leap, their fingers trace intricate patterns in the air, and their eyes alone perform whole dramas of rage, sorrow, of exquisite pain and the deepest happiness.

Their steps take them in ever-widening circles and the walls of the room move outwards to accommodate them. They swirl past me at longer and longer intervals, passing in a rush of tinkling bells and rustling silks. The room grows outwards until it presses up against a bank of clouds and looks out on the blue sky. The music beats faster and faster and Nazeer and Baby spin by at lightning speeds until they become a blur to my eyes, a flurry of colour: reds, golds, ochres. As I watch, the colours swirl away into a cushiony white cloud, and the dancers are enfolded and gone in a light puff of breeze. At once, the music dies, fading into a faint tinkle that falls away into silence.

The walls of the room move back once more. The silence presses up hard against my ear, making it echo loudly in my head. I miss the music, the dancing. I am in the mood for a celebration and I wish my grandparents could have danced for me all day, but when I look up, I see that Nani is asleep. Her head rests on the cushioned back of her rocking chair. The chair is still. She looks exhausted. From all that dancing, I think, and I leave her to rest, skipping down the stairs to the kitchen where my mother is busy among her pots.

"Did Nani dance a lot with Grandpa?" I ask brightly.

"She could do a few steps, but I never saw them dance together.

She was so busy with her politics, so busy with taking care of everybody's business that she didn't have time for anything else."

"Maybe she danced with him before you were born?"

"Maybe. Why are you asking about this? She didn't get up from her rocker and dance for you, eh?" My mother laughs. She is also in a mood for celebration and it has made her talkative, throwing her memory back to her young days, letting the past draw itself up and breathe again between the fire and light of the kitchen.

"Ma was always the one for being serious minded," she says, stirring a big pot of curry gravy, then turning the flames down to let it simmer. "It was Pa who brought bellies-full of laughter into the house with his merry dancing and joking. That's why he liked what he did, buying this and that scrap from everybody and reselling it. He liked talking up everything – even useless bits of scrap metal – 'til his buyers thought they were getting the crown jewels themselves! 'It's a gift, Shabhan, a gift to take something ordinary and shine it up bright. You give it new life.' I used to look at him with wonder as he took a set of rusty car hubcaps, rubbed them up on his sleeve and told me they were discs of silver that were once the wheels of the chariots of gods that flamed across the sky.

"Oh, the stories he told and the promises he built up in the air for me and my mother: the house he would build, the cars we would drive, the pretty clothes we would wear. It was always going to happen tomorrow. He had a pack of cards that he used to read every morning that would set him up with his fortune for the day. The cards were always promising him money in millions. The turn of his fortune was always just a day away, so he woke up every morning thinking 'Today is the day'. That's what kept him going all those years, but it never happened, never happened.

"The truth is, catching his hand like that didn't bring in much money at all and Ma got more and more angry. 'You're just playing at life,' she used to tell him. 'But life is more serious than all this catch-hand business you're doing, You have a wife and child and a home to look after and all day you're just running off your mouth about all this junk you're trying to push off on people. It's a waste of time!' Her mouth would shut down into a hard, thin line when she talked like that and I used to run away and hide and cover up my ears.

43

"One day when he was turning up his cards to see his fortune, Ma picked them up – every last one of them – and threw them out the window. The house was a mad house that day. She told my father: 'Your kind of talk is cheap and empty; it piles up to a whole heap of nothing. I'll put something heavy and solid in your mouth instead. Come! Tonight you can go and talk to the people at the sugar plantation; they have problems with the manager; he's trying to get them to cut and load the sugar cane for one set of pay, but that is work for two sets of people and two sets of pay. They're trying to rob the people and we're going to help stop it.'

"I remember how Pa dropped down his head into his hands. You would think he was praying, except he was not a man who went to the mosque except on Eid day. When he looked up again, all the life that used to dance at his eye corners was gone. His face looked like it was set in stone, real heavy granite stone. Pa knew all the time that his lil buy-and-sell business couldn't make ends meet, but he was like a lil boy trying to get away with as much playing as he could. That day, my mother took a man's weight and threw it on his shoulders and when he stood up and followed her to the kitchen his feet sounded heavy-heavy on the floor.

"That night was the first time he stood up on a stage and spoke my mother's words. It's true she didn't get any real pay for all her advice and work, but if the people got a raise of pay from a strike she organized, they would put together some money and bring it for her. My mother would make a fuss about taking it but they used to leave it on the table and God-bless her until she couldn't refuse. And besides the money, they always found something to bring whenever they crammed themselves into her kitchen. They would pick something from their kitchen gardens, so our house was always packed up with pumpkins and mangoes and cassava, or they would bring shrimps fresh from a morning's catch, and eggs, and even chickens. We had so many chickens one time, Pa had to knock up a pen for them in the back yard. And so it went on for years until Pa's head turned white all over and he jailed himself up in his room."

My mother stops and sighs and sweeps a hand over her face. In a soft voice, she adds, "Then he went and did it – choked off her words for good and all with a rope."

Abruptly she stops any further questions from me. "Come, help me peel these potatoes, girl. Dinner will be late if we don't hurry." Her mouth has shut down tight and I know there is no use trying to pry anything more from her.

At that moment, my brother and sister rush from the kitchen with their hands round their throats shouting, "Look, I'm choking! Aargh!" They must have crept up and heard Ma's last words.

She sucks her teeth softly and mutters, "Those children need some good licks. They think the past is just a plaything. But time enough for them to understand all that happened in this family; they're small yet and that story will just weigh down their lil shoulders now."

I want to tell her that I am old enough to bear the weight but she has stepped away from the story. I shiver in the hot kitchen, keeping my tongue silent and letting the cooking noises take over as we make the roti, me rolling out the soft dough and Ma, with quick turns of the wrist, turning them over on the tawa, rubbing them with ghee until they glisten then wrapping them in a small towel to keep them soft and warm until dinner time. Then my father calls out to me from the shop, "Aleyah, Aleyah, come here a minute."

He has read the newspaper story to the last of his customers for the day and they want to congratulate me and wish me well. They are kind people. The stories that linger over the tragedy that shook our house are retold now with understanding rather than malice. My grandmother's silence is accepted as rightful penance for her sin, and they look on my mother and father as good children who are taking care of their family worries with correct fortitude: they have not bruised the neighbourhood with bitter talk, or thrown their mother out to suffer among strangers.

"You're from a nice family, child," says Aunt Gwennie, one of my father's regular customers. Her head is, as always, wrapped in a calypso-coloured scarf and she pulls at it steadily to make sure that her hair is covered. "You make sure God is in all your footsteps."

"Amen," another customer adds.

"You walk the straight and narrow, child, and you're bound to succeed."

"God has given your family a whole lot to bear and they've done their duty well," Aunt Gwennie says. "You see and don't make their hands fall now."

"Praise the Lord!"

I smile broadly at their good wishes and nod my head, covering up the big fear that has settled in my stomach. Now, I think of all the pictures I have seen of England, of the endless green fields that butt onto milky-grey skies, of its giant-sized buildings and snow-covered streets busy with people in heavy coats. In movies, they look weighted down, anchored, insulated against the cold and everything else in the world. I try to imagine myself in those streets in such coats and scarves and hats but cannot, not while the bright sun touches my skin with warmth. I fear the worst and take my fears to my grandmother's lap. How will I live among strange people with their cold weather and strange foods? What of their white skin and light-coloured hair and eyes? How will they view me? What if I fail my course? What if I get lost?

I heap my questions all around her as I had once heaped my dreams, and she hums and says nothing. I talk on and on, fretting about everything, but I stop when her humming fades away and brings a sudden silence.

In a clear, even voice she says, "When you were born, the whole world was spinning round in your eyes. How could you ever lose your way?"

Nani stops talking as suddenly as she began. I look around and see my mother standing in a doorway. "I heard her talking; it's so long since I heard her voice that it drew my feet here without me even asking them," she says. "When you're gone, Aleyah, we won't hear her voice at all. You're the only one that can draw her out and even that doesn't happen too often. Her mouth will stop itself up forever."

"She was telling me not to be afraid," I say.

"She would. She was never afraid, at least, not until your grandfather went and hanged himself. Now, she sees his body dangling everywhere she looks, even at the bottom of the plate she eats from. Now she wants you to pick up her braveness and carry it on. If we believed in reincarnation, you'd think she thought that you were herself reborn, that you're her karma."

"But, Ma, you have to die first for your soul to be reincarnated."

"I know, Aleyah, I know."

My mother hurries away from the questions in my eyes. She hurries back to the kitchen where she starts to chop up vegetables furiously.

Maybe my impending journey is pressing me to tidy up the past – as one puts things away before setting out, to make the homecoming easier. Maybe I feel that my shoulders have grown wide and are ready to bear all of our history. However, if I ask too many questions, my parents simply pull their blanket of silence closer, or shrug their shoulders and turn away.

But there is always Great Aunt Khadijah and her busy prattle, and when she descends on our house with her brood of grandchildren one Saturday, a month before I am due to leave, I tune in to every scrap of her conversation. Her chatter, which skims and shifts from subject to subject without drawing breath, is bound to let fall some detail, some comment.

When they arrive, my great aunt and her grandchildren turn the whole house upside down. There are big pots cooking in the kitchen and a happy commotion in every room and in the yard as the children, led by my brother and sister, play games that involve much shouting, running, and jumping up and down in the air. The day becomes even more riotous when Great Aunt Shamroon joins us with Great Uncle Rayman leaning on her arm. My great uncle is sickly and Great Aunt Shamroon fusses around him like a bright bird pecking and feeding her charge. How fortunes change, I think, as I watch my great uncle to see whether he notes the irony of his situation. But he is placid, content, and arranges himself comfortably wherever he sits, as is the due of one who is ill and deserving of sympathy. And for all that my great aunt fusses over him, if his hands flutter and signal her to sit and be quiet, she folds herself quickly into a corner and is still, like a child reprimanded.

I recall the many sessions of complaint and commiseration in our kitchen.

"It's how my mother was, and her mother before her and before her and before her," Aunt Shamroon would say to explain her helplessness. "What to do, eh? What things you want, I should say? My tongue only knows what it has learned. It doesn't know any better." I had heard her talk like this many times when I was a little girl, but it is only now that I hear how her voice falls away into a long sigh and see how she shrugs her shoulders and sweeps her hand across her face.

"You just have to take things as they come, that is all," my mother would say on such occasions.

"You're so lucky Shabhan. Not many husbands are as good as Saeed." This is Great Aunt Khadijah. Her husband had not been an easy man to live with and before he was struck down suddenly with a heart attack at forty, my great aunt had spent a good many tearful nights with my mother complaining of his meanness and his tyranny.

"He's watching me all the time," she used to say. "I can't step out of the house without a whole heap of questions, like I'm a criminal or something. I don't know what he's so afraid of, what he's guarding so!"

"Yes, Shabhan is lucky. Most men think you're there to pick up after them, to pick up their clothes and their bad ways and wash everything clean," Great Aunt Shamroon says.

My mother would offer a sympathetic ear and cups of hot tea sweetened with condensed milk, and by the time they were ready to return home, her aunts would be counting their many blessings, though even here there were further comparisons from Aunt Khadijah. "At least Aziz doesn't drink or smoke or go with other women or beat me the way my brother beats you. What to do, eh, what to do?"

It is late in the afternoon and the day's visit is coming to an end. The house has quietened down. My father and great uncle are in the back yard talking and laughing under the mango tree and the children have scattered around the neighbourhood; they will find their way home come dinner time. In the kitchen the women rest their thoughts, each turning over the memories before her eyes. They have few secrets from each other, have seen each other through so many crises that words are not always necessary to frame their conversations. It is a comfortable silence, the kind that pillows thoughts and, I am hoping, loosens the tongue. From the edge of the kitchen doorway I watch the light leave the kitchen, making my mother and her aunts appear ghostly in the patchwork of shadows. I draw in my breath and hold it so as not to make a sound. The least rustle would give me away. I wait, it seems, for an eternity as the light continues to slide away from the edge of the afternoon. Then my ears perk up: I hear a sigh. It is a long, doleful sound and it is followed by Great Aunt Khadijah's voice.

"She was too hard-ears, stubborn like a mule," she says, picking up a story that has been told and retold so many times it needs no introduction. From the corner of my eye I see my mother and Great Aunt Shamroon sit up. "How many times I told her to leave those books alone, even up to her wedding day when she looked so pretty like a rose. But she would just laugh at me and say that Nazeer likes to listen to her reading, that he is not an old-fashioned man and he likes that she reads and has ideas of her own. And she would just flounce herself away from me!

"Well, what could I or anybody say, eh? And it was true, too. Nazeer used to come every single day and sit at her feet and she would read her big words from her leaflets and books and he would just smile and smile like it was blessings from an angel. He didn't understand a word she was saying, but he felt so proud that this bright, so-pretty girl had picked him that he just couldn't keep his head on straight. Who could blame him, eh? I tell you that man was on the cross from day one."

"And he died on that cross," Great Aunt Shamroon says.

"You could say so. By the time he found out the price he had to pay, it was too late. The cross was too heavy to bear. For him and for her. And for you too, Shabhan. How you were bawling down the place that day. As soon as I got the message I rushed over here and saw you holding on to her and screaming the place down. All she did was stare into space, to the place where they found the body hanging. They had cut him down and laid him out on the bed, but she was still staring into that vacant space and humming like a busy bee. I screamed at her, I had such a passion in me. I was shouting and screaming at her. 'What happened, Baby? What did you go and do?' I was even telling her, 'I told you so, I told you to leave those books alone. You went and shamed him and that wasn't enough? You had to go and kill him, too?' Allah, forgive me for the things I said."

49

My great aunt casts her eyes to the heavens and pauses before she continues. "The house was full of people, god knows who. They had come to stare at the hanged man. So I hauled her away. I hauled her away from you, Shabhan, to the next bedroom and I sat down with her quiet-quiet and I quieted down myself, too, and I started to talk to her like she was a little baby. And she started to rock herself – back and forth, back and forth – and she was whispering prayers, and when she turned big, staring eyes on me, I knew then that her eyes had turned in on themselves. Her eyes were looking at me but she was seeing nothing. Nothing! My little baby sister, my sweet baby sister had gone blind!"

My mother and Great Aunt Shamroon gasp. I hear sobs and see Great Aunt's Khadijah's bosom heaving and shaking.

"They say things like that happen when the mind gets a shock so big it can't bear it," says Great Aunt Shamroon. "There is a story that the Prophet Mohammed – peace and blessings of Allah be upon him – once went to see a friend who had died, that he closed the eyes of the dead man and said that when the body is seized, the eyesight follows."

"My mother wasn't dead!" my mother says sharply.

"I don't know, I don't know. All I know is that she wasn't seeing me any more," Great Aunt Khadijah says, still sobbing.

"But what did she say to you?" my mother asks. Her voice is trembling. "Up to now, I don't know all that happened that day. I went to the market and when I came back my baskets were full, my father was dead, and my mother was hunched down in a corner staring up at him, but I still don't know what really happened. Do you know, Auntie? Did she tell you?"

Great Aunt Khadijah sighs and shakes her head. "There are things, my daughter, that should go to the grave and wait there for the Day of Judgment."

"Auntie!" My mother's eyes are wide with fear. "What are you saying?"

My great aunt sighs again then places a calming hand on my mother. "I sat with her a long time like that, all quiet and with her humming prayers. I felt so sorry for her, so sorry. I sat there and remembered how as a little girl she was always bright and laughing. Then she touched my hand and I watched her mouth opening and shutting over words that wouldn't come. I remember how I stopped up my screams then, because I thought she had gone dumb too! But I hauled up all the strength I had and kept my backbone straight and I patted her hand to quiet her down, and then she leaned up close to me and I heard her voice come out in a lil-baby whisper and she said to me, 'Oh, sister, sister, I've gone and done something so...' "

By now, my head is right around the kitchen door and I am leaning forward, bending over double from the waist so as to catch every last word, and stretching out my ear so far round the door jamb so as not to miss even a whisper, that I lose my balance and fall head first into the kitchen. I hit the floor with a dull thud, falling full length and face down. My nose hurts and my shoulder hurts and I feel a bruise on my knee, and before I can pick myself up, my mother is holding me with gentle hands and scolding me all at once. She searches my face and arms for bruises, then sits me down and makes me a big glass of sugared water to soothe the shock. When she asks me if anywhere hurts, I shake my head.

"It's only her ears hurting," Great Aunt Khadijah says smugly. She has regained her blustery, big-mouth ways. "The doors in this house have big ears, eh Aleyah? They want to hear everybody's story."

I sip my sugared water and feel my ears get hot.

"And what will you do with the story, girl?" my great aunt continues. "You think you turn a big woman now, eh? You think you're like your Nani now that you can read big words? You better don't make the mistake to think that all that high-up education is everything in the world."

"Oh, Auntie, leave her alone," my mother says.

"Well, she's growing up, Shab, and one day she'll find out that if she's not careful this life can throw a big heaviness on your back and all you can do is sit down – braps! – right in the middle of it and end your days right there. You better listen to your mother and daddy when they talk to you and don't be hard-ears like your Nani was."

"Aleyah is a good child, Auntie. She doesn't give us any trouble," my mother says, smoothing back the hair from my face.

"Well, Shabhan, you see and make sure that she doesn't bring trouble on her own head. Soon, it'll be time for her to marry, so you and Saeed better make sure you make a good match, find her a nice Muslim boy and …"

My mother cuts her off. "Auntie, these are different times. Aleyah will choose a husband for herself."

Both of my great aunts make sounds of protest at this and Great Aunt Khadijah looks closely at me and says, "You'll let this girl child go off and make a decision like that on her own? Not me! All my children had to listen to what I had to say – and look at all my nice-nice grandchildren, eh? Even if they find a boy or girl that they like they still have to get approval – just like our parents did for us – or it's nothing doing. No, sir! You and Saeed better know what you're doing. You mark my words, Shabhan."

I blush. The talk of marriage and husbands is making me squirm and I press myself back into my chair and hide my face in the big glass of sugared water.

My mother says, "Oh, come, there's time for husbands and so on yet. Now, it's time for her books."

"It's the books that worry me," Great Aunt Khadijah mumbles.

"The words are heavy-heavy," Great Aunt Shamroon adds.

"They carry the weight of the world."

"And the weight can crush."

"And kill."

"Oh, shush, you two," my mother says. "You're like two jumbies in the dark." She gets up and turns on the lights. The sudden electric glare kills my great aunts' conversation and acts as a beacon to bring everyone in from outside. The kitchen fills up in seconds and the noise gets so loud that I slip away upstairs and enter Nani's quiet world.

I sit on the floor and place my head on her lap and she strokes my hair gently. I want to ask about love and marriage. All I know of these are the stories I hear. There is the grand passion and there is the tragedy. There are the classic tales of *Anna Karenina* and *Romeo and Juliet* and *Wuthering Heights*, and there is Nani's story, and all the stories that I hear in the market, stories that travel from ear to ear with weeping and sorrow for company.

At school there were boys who made my heart ache and draw itself in so tight that I could hardly breathe. Each in turn would appear so handsome, so nice, but if they looked my way I would feel my face go hot and I would hurry away. I'm no beauty like my grandmother had been, nor did I have my mother's prettiness. There is much of my father's solidness about me. I am short and round-cheeked, with eyes that are set wide apart. In every mirror I see that my eyes are small, my nose big, my mouth wide, and my neck much too short.

But I have seen how my friends, Sita, May, Pammie and Cheryl – all of them – preen and simper, inviting the looks to linger. They titter and giggle in chorus, throwing back looks from the corners of their eyes, managing to appear shy and forward at the same time. When they walk away, they're like so many graceful gazelles, knowing that the looks will follow them. I have to wait for my heart to uncurl and return to its steady thrumming so that I can breathe again. The thought that one day my heart might stay in a tight fist forever fetches in a chill from the night air and makes me shiver.

My head is restless on Nani's lap and she pats it gently, making a shushing sound and, though I have framed no question, she says, "It's all there is, Aleyah."

"What do you mean, Nani?" I ask, turning to look up at her.

"It's life."

"But the pain, the unhappiness?"

"And the joy, my child."

"That's the heaven but what of the hell?"

"Life is heaven, and life is hell."

"So, we cannot choose?"

"We always choose."

Her voice is steady but, as if exhausted from a great effort, Nani brings the lids down on her unseeing eyes and falls asleep.

As the day of my leaving draws nearer, the house becomes quieter. My brother and sister walk about on softer footsteps, and look at me with eyes big and round with sadness. I shall miss them. I would like to be there to see them grow up tall and strong and beautiful, as I know they will, but I will have to be content with viewing them from a distance and watching them grow in startling leaps through photographs.

My mother tries not to look at me when she speaks, framing her words in formal questions and statements, as if I am a stranger who must be properly addressed. My father sits on the high stool behind the counter in his shop, licking the end of his pencil and making lists of things that still have to be done: travel documents to be picked up, warm clothes to be made or bought, airline and taxi arrangements to be finalized. He keeps busy and has taken to greeting me with big, blustery laughs. "Aleyah, Aleyah, my girl, what're you doing today? Do you want to go into the city with me? It'll be a nice drive." He acts as if I were a visitor, someone who has to be entertained.

Stranger still is the Koranic function my parents organize for the weekend before I leave. Strange because we do not usually observe the rituals of our religion, and, except for Nani, the reading of the Koran and the saying of daily prayers are alien to our household. We keep up the holy days and holidays but they are little more than excuses to gather in the family for feasting and celebration. But now my parents seek comfort in the singsong reading of the Koran and the chanting of age-old Arabic prayers. I lay a white lace orni over my head and place my palms side by side like an open book, and follow the moulvi's prayer as he asks Allah to grant me success, and protect me from the temptations of the world.

The whole family has come, my friends from school, neighbours, even those who are not Muslims. Nani sits through the prayers quietly, giving way to the moulvi and listening to him as he leads the chants. I have heard her sing all of them in her whispery way. In the moulvi's strong voice they lose the quavers that make them her own, personal music and, for all the richness of his bass tones, it is Nani's breathy chants that I will always remember. I sit next to her during the sermon when the moulvi talks of the journeys of the Prophet Mohammed, the battles he fought defending the Faith, and the trials he faced during his lifetime. I listen with half an ear and reach over and hold Nani's hand. It is dry and delicate and I hold it gently, sensitive to its frailty. She knows that I am leaving in a few days but she has said nothing to me. Perhaps, there is nothing to say. Perhaps, I am to discover my future without encumbrance of promises or predictions.

Just then we gather up our hands and lift them before us for the final dua, the prayer to close the reading. Nani's lips move as the prayer is said. When it is over and I raise my hands to my face at the ameen, I feel her hand light on my hair, gentle as a whisper.

As my departure draws even nearer, my mother gives me advice on keeping warm and eating well and keeping to my books and being careful about the friends I make. Her tone is brisk, a quick-march of commands. She avoids my eyes and stores up her emotions behind her no-nonsense manner, but every now and then she steals a look at me from the corners of her eyes and her face softens. I know that if she ever starts to talk about my leaving and what her heart feels, her tears will be unceasing. So I let her talk on and on about wearing a good coat and keeping my head covered and being careful not to catch colds, and I hear how hard it is for her to watch me go and how she is steeling herself against the day I leave.

The day before my journey begins, I look at her steadily, forcing her to stop talking. She sits down on my bed and holds her head in her hands, her words cut off in mid-air.

"I'll be okay, Ma," I say, taking her hand.

"I know I mustn't hold you back but …"

"I know. It's hard. For me, too, but I'll be back soon."

"I'm so afraid that you'll …"

"I'll be safe, Ma."

"You'll grow up and …"

"And I'll always be your Aleyah, you'll see."

She manages to smile through her tears and I hold her close. Her head is on my shoulder and mine on hers and we stay twinned like that for a long time feeling the beat of each other's hearts.

As if in empathy with my leaving, the heavens open and pour down rain all day without stopping, and into the night, my last night at home. The steady thrumming of the drops on the zinc roof is as calming as a lullaby and I fall asleep to its sound. But hours later, I awaken to a loud banging. A window has blown open somewhere. I follow the sound to Nani's room and I go to shut the window. Nani is fast asleep and I sit on the edge of the bed and look at her. I smooth her brow. The skin is folded in deep ridges.

I must have been stroking her brow for several minutes when I look up, frightened by a quick-fallen, chilling silence. The wind has dropped and there is a break in the rain. Not a leaf stirs, not a star twinkles in the heavy darkness. The world holds its breath and I fear that nothing will ever move again. My hand stays frozen on my grandmother's brow. I, too, hold my breath, knowing with a deadly certainty that a crash of thunder will split the world apart in one second, two seconds, three seconds. I measure off the time in the dark, and as the seconds mount it comes: a white light crashes through the window I closed and splinters fly about the room. A long lash of rain whips through the broken glass, drenching everything in the room. A howling wind follows and thunder rolls on the roof and stays there, unmoving, with a savage, threatening rumble. Nani is still sleeping peacefully. I put my head next to hers and cover my ears to keep out the wild roaring of the storm. I hang on tightly to her, thinking it will be over soon, that such fury cannot last forever. Just as I think this, the door of the room bursts open.

My grandfather, Pa Nazeer, stands in the doorway. His white hair, grown long, is lifted by the wind and surges around his head. Nani is now wide awake, sitting upright, her back rigid. My grandfather looks straight into her eyes. Her unseeing eyes hold him in their sight. As he comes closer I notice that he holds a piece of rope in his hands. He is playing with the rope. It is fat and frayed with wear. Once it may have tied bundles of sticks, lashed a loose picket fence to a post, or hung a tyre swing for the neighbour's children. It has had its uses and now my grandfather is playing with it, turning it, twirling it, twisting it in his hands. He holds the rope taut and lets it slacken. He wraps it around his hands, then loosens it and wraps it around his hands again. He comes closer to the bed. Nani sits unmoving. She watches him. Her eyes never blink.

He is laughing. I see his mouth open wide, hear the scrape of sound from his throat. He says in a quiet voice, "Look here, Baby. I have the rope. It's long enough, Baby, long enough to fetch me away. Now, watch this."

And as if the wind has picked him up and thrown him to his task, my grandfather rushes forward, grabs a chair, stands on it, makes a small loop at one end of the rope, throws it over a beam, catches the loop and pushes the rest of the rope through it. He draws the rope taut around the beam, pulls on it to test it, wraps it three times around his neck and knots it. He levers himself up on the rope, kicks the chair away, then lets his body drop in one quick, sudden moment. It jerks once, twice, and then is still.

At once, the wind drops, the rain stops, and the thunder rolls off the roof. I scream and scream and my grandmother does nothing but stare at the body that dangles. It is being blown ever so slightly this way and that. His head has dropped to one side and the body sways before us, now with its back to us, now turned around so we can see his face. His mouth hangs open. His eyes stare. Nani's eyes stare back. She whimpers and I hear the faintest rustle of a hummed prayer.

I shout, "The rope? The rope? You gave him the rope? Tell me! Youyouyou?"

My fists pound her chest, pound the skeletal cage of her ribs. I want to tear at her, tear away her silence, and hear her scream as well. But she does not cry out nor defend herself. She sits in the bed with her knees drawn up and hums and stares at her husband. I want her to die. I want her to hang like my grandfather. I want to put a piece of rope in her hands and watch her throw it over the beam and knot it. I want to see her body dance in the breeze.

I pound at her chest again and scream, "Youyouyou?" She doesn't raise her hands to fend off my blows, to stop-up my screams. She sits in the bed, unmoving. She stares into the night. She never blinks. Nothing in her body moves except for the slight rise and fall of her chest.

I fall back onto a pillow and lie there exhausted for I don't know how long until, from behind closed lids, I sense the lightening of the sky. I open my eyes. Dawn is spreading. There is no sign of the storm of the night before. Everywhere I look is bright and peaceful. I think, though, I see the faintest spectre of a hanged man suspended in mid-air, ropeless, but I blink and it is gone. I sit up, sure that I have imagined it, that all I saw was but a trick of the light.

Nani is asleep beside me. She looks so rested, as if she has not stirred all night. The morning sounds of the house are starting up. My mother is already in the kitchen, my father is in the shower, and my brother and sister are rushing about the house. Nani sleeps on and I lie there wondering whether I'd had a bad dream, but no one puts their head around the door and says anything. Outside, there is not even a ripple of cloud to break the sky's blueness. But as I cross the floor, I tread on something soft. I reach down and pick up a small bunch of threads. They are pale gold and coarse. Directly overhead is the beam where my grandfather threw the rope. I take these strands of rope to my room and put them away carefully in a corner of my suitcase.

My father will travel with me to the airport. I am to say my other farewells here at home. At breakfast we sit together but hardly speak, hardly eat. My mother looks mournful, and my brother and sister are silent. It is the first leave-taking for the family and we are all awkward. I hug my brother and sister as they set off for school and it is not until they are out of the gate and way up the road that I allow myself to think that this is the last time I will see them for several years. When I see them again they will be almost grown up, strangers. I will not see them stretch out and take on adult ways and adult voices. I wave to them but they have already turned the corner.

Leaving my mother is hardest. Neither of us can say anything. She passes her hands over my head, over and over, to smooth my hair. She cries. She pats my back. She holds me close. Once more, I feel the faint beat of her heart against mine, and I think of how I knew that heartbeat even before I was a conscious being. I have no words to leave with her; she has none to give me. I can only hold her close and our faces are wet against each other's. My father parts us, gently, then picks up my suitcase and takes it downstairs and out to the waiting taxi.

I am alert to every movement that has to do with my leave-taking and when I hear the thump of the suitcase as it is placed in the trunk of the car I reach out and hold my mother close once more. I close my eyes and shut out the world and hold her, wanting to feel this safe forever. We only let go of each other when my father returns and says in a soft but firm voice, "Aleyah, we'll be late."

I turn to Nani. She is sitting in her rocking chair and looks her usual self, as if she has spent an untroubled night, and the storm, the screams and the knotted rope have never been. I remember my grandfather's words and see her cowering in a corner of her bed. I see myself angry and full of rage. Now, looking at her calm face, her quiet hands, I am not sure what I was angry about, so I shake off my confused thoughts and try to find all my old tenderness for her. But I cannot push the shadow aside from my heart so easily. I kiss her cheek and feel its dryness. I hold her close and feel her frailness. I let go and know that she watches me as I walk to the waiting car. As the car pulls away, I am just as sure that she hums a prayer that rises far beyond the roof and touches the sky.

During the hour-long drive, my father says little. He holds my hand and stirs up some words of advice on dressing warmly and eating well and paying attention to my studies. I hear his voice but hardly listen as I look out on the passing countryside: the even green of the rice fields, the sugar cane rising like golden shafts of light from the brown earth, the modest houses of the villages that front the main road, set amidst coconut palms or bougainvillea run wild, and over all this, a blue sky, bright and clear as a jewel. I shall miss all this. I do not look at my father but hold his hand tighter. There is an answering pressure on my palm and, as each bend of the road draws me further and further away, I knot it all into a corner of my memory for safekeeping.

CHAPTER FOUR

I draw my eyes in to fit the cramped landscape. It presses up hard against the shuttered window of my room. A heavy mist hangs from dark clouds and draws in the horizon right up outside the window, right against the tip of my nose. I peer into the mist, trying to roll it back so that I can see the shapes of the next door houses, trees, anything, but it stays there unmoving. I pull my dressing gown closer and wonder at a world that keeps all its shapes and colours shrouded and secret. This is so unlike home where windows are flung wide to catch the light, the air, the heat of the day, and are kept open at night to frame the stars. Here, everything is shuttered and cold, still and sodden. The sun is little more than a watery orb that steals over the backs of clouds and disappears into the night without spreading any of its heat. I long for blue skies, and rain that drums on zinc-topped roofs and bright green trees that spread their leaves high against the heavens. I sigh and turn around to face my small room. Its walls clamber with roses, all of them pink and fat and hanging lazily from snaky vines.

My mother would like this prettily pink wallpaper, she would run her hands over it and smile. I miss her gentle face and, missing her, the roses tremble as my eyes fill with tears. I would give anything to hear her now, even if her voice was pitched to a sharp edge with a reprimand aimed at me. I miss my father, too, miss his big laughter. And my brother and sister scampering about the house as quick and busy as mice. I miss their giggles, Nani's humming, my mother's clanging pot lids, I miss all of it and press my wet face into the pillows. They smell of cold, shut-in rooms and I think of Nani's lap and her soft scent of baby powder and Pond's Cold Cream. I close my eyes and let my tears flow. But, just then, there is a soft knock on my door. It is Katu. She places a gentle hand on my shoulder.

"I was a mess, too," she says.

"Does it get better?" I ask.

"No, but you get used to it. Writing and receiving letters, photographs – that helps. But the feeling that you're cut loose from everything that you are, it's always there."

Hers was one of the four faces that looked out at me from the doorway of the narrow, redbrick house when I arrived yesterday. I had flown through the night and been set down into the middle of a morning of grey light and a thin drizzle. Everything appeared as smudges against dark clouds and, through the windows of a speeding taxi, I had shut out the blur of heavy stone houses and hurrying cars and let my tiredness overcome me. The official from the Guyana High Commission, who had met me at the airport, gave up her attempts at conversation. I awoke from my doze only when the taxi slowed and rounded a tight corner into a narrow street lined with narrow houses, all built of red brick and sitting back from front yards filled with trees that were putting off their dead leaves. We stopped before a house with a big, red door, and when it opened, there were brisk handshakes before the official left. It was then that I had stepped into the warmth of the smiles of the women at the door, had curled myself into a big blanket spread over my cold shoulders, and had sat back and let their bright chatter flow and billow around me.

There was Miss Wickham, with skin white and crinkled like tissue paper. She looked after the house and garden and "you gels", she said, handing me a cup of hot, sweetly spiced cocoa. Then there was brown-skinned Cassie. She was a big girl: big voice, big laugh, big hips, big hair. She answered my questioning look with, "I'm from Barbados". Next to her, half her size, and with a voice made small by shyness, was a young woman who peered out at me from behind large, black-framed spectacles.

"I'm Vindi Sanjit," she said, her tongue twirling around the English words, giving them a foreign shape. "I'm from Bombay."

Then there was Katu, sitting on the arm of my chair. "Mulikatu

61

Ajala," she said, then laughed and added, "but everyone calls me Katu. I am from Lagos, from Nigeria."

She seemed carved in ebony, honed and burnished. Every curve, every plane, every feature of her face followed classic proportions, but what drew you to her was her grace, the careless ease with which she carried her beauty. She smiled and I felt at ease, welcomed. Now she crosses my room to the window and says, "The mist will lift. The sun will come. We must make the most of it, yes? When the winter comes, the sun, it puts its face away in long night times."

She turns away from the window and heads for the door. "Come, get dressed. Wear a jacket. We'll have coffee, then I'll show you around, take you to the campus. It's just a little walk. The mist; it'll lift," she says, smiling.

She is reading for a first degree in Fine Arts, Vindi is studying for her masters in Physics, and Cassie is also doing a masters in Education. Katu tells me all this as we set out on a tour of the neighbourhood. "Vindi is shy; she keeps to her room most of the time. She has all her little gods lined up on a shelf. She prays every morning, does her pooja in her room. She's real quiet."

"Now, Cassie," she continues, "Cassie dances and sings all day to the music from her radio, and she parties all weekend with a whole parcel of friends. She says you Caribbeans are party people! But for all that, she's top of her class and she'll graduate with first class honours."

Katu takes me along the quickest route to the Economics Department where I need to get registered the next day. The buildings are all rectangular, built of exact grey stones, with corners so precisely squared, they seem razor sharp. The windows look out on neat quadrangles where trees are planted so as to be equidistant from each other. Everything is so precise, the result of meticulous planning; so different from the wild lushness of home where houses, trees, fences all go their own way.

Katu notes my wide eyes and laughs. "Different?"

"Everything is," I answer.

"That's much of the adventure," she says. "Yours is just beginning. Two more years and I go home."

She sees the question in my eyes and continues, "To my family, to teach art at an all-girls college in Lagos, to marriage." She says this, then stops abruptly.

"You're engaged?" I ask.

She does not answer directly but talks on about her family as we walk back home. We pass rows of brick houses with steps leading up directly from the pavement to front doors. Every gate, door and window is shut. Each house stands in tight isolation, and I know not to expect the free and easy comings-and-goings of home where people drop in all the time and a day can pass in the lazy meandering of one conversation after another.

We pass a small park with clumps of trees and swings and slides, and small children bundled up like tubby bears playing under the watchful eyes of their mothers. There are shops selling vegetables heaped in bins – cauliflower, broccoli, Brussels sprouts, Katu tells me. I think of my mother's quick kitchen knife that knows which way to cut and slice breadfruit, plantain, squash and callaloo and I feel doubtful that I will ever learn to chop these odd-looking vegetables and learn the different ways to cook them.

My thoughts flit in and out of Katu's conversation. She tells me that her family are Muslims and that she learnt her kalma and namaaz as a child and performs some of the daily namaaz in her room on a prayer mat laid out to point east to the Kabbah. "I recognized your name as Muslim when your embassy people came to arrange your stay," she says.

I nod and start to tell her about my family, but find my voice breaking away and ending in unfinished phrases. Katu puts a comforting arm around my shoulders and picks up the conversation again, telling me about her engagement to a civil servant who works in the Finance Ministry in Lagos, a marriage negotiated by their families. Katu will marry as soon as she returns home. Her husband will climb high in the government, maybe even become a minister. His family has the right connections, she says, and the artfulness to survive violent changes of government.

I tell her that it must be nice to have her life so well arranged, and she answers immediately, in all seriousness, "Oh, my father has told me already that when you go – when you get married – you don't come back."

"Doesn't that make you afraid?"

"No. You marry knowing it's for life; all other choices are closed to you. There is peace in that kind of finality."

"Like death?" I say without thinking, but Katu only laughs.

"Oh, death is not so bad when you believe. It opens the door to Paradise." She says this just as she opens the big, red door of our terrace home and we catch each other's eyes and burst into laughter as we step into the narrow hallway and race up the stairs.

She is so beautiful that I expect her fiance to be a prince among men. I could not believe that her parents would demand anything less for their exquisite daughter, so I am disappointed when she shows me a photograph of a young man with a pudgy face, big white teeth, and eyes that are already lost in an oily fleshiness that betrays a degree of self-indulgence. I murmur something non-committal and Katu laughs again. "Oh, I know he's no beauty but my parents says he's kind and will work hard to make his family comfortable."

"Do you love him?"

"I hardly know him at all. We met briefly before I left. But I will love him when he's my husband. Love grows, my mother told me. She says the best kind of love is the one that grows slowly rather than the one that bursts the heavens with fire, because that one burns itself out as quickly as it starts. My mother knows about the world. She has brought up six children and she and my father, they live well. I want to be like her."

"Have six children?"

"Yes, why not?"

"And your art?"

"That has its place. I expect I shall always paint, but my husband will want sons. And I want daughters."

"They'll be beautiful like you. And will you bring them up to bear sons, too?"

"I expect so. It's how it's always been."

She laughs and places me in a patch of light and begins to sketch a portrait. "Hold still," she says, making deft strokes with a soft pencil onto a sketchpad balanced on her knees. Her hands move swiftly to lay down lines and curves and shadows and, within minutes, she has a drawing. When she hands me the sketch my breath stops. I know nothing about art and its techniques – all I know are pictures in books, and on the calendars that hung on the wall of my father's shop. What I hold before me – the fine mesh of lines, here heavy, there light – makes me put a hand to my face to find out if I am nothing but a figment of light and shade.

"Katu!" I hold the drawing at arm's length and watch how the pencilled diamonds – clustered to shape my eyes, my cheeks, my hair – dance in the window's light.

She smiles. "It's good? You like it?"

"It's brilliant. I've never seen anything like it."

"It's why I got the scholarship. My style and technique, you know."

"You must draw and paint. I'll have it framed," I say. "One day, when you're famous, it'll be worth millions!"

Katu laughs and shrugs, then asks. "So what is your brilliant idea? Why did you win a scholarship?"

"Oh, I only want to change the world." I laugh.

"How?"

"I haven't worked it all out yet, but I have this idea that this measuring of wealth in monetary terms must be stood on its head."

"An economist who does not pursue the accumulation of wealth. Hmmm."

"Oh, no, no. There must be wealth, but should wealth be money or should it be an accumulation of happiness, peace and contentment?"

"Money doesn't buy happiness, eh?"

"Corny, but exactly. We learn about selflessness and goodness from our cultures and work in a world where the rewards lie in making money through selfishness and greed."

"So, what's the answer?"

"Don't know yet. There's a gap between the ideal and the real. Can it be bridged? Can God and the promise of Heaven be the centre of an economic structure?"

"Wow," Katu laughs. "Well, you change the world and I'll draw it."

We laugh and I look out of the window where the grey light deepens into darkness. My mother would be putting dinner on the table. She has made roti and a stew of potatoes, shrimp and bora and my sister is helping her lay the plates. My father comes in from the shop and I hear my brother out in the yard, shouting, playing with friends.

"Take this up to your Nani," Ma says to my sister, but Shaireen pulls away from the plate of food.

"She only wants Aleyah. She doesn't like me." My sister pouts.

"Well, Aleyah is gone and you …"

"No. I'm here! I'm here!" I rush in to grab the plate from Ma's hands and run up the stairs.

"Aleyah, Alli. Where have you gone?"

I am about to answer when Katu pushes her face up close to mine and laughs. "You were far away. Who were you thinking of? Do you have a betrothed, someone picked out for you back home?"

"No."

"No?"

"I shall make my own choice."

"Ah. You'll fall in love with a prince and marry and live happily ever after."

"Yes, why not?"

"My mother says that is just a fairytale. She says the real love story begins with the wedding, not ends with it."

"I shall only marry when I fall in love."

"You believe, then, in fairytales."

"Yes, I shall await my prince!" I sweep across the room with my arms flung wide as if to gather in all my little-girl dreams of castles and golden carriages and splendid gowns. "What is life without dreams?"

"Dull and flat and ordinary," Katu says, as she takes my hand, and we spin round and round the room until we are dizzy.

I see my grandparents dancing. I see them looking at each other as lovers, see them looking with wonder at their baby girl, then see them split their world apart with a raging fury. A rope dangles from the cloudy sky that presses wetly on the windows of Katu's room and I shudder.

"Are you cold? I bet Miss Wickham has turned down the heating again. They like it cold." Katu runs down to the hallway to check the thermostat and I hurry back to my room and creep under the heavy, down quilt. It weighs me down into the hummocky middle of the narrow bed. I do not know how I will survive this cold that drips on the spine like ice. I do not know how I will survive. I do not know how. I close my eyes and fall into a deep, dreamless sleep.

As the months pass, it is only the letters from home that wind down the days. They bring with them a world of slower rhythms, demanding that I give time to the unhurried voices of my family. Without the letters, the days would run together in a continuous blur, each falling headlong into the next, the grey mornings yielding to sunless afternoons, I hurrying through the dark to sit at my small study table to read over the notes from my classes. Our timetables keep us out of each other's way and it can be days before I pass Katu or Cassie or Vindi in the hallway or kitchen. Even then, there is only time to say something fleeting before we rush off in different directions to lecture halls or libraries or tutorial groups. It is only when I scurry into the warmth of the hallway and see the big, brown packet lying on the table, with stamps tiered like medals, that the winter lifts and I feel the sun on my face and remember how a day can idle itself away in long hours before putting away its light.

I'd throw the letters on my bed, spread them out before me, and flit from one to the other, following a sentence from one with a paragraph from another, weaving together a conversation about nothing at all, nothing more than small events of the day, yet finding in that nothing all that lies at the heart of the world.

"Your friend Pammie dropped by today to ask after you," Ma writes in her careful hand, all her letters large and round. "She is going to have a baby but she still looks so baby-faced herself with her chubby cheeks. Then I remembered that I was younger than her when I had you! Funny how it is only when you look out at other people that you see your own self so clearly."

"The shop is doing well. Everything is quiet at home," my father writes. His words are formed with long, thin letters that slope forward as if hurrying up to get across the page. "Shaireen helps your mother in the kitchen now and Mansur sits with me in the shop sometimes – but only when he's not too busy playing cricket with his friends. They're trying to be more grown up. I think that when you were here they felt they could get away with being small children forever."

"I can't even imagine you being married yet, and here was Pammie all big with her baby and making big-woman talk so easy-easy," Ma continues. "She told me that her husband got a job in Georgetown selling insurance so they will be moving there. That is why she came by – to tell me that and to ask how you were. I told her you were keeping busy with your books and studies."

My eyes shift over to another letter and Shaireen breaks in with a string of questions. Her hand is all curly and cursive and she dots her i's with little stars. "Have you seen snow as yet? Is it cold? Is it heavy or does it float down to the ground on fairy wings? What does it taste like? Write and tell me everything."

"Tell me about the university. I will go to one, a real big one, one day. I am going to be a scientist. We made an explosion in the lab today. It went up with a big ka-boom!" Mansur writes. His short sentences burst with excitement and I laugh, imagining the shine in his eyes when he wrote them.

When I turn back to Pa, he tells me how much they miss me. "Even the house knows there are footsteps missing. It feels quieter somehow."

"We all miss you," Ma writes. "Nani, too. Since you left, she has made not a single sound except for her humming-humming. She is well, Allah rest her soul. You take care of yourself and keep warm."

Write soon. Write soon. All the letters end like this and I leave them strewn on the bed beside me and lie back and compose long replies opening all the secret spaces of my heart. But when I pick up my pen to write, I set down the humdrum details of classes, snowfalls or my health, and the secrets fall between the lines where their eyes will have to look for them.

I write to everyone, except Nani. Each time I make the attempt, I see my grandfather's body dancing in the breeze, and I push away the pen and paper and pick up some heavy tome on macroeconomic theory, focus on Say's Law, or delve into Keynesian growth theory and Malthus's population principle. As

68

I plough through the pages I find that the arguments fill up the quiet spaces of the night and keep the darkness outside my window, safe from old ghosts.

One evening, though, as I put away my books, my hand brushes against a letter from my mother, one she had written months before, one that I have taken out and reread in thin morning light, and again in the long, bright evenings of my first London summer. My fingers hover over it for a moment but I slam the drawer shut on it. The truth is I do not need to read it any more; I know all the words by heart and before I fall asleep I hear Ma's voice in my ear: "Write to your Nani, Aleyah. She misses you. You know she has a big cry inside her, but since you were a small girl you could always make her laugh. I have this big fear that if she never laughs again she will fall down inside herself for good and all. So write to her, daughter, just a few lines. I will read them to her if she will not let her eyes see them. It will make her smile again."

The letter is there again, brushing up against my hand when, on a weekend that looks set to be a dreary drizzle of days, I pick up *The Communist Manifesto* and settle down to read. I push the letter to the back of the drawer and try to lose myself in Marx's and Engels' stirring rhetoric: "The lumpenproletariat, that passively rotting mass thrown off by the lowest layers of old society…" But the arguments, for all their insistence, give way to my mother's soft words about Nani's big cry, and when I turn back to the stark language of the book before me, it breaks up into brightly coloured leaflets that proclaim in big, block letters: "Every class struggle is a political struggle"; "Working People Arise"; and, "Workers of the World, Unite".

They were my grandmother's, these bright slogans. They were written to stir the poor who pressed themselves into her small kitchen. Their voices reach clear into my rose-covered room on a wind that lifts the lace curtains at the window above my desk and makes the pages of the book flutter. Out of the clamour, individual voices speak.

"Sister Baby, I've been working on this sugar plantation since I was born and I can't get even one lil piece of land to make a home for my family."

"They keep us poor and powerless."

"Bullies!"

"I want to get some land, something to give to my children."

"We not asking for charity."

"They keep us weak."

"They keep us beggars."

"So they can stay masters."

"Now, you listen to me!" This is my grandmother. She is small, yet in that room, packed with tight-muscled men and heavy women, she leads. The fight in her fisted hands fires her eyes and gives power to her voice. "You're right; but they're only strong so long as you're weak. We'll show them how strong you are, show them that you're from a proud people with a history rich with powerful gods who created the heavens and the earth before their gods even drew breath. We'll show them that you know the dignity of work, and that you have the strength of all the workers of the world at your back when you say that you want – no, you demand – dignity and fairness. You are not alone! Together you have power!"

Her fist punches the air. Everyone has stepped back. They press themselves against the walls to create a circle around her. And there, standing in its centre, she tells them of the struggles of workers in other parts of the world, how they face their bourgeois masters and vanquish the enemies of the people. But the victories the poor seek in my grandmother's kitchen are small ones and they shout and clamour until she draws back her words from all those foreign places.

"Is only a little ease-up in our lives we asking for, Sister."

"That's not plenty to ask after all these years of breaking our backs."

"Fair is fair."

Pressed in by the crowd, my grandmother's hands fly about the air as she talks, then are plunged deep into the pockets of her apron. An aproned leader. I smile at this, and my eyes travel beyond the kitchen window to the back yard where, under the mango tree, my grandfather sits with his hands between his knees, his head bowed. I know he is not in prayer. His eyes are restless. They roam the horizon, fall back to his feet then fly up to the horizon again. They look pained, resigned. I hear him sigh. Then one short command calls his eyes back from their wandering.

"Nazeer!" It is my grandmother's voice. It cuts deep into the air. My grandfather gets up and slouches into the kitchen.

"Nazeer will go with you tomorrow to meet with the manager and explain your position. You will not fail as long as you remember the points you have to make. I'll let Nazeer know all that we talked about," Baby says, bringing the meeting to an end.

Everyone shuffles out and Nazeer sits down on a bench and watches his wife get busy with her pots. "The manager is doubling the rent for the rice beds and the water they're supplying from the plantation," Baby tells him. "They're squeezing the life from them, these poor people. The union isn't helping; this is too small-time for them. They're busy with big-shot affairs in the city."

My grandfather says nothing. He watches the floor around his feet as Baby instructs him on the petition he is to make. As she talks his shoulders bend and buckle, and her voice grows faint, flying off on the wind but I am almost certain I hear her say, "'These labourers, who must sell themselves piecemeal, are a commodity, like every other article of commerce …'"

The wind fetches her words away altogether and I hear myself reading aloud, "…and are consequently exposed to all the vicissitudes of competition, to all the fluctuations of the market."

Outside, the rain continues to drizzle against the windows, making me long for home where on rainy days, when I was a little girl, I would sit at Nani's knee and create dreams that danced among the raindrops. I often wondered whether she had a grandmother to dream with, but all I know of her are the bits and pieces put together from scraps of family conversation.

I know that her parents, my great grandparents, worked on the sugar plantation at Leonora on the west coast of the Demerara River. Nani's mother was a weeder, and her father, a cane-cutter. Their long years of work piled up and, in the end, weighted down their poor coffins into patches of earth. They made much of little and passed the little on to their children. It was a hard life but they accepted their lot. They were not ones to raise their tongues in protest so it cannot have been from them that Nani got her rebel spirit. Perhaps that came from her grandparents. They were the ones who had travelled across the seas from India, cutting their ties with the past and adventuring into a whole new world. That would take spirit and daring – to stand at the stern of a sailing ship and watch the land of your ancestors disappear from view, possibly forever. It had to be their blood that made fists of her hands and placed the fight in her shoulders.

I put away my book and when I stare out through the window I can see her there, sitting in her rocking chair, still and quiet, with her hands prayer-folded. Without giving it a second thought, I pick up my pen and start to write: "Dear Nani ..." The letter is long. I do not know whether she will let her eyes read it, but Ma will read it to her, read to her about my classes, the house where I live, about Katu and how beautiful she is, about the long summer sun and the short winter days. I tell her about the friends I have made, especially about Jeremy who sits next to me in several classes. His father is a doctor, a general practitioner, in Manchester, and he has an older brother who is in the airforce, training to be a pilot. His mother paints pretty pictures of the countryside and sells them at country fairs and bazaars. I pause. I want to tell Nani how I almost told Jeremy about her, but my pen lifts itself away from the paper. We had been talking of our parents, our homes, and were amused at how similar the patterns and movements of our lives were.

"Father works, mother keeps house," Jeremy had said. "And you, Aleyah? Will you go back and keep house, too?" He had asked the question, then answered it. "No, you'll be a crusader, you'll set about to change the world."

I had laughed at this and listened to him continue, "Yes, yes. There's a fight in you. I see it when you argue a point."

That was when I had wanted to tell him about Nani, to tell him about her fight. I had wanted him to tell me that the rope that dangled from the sky was a relic of the past and not a portent of the future. But I had looked at his open, laughing face and had moved the conversation on to other things.

My pen goes back to the paper and I write no more about Jeremy. I tell Nani, instead, how the leaves turn brown and red and gold outside my window as the trees bare themselves for winter.

As I write, I realize that a year has slipped by. Nani, I'm sure, will have been unaware of its passing but, for me, it has brought the crackle of autumn leaves underfoot, my first experience of snow and boots that stretch all the way up to the knees, the smell of new grass in the spring, summer and the burst of ripe strawberries in my mouth. Sometimes I feel like a child in a dreamscape, a place where every turn could surprise. I tell Nani all this, fold the letter over and tuck it into an envelope. For a moment, knowing the words will be read under brilliant sunlight makes me feel close to home but when I glance outside the feeling is gone as quickly as it came.

Their world has not changed much. I know this from their letters and photographs, and I wonder what they make of the snapshots that I send. They must think that I have changed, that I must be growing away from them like a tree leaning towards a different slant of light. But the truth is that I have not changed at all. My mirror still looks back at me with the same plain face. Once Katu tried to colour it with brushes and sponges dipped in powders of pink and copper and red. She made me arch my brows and suck in my cheeks and pout my lips, but I pulled a face when she was finished and daubed at the make-up until it was a lurid mess across my cheeks.

"You're afraid to be pretty," she said, her voice sharp and indignant. "Why?"

"I will be when I'm ready."

"Ah, when the prince rides up."

"Uh-huh."

"And isn't it Prince Jeremy?"

"No, no, no!"

"No? He was so shy and nervous, shuffling his feet about at the door when he stopped by to see you yesterday. He likes you and you know it! Aleyah, come on, tell."

"There's nothing to tell. We're just good friends."

"Uh-huh," she said and smiled again.

Jeremy and I had taken to going to a pub near the campus, the *Fox & Hounds*, for a drink after late afternoon classes. He would sip pints of bitter and I would nurse a lemon squash and watch him laugh. He's tall and thin with sharp shoulder blades, has a long narrow face and dark brown hair. He's not handsome but his eyes light up when he laughs and he has an easy manner that charms. I suspect he likes me because I pique his interest, give him an attachment to the outside world, but he does not draw attention to our differences, and I like him for that, for not making a fuss filled with words that say "exotic" and "colourful".

I did not tell Katu how my breath stopped when he first looked at me and I had seen his eyes grow intense, become pinpricks of light. It would happen sometimes when he smiled at me and I would feel my voice tremble and my heart tighten with its old schoolgirl fear. I would look away and wait for his eyes to release their hold so that I could breathe easily again.

"So what do you two talk about? Economics?"

"Everything," I answered, thinking how I would rush the conversation away to topics of the day, to the weather even, and wait to see Jeremy's shoulders ease themselves into a comfortable slouch, see his eyes shift away to take an interest in the men playing darts at the far end of the room. Then I would move in with bright chat that would keep his eyes laughing.

"Everything? Like future plans?" Katu asked.

"No, no. Oh, you're impossible," I said, dismissing her teasing and thinking how for all his easy laughter and charm, I could never place Jeremy in our shop chatting with my father, or listening to Nani's hum, or running after my brother and sister in back yard games. He would never fit into our landscape, was not made to move about on hot, parched earth or through fields drowned with rain, so I had continued to edge my eyes away from his long glances until one day I had heard him sigh and ease down more comfortably into his chair. He had smiled at me and thrown up his hands in mock surrender. I had taken his hands then and laughed with him. Now, he is the one who looks away quickly if I ever find his eyes holding me in a steady gaze.

"We talk about the world. How it could be fixed," I said to Katu.

"Ah, idealists."

"No, realists."

Katu raised her eyebrows. "Just maybe, the world doesn't want to be fixed? It's not perfect, because we're not. It's only we – artists – who can create the ideal and that only from paint and plaster."

"So, blind acceptance of Fate?"

"No, no. But is it fixable?"

"We can't give up. Others have tried. We can't disappoint them."

Katu's ear picked up a wistfulness in my voice and she raised her eyebrows again. "Aleyah," she said softly. "What others?"

I looked at her and smiled. As with Jeremy, I wanted to tell her then about my grandmother, about her blazing beauty, and how her cheeks, too, once made curves that were perfectly rounded. But Katu would want to know everything and I would have to tell her that the cheek has collapsed onto the bone beneath, so I just looked at her and shrugged and let her question slip away over my shoulders.

Perhaps, I let it go because I, too, do not know whether all hopes and ambitions must end this way. I am reminded of this when a letter arrives from my mother, a lone letter in a blue envelope: Great Aunt Khadijah has died. Alone in my room, I remember her laughing face, her hot-mouth, her bustling figure. She had a stroke and spent several days in hospital, Ma writes. "Even with half her face fallen away and her words coming out all slurry, she gave the nurses a good cuss-down from morning 'til night. I had to cork up my ears with my hands. I never heard such language in all my born days. She wanted to go home. Nobody could get her to change her mind so the doctors just shook their heads and let her. And the very next day, she was sitting on the settee in her drawing room and one of her grandchildren went and jumped in her lap and that's when they found that she was gone. Just like that, she was gone. Aunt Shamroon said she knew it was time, that was why she wanted to go home. She had a big funeral. Everybody came. We took your Nani and I swear, when she stood by the coffin, her eyes did look and see her sister's face for the last time. She has gone so quiet now. Even her prayers are barely a breath. Write to her again, Aleyah. She liked your last letter. She even smiled."

Everyone will miss Great Aunt Khadijah but Nani will miss her most. Only her sister knew her secrets and now that earth has closed over them, Nani is alone with all that happened. And we shall never know any of it unless one day she uncovers the words that she has clapped down hard under her tongue.

CHAPTER FIVE

I throw the letters into the air to fall any which way and watch them settle on the grass. A passing summer stroller looks away quickly, not meeting my eye and I scramble to pick up the letters before they are blown away. Once my family's letters brought the sun, but now their world has turned shadowy and dark, making my mother's hands tremble and my sister's push across the page in jagged lines. Just weeks before, Shaireen was telling me about a school fair and Mansur about winning a debating competition. I had seen him with his chest puffed out and his head held high. Now their words shake the pages with fright.

"Rigged! The elections were rigged and so barefaced!" my father writes. He has pressed so hard on the paper that the ink has spurted in little blots. "They even hoisted the dead from their graves to vote, to put jumbie exes for the PNC, and now their leader, the Kabaka as he calls himself, is king!"

"We just have to lock up our mouths and stay easy, or else who knows what could happen to us," Ma says, all her words wobbling about on the page, running scared, looking for a place to hide.

When I think back to their recent letters, to their talk of the elections and what the politicians were saying, I cannot remember any phrases that warned of danger. But those signs must have been there and they must have turned their eyes away, not wanting to think that the danger could be real and that it could move in so swiftly.

Their words hurry off the pages, paying no mind to the peaceful scene before me in these gardens in the square. Even if there is a fine drizzle, the strollers will all be here again tomorrow to throw breadcrumbs to the birds and smile and talk about the weather. But this calm is shoved out of the way by the words that rush from the letters. "There is a militia of young men, his supporters," Pa says. "All of them are black. They stamp about the place in heavy boots with their faces screwed up tight and ugly. Brutes! They would shoot down their own mothers if the Kabaka ordered it. And since our man Jagan is buddy-buddy with Castro, nobody bothers with him when he goes about complaining. The Americans and British don't want a Cuba in South America, so they rest their heads easy and look the other way. And the Kabaka, he just puts on his snake-oil smile, and takes them for a proper ride. They think he is the lesser evil, but they are true-true fools if they think so. Ha!"

"You stay there safe, daughter. We are too glad you are away from all these worries," Ma writes. "You study your books. We are out of the way in our country town, so we sit down quiet and try not to breathe too hard."

Just then there is a shout, a sudden noise, and I look up startled, expecting anything, but it is only children chasing after a ball. There is nothing here to frighten them. Shaireen writes how she and her classmates stood at the roadside waiting for the Prime Minister to pass by in his open-topped car. "It was so hot and we were thirsty and, when he drove past us, he had on a silvery suit that was shining so bright in the sun we had to shade our eyes to look at him. He was wearing black, goggly glasses and we couldn't see his eyes. He looked so like a night jumbie, I was trembling all over. We were so hot and thirsty and tired from standing up in the sun. We waved and cheered like we were told to do and he put up a hand and waved back and when he smiled his mouth was all pulled back to show his teeth. Alli. Alli, I was so frightened."

Mansur's lettering is different too, swaying backward as if in retreat, but he sounds more tired than frightened. "We have to spend hours at the National Park doing stupid mass games," he writes. "We have to perform for the Comrade Leader at some celebration soon. We have to get up early and go by bus to the city to the park and spend all day holding up big cards and flipping them over to change the colours and patterns to make pictures to some kind of soldier music. I am in the one that forms a picture of his face. I have to stand up in his eye all day. My arms get so tired. Why can't we just go to school like before?"

77

Every month the letters come with more news of hard times. "The Kabaka decides everything for us now," Pa writes. "Even what we eat."

"Flour and so are getting scarce and he says we must use rice flour. But how you can make cake and roti with rice flour? That flour can't hold together," Ma continues. "He is no cook," she writes and I cannot tell whether she has attempted a feeble joke.

But I am sure of Pa's anger. His fists are bunched and his knuckles, white. "The truth is that they're stuffing up their pockets with the country's money good and proper, chartering whole jet planes to fly everywhere and so on, so there's nothing left to run the country with." Ma tells me again how "We all rest easy knowing that you are safe in a safe country. It is one less worry on our heads, daughter. You take care of yourself and keep well. All of Allah's blessings be with you."

But I am even more alarmed by what I do not hear from them. It is evident our small country town is not a safe place, even if you keep your head down. As I'm leaving the library, I catch sight of an article in the *New Statesman* about Guyana that details the phenomenon of "kick-down-the-door" crime in the rural areas, mostly targeted at Indians by AfricanGuyanese gangs. I go to sit in the square to try to recover my composure, but all I can think about is Ma and Pa so vulnerable in their shop. I want to be with them.

I sit silently for a long while, feeling the shadows lengthen. I shiver and pull my cardigan closer around me. Then I remember the note from my professor asking me to call in and see him in his rooms, and Katu: I'd promised to be back early to help her pack.

In Professor Roberts's gloomy room, my breath is still coming fast but my hands are folded calmly on my lap.

"If you're going to turn the world on its head, you'll need to take your studies further – a masters and then a doctorate – and you need to have some practical experience. You must have deduced by now that your ideas run counter to received economics and you'll undoubtedly find yourself battling against the world to prove ..."

In the growing dark, Professor Roberts cannot see me suck in my breath and hold it. I have never told him about Nani.

"It's not a new idea that economics must fit itself to cultures and not the other way around, or even that goodness and altruism – God, if you like – should drive economies. But you will have to recognize that ultimately they must be embodied in a political programme that can win the assent of voters, and work with entrepreneurs if the society is actually to create wealth, if they are to be in any sense realizable. Your ideas will require the wholesale re-education of people. Priests as leaders rather than corporate managers? Iran? But is that not a return to Medievalism? You see the problems before you?" He waves his hands. "Yes, I know, I know you do not mean God in the strictly religious sense but, you see, that alone will create enough controversy and …"

He is a silhouette against the window but Professor Roberts still does not reach to turn on his desk lamp and we sit in the dark, he talking softly and sucking on the sweet tobacco of his pipe and me with my hands neatly folded in my lap, holding my breath and seeing Nani framed by the window. In the darkness outside I see a golden glow and I want to laugh at the piles of pumpkins, some split open to show the golden insides, the flat cream-coloured seeds spilling everywhere. Baby is laughing as Nazeer cuts through the green-gold skins and golden flesh, one after the other.

"Girl, we're going to live on pumpkins forever!"

"And become golden!" Baby throws her arms up wide and laughs again.

"Yes, the golden couple. That's us."

"We'll look shine-shine in the sun."

They continue to laugh, then Nazeer says, "This is alright, Baby girl! People bringing pumpkins and squash and eddoes and everything just for standing up and talking for them. Yes, Baby, this is a nice-nice thing."

"But we can't live on pumpkins forever." Baby's voice has turned serious and Nazeer pauses, his knife poised above the last pumpkin, the blade glistening. He holds the knife like that for one moment, two moments then puts it down and leaves the last pumpkin sitting uncut, among the golden, glistening flesh of the others.

"Cut that one yourself," he says, walking away, disappearing into the darkness.

79

In the room Professor Roberts is haloed by the desk lamp that he has at last turned on. "Your masters, then a doctorate," he says, sucking on his pipe. "Any ideas yet for your thesis?"

Pumpkins. Piles of plenty. The glow of wealth.

"No? There is time," he says.

No, there is no time, I think.

"You were saying – your ideas about an economic framework that could check the rise of dictators in the developing world. Hmm. Could be something there."

Too late, too late. "I really don't think I can stay beyond the end of my degree," I say. "I've told you how bad things are back in Guyana. I need to be with my family."

"I understand your fears for your family, Miss Hassan, but your work is here now and there is much to do."

I must go, I must hurry.

He opens a drawer and says, "You need to test your ideas, see how they work, or don't work, in practice. That's why I think you'll like it at World Aid."

He smiles and talks of the future while I tremble like my mother and feel the fear of my brother and sister. My father spreads his hands as wide as a barricade before us and Nani turns abruptly and looks at me before turning back into the night. I have never told Professor Roberts about her, nor about the fragility of a world that breaks from being held too tight, of words gone wrong, and a length of rope as long as eternity. We have only talked about economics, argued rather, since he believes that the world works best when it fits itself to systems for creating monetary wealth. I always counter, questioning his definition of wealth itself.

He tap-taps his pipe against the ashtray then hands me a business card. "World Aid is a young organization, just twenty years old," he says. "It helps poor communities all over the world, but never imposes itself on people. They listen, work to under-stand the people and their culture, then they co-operate with them to design projects that will work best for that community."

"The pieces do not fit," I say, the words coming unpremeditated into my mouth. They refer, I think, both to how I feel and what is going on back home.

Sweet tobacco and words that fall gently in a lamplit room do not sit easily with soldier's boots, pointed guns and kick-down-the-door crime. Professor Roberts puts up a hand, so he must have heard my distress this time.

"Think about it first. Rushing away would be a solution for now only, so think carefully. You could intern with them next term, then who knows, maybe a job? You'll like Ms. Nath. She's the director. An altruist at heart," he says, then adds, chuckling, "so always in need of help with balancing the budget. I have told her about you."

He grows serious. "In a few years, you'll be ready to return home, and by then, maybe your country will be ready for you."

I walk away into the summer night, pulling my cardigan close again. "I must hurry, I must hurry." My breath is short. "Hurry, hurry." Streets, buildings, fences fly past. I feel a scream rising in my throat, but it is shut-in, silent. I stop and look around thinking there is no one to hear it anyway. Would Nani? Would she hear it and think it was her voice and put a hand to her mouth to stop it up? At the house I want to run up the stairs to my room to sit in the dark, but Katu is there, with her door open, waiting for me, surrounded by suitcases, all open and half packed. She is returning to her family, and to her marriage. From the open doorway, I watch her fold and lay each piece of clothing carefully in the suitcases. She is to marry a month after she returns and all her movements flow one into the other, seamlessly. Everything is arranged for her; there is nothing to jerk her to a stop, not even a hesitation.

She will make a beautiful bride, I think.

"Where were you? I leave tomorrow and I may never see you again." She circles me in her arms. "You are trembling. What is wrong?"

"I'm cold."

"But it's warm tonight. Look, I opened the window."

"The sun has gone." I step over to the window and pull it shut. Katu looks at me. "Is it home?"

When I do not answer, she rocks me like a baby, making shushing sounds. I shall miss her gentle ways.

She must not know that everything has changed, that inside me is only darkness and confusion, that no weddings happen there, not even hers. Only a week ago she had shown me how to wrap the gele and drape the ipele on my shoulder and has promised to send me some of her wedding material so that I could wear the gele and ipele on her wedding day and be part of her bridal party.

I had sat before her mirror and balanced the gele with its peacock fan of pleats on my head. We had giggled like schoolgirls and Bea and Vivi had joined us and tried on the gele too. They had come a year ago, two Filipino nursing students who had taken Vindi's and Cassie's places. They were small and light as dolls and the gele kept slipping off their long, silky hair. Our giggles had attracted Miss Wickham and she had clapped her hands in delight, thrown the ipele over her shoulder and stepped regally around the room.

"Shhh," Katu says and wipes my eyes dry. "Shhh. You're right; it is cold tonight."

The next day, she is gone, waving like a princess and disappearing when the cab rounds the corner. Bea and Vivi and Miss Wickham are there on the front step too, waving.

"Come, gels, some lemonade. It's going to be hot again today," Miss Wickham says, but I pull my cardigan close around me and settle into my room, shutting the window tight, and watch the snaking vines climb and climb, weighted down by the fat, blooming roses.

Miss Wickham calls up the stairs, and Vivi and Bea knock on the door. Shouting, pounding noises, footsteps up and down – too much clatter. I put a pillow over my head.

The cold and grey stay for weeks, slouching along with me everywhere I go, even when the package comes from Katu, with a long length of fine cotton, ivory in colour with geometric patterns of gold. I draw it out slowly and cut it to make the ipele and gele, but cannot make myself feel the joy of a wedding. I sit before my mirror and tuck my hair into the gele as Katu had shown me. The turban looks like a fluffy confection on my head, with its crowning fan of pleats, something I might have made up in a sky dream as a child. I had married many times as a child, always dressed in bright, spangled gowns, and wearing smiles as broad as my face. There were never grooms in these affairs – events that starred me, my gowns, the chandeliers and marbled halls. This seemed prophetic now. Jeremy and I had long since drifted apart. Our silences when we met had grown longer and more uncomfortable.

Now I peer closely at myself, wondering at my face and how it might seem to others. Long nights of study have given me tired eyes and harsh winters red, dry cheeks, but it has changed little over the nearly three years I have been away from home. At the beginning of my second year I cut back my hair like the wisteria and rose bushes that Miss Wickham prunes. I took the large pair of scissors from the kitchen and cut it straight across the bottom and got rid of its bushiness. But my face has not changed at all. I feel that I could slip back home, live within those walls once more and no one would know that I had ever been away. They would look into my eyes and know that they had not yet measured the depth of the world; they would look at my face and see that no real experiences had yet sculpted contours to my cheeks. I would be found out as the daughter who had left home all wide-eyed and baby-faced and returned the same.

Perhaps, working in the real world might change all this. I dig out the business card Professor Roberts gave me and telephone Ms. Rani Nath.

"Yes, Ian and I are old friends, or foes, however you wish to see it," she says, laughing. "Oh, the ideas of that man! He thinks people must bend themselves to nicely thought-through academic theories. We know it's quite the other way around, don't we?" She laughs again and tells me to come by her office in the morning.

She is a small woman, five foot nothing, but because she is always on the go, talking, walking, her arms flying and wheeling through the air, somehow she appears larger. Over the next few years, I get to know her well, know all the colours of blue she wears. It is her only colour. She wears saris of royal blue, sky blue, the turquoise of the ocean, and blues that are steeped in the colour of midnight. "Who can argue with the colour of the sky?" she would ask, laughing.

But our first meeting is all seriousness and Miss Rani, as she is known to everyone, questions me about my ideas on everything: economics, politics, religion, my career and myself. I think I sound brash, rushing about and grabbing at every thought that comes into my head. Miss Rani's face remains closed, composed, and I feel that her steady eyes are noting every nervous laugh, every hesitation.

"Sounds like they need your help back home. Ever thought of going into politics?" she asks when I stop to find my breath.

"No, no, I could never be a politician. The power goes to their heads and they become corrupt. I just want to help people improve their lives, to do better."

"But that, my dear, is politics, and you're too young, anyway, to say 'never'. But I can see why Ian recommended you to us. We're very careful about who we recruit because we're very serious about being respectful of other people's ways. We have no time for the kind of help that is tied up with advice about what's good for you. So, yes, you can spend a few hours a week as an intern with us this year and when you graduate you can become an assistant development officer. Probably part-time, and we'll work out a schedule so that you can continue your studies. You must get your masters. Economics? Political Science? Have you thought about it?"

She is talking very fast, and I am about to say that my scholarship only covers my first degree when Miss Rani adds, "Ian and I have discussed this and think we can recommend you for a grant from the university you will attend – the London School of Economics? That plus grants from World Aid itself, and, maybe, even the British Government through its Overseas Development Office – that should see you through. Ian expects you to graduate at the top of your class, you know. He thinks you'll make an important mark somewhere, someday."

Miss Rani laughs and I swallow hard, pressing myself into the back of my chair. I had expected to return home and become a civil servant, overseeing such projects as installing a new water pump for a village well, adding a canal or bridge to a rice field, building a new cottage hospital for a riverside town. It would be reward enough to make a difference to the lives of small communities around my country, to see fresh water spring from newly fitted pipes and children skip their way down evenly paved roads to a village school. It would make my parents proud. In truth, it was to be a life remarkable only for its ordinariness. I would sit once more at Nani's knees and tell her about my projects, so that she could see the hut-shaped hospitals and schools built in forest clearings, or the spread of new farms funded by some global agency. She might even smile at all the pictures I would draw for her, as she did when I was a child.

I manage to nod and mumble some words of thanks to Miss Rani before I find myself outside, walking through the summer air, stopping to look in shop windows, catching the reflection of myself, smiling. When I arrive home, there is a packet of letters on the hall table and I sit in the sun in the drawing room and read my family's news. Their letters have started to lose their panic. They sigh instead, and family news and events have drifted in again to their conversation. They even joke about the Kabaka now. He has moved into a large colonial house next to the zoo, my father writes, and now everyone calls it the Big Monkey House. His words dance with laughter before they settle down to tell me about the people who have formed small groups to fight the dictator. "Some of them are good men. There is one young black leader, Walter Rodney, who is hitting out at the Kabaka at every turn. He is a good man, a historian, and he knows what he's talking about. Crowds and crowds of people go to his meetings, so I don't see how the Kabaka will let him live.

"Look at this, Aleyah. Look how easy-easy I can talk of such things, of one man killing another! I have never in my life even thought of such a thing and now it can fly out of my mouth just so – that the Kabaka will kill Walter. And when Walter goes, it ends, because many of the people around him are the Kabaka's old pals, people from the middle-class city set. It's not the corruption and terrorism and racism and brutality and breakdown of every-thing that vex them. No, no! They're vexed up because the Kabaka has gone and taken away their electric lights, and water from their showers, their Christmas apples and grapes. He even went and banned Christmas! I'm not joking. He said Father Christmas is a white man, so there's none of that any more. He said there are no pine trees and snow in Guyana, so all their artificial Christmas trees and twinkle-twinkle fairy lights – banned! He put up one long, ugly Long Lady in a corner of his house with gifts all round her and told them that this is how they must do it, that Christmas is a local thing. So the boys round here got smart and built Long Ladies to sell to the city people. I think the Long Ladies are too glad. They retire now. Since I was a small boy they had to go and dance up in the streets every Christmas time, but now they can just stand up in the drawing rooms and receive gifts like the mistress of the house!

"I swear if the Kabaka gives these big-shot city people lights and water and Christmas, their revolution will be done and over quick-time and everybody will be smiling. Should I laugh or cry, Aleyah? Why do I feel like I want to do both?"

I hear my father sigh as he puts away his pen and my eyes drift over and pick up my mother's line that Allah never gives us more than we can bear, daughter. "Everything is breaking down more and more and you can't get jobs, or foodstuff to sell if you don't have a party card. Did your father tell you he has a party card? He had to get one. It's only the government has any foodstuff to sell now – split peas, onions, even sugar and rice that we grow here! Without the card you can't get anything. So he's a member of the Kabaka's party. So the card says. We have to do what we have to do, eh? This is no time to make style about what we believe is right, Allah forgive us."

I can see my mother raising her eyes to the heavens and I hear her sigh, but when I turn to Mansur's and Shaireen's letters, they are laughing and calling me over to look at their friend, Ramesh. "He went into a big hole that goes all across the street – splash! – and the bicycle tumbled in and he landed in the mud," Mansur writes, and my sister picks up the tale, "He didn't know the hole was so deep because it was filled with water. The whole street is holes now and when it rains it's like a big trench."

"He looked like he was made from mud. We call him the Mud Man, now. It was so funny. And his bicycle got drowned. We had to get a rope and pull it out like it was a big fish. You should have been here," Mansur continues, and their laughter lifts off the pages and spreads itself out in the room.

The warmth spreads into my reply to them and when they write back I find it there again. "Nani had a smile so wide," my father writes, and I can see him stretching out his hands, pushing his fingertips out to their furthest length, "when she found out that you will be staying on to do your masters in Economics. Her humming got so loud that the neighbours wanted to know why we had turned up our radio so loud. It's true! They couldn't believe it was Nani's voice standing up so strong after all these years. She has got quieter again, but she is too happy to know that you are going to ask all these things like how come the world is letting women waste all their talents and so on, and how the world has to change the way it thinks."

"It all sounds so big and important, daughter. All I ever wanted to do in life is to look after you all and see you all happy," my mother writes. "But you do your work. Your father is so proud, he's killing everybody who comes to the shop with talk about your thesis and your new work and things like that. It's different times now for all of you with your education and so on. Shaireen is talking about going away to study, but I don't know – all she really wants to do is to make merry and dance. Like Pa. She looks so much like him, too, and now that she is a young lady, I see how the boys round here are looking at her. She thinks I don't see how she smiles at them from the corners of her eyes, but I have my eye on her all the time even when she thinks my back is turned."

I hold the pages to my breast and close my eyes to stop the roses from climbing all over them, so that I can see instead my mother and father, Shaireen – a young lady! – and Mansur, almost a teenager now, and Nani, singing loud enough to disturb the neighbours. I laugh and hum one of Nani's tunes, letting the sound climb.

I met Dean shortly after I started working at World Aid, at a fund-raising dinner for a sister charity that Miss Rani supports. "My invitation is for two. Come with me. It's time you got out and met some people, you know, other than university types. We might even find you a nice young man," she said, but seeing how I rolled my eyes, added, "No, probably not. By the time they're rich enough to be a little charitable, they're too old. But, just maybe, there'll be a rich *and* charitable young man, eh?" She tossed the border of her sky blue sari over her shoulder and was gone. "Be ready at seven."

I was ready when Miss Rani arrived, but she stopped me at the door and looked me up and down. Without a word, she stood me before the hallway mirror and dove into her beaded evening bag for her lipstick, powder and a tumble of little jars and brushes. When she reached on tiptoes for my face, I leaned forward. I sensed the hallway filling up but no one spoke. I felt my face being patted, my cheeks rubbed, my eyelashes brushed, my lips rouged, and my hair being brushed and fluffed and sprayed.

"Ooh, I always knew she was a lovely girl," Miss Wickham said, clapping her hands.

"It's like Cinderella going to the ball," Bea said.

"Where she'll find her prince," Vivi added.

They clapped their hands and giggled, and when I looked in the mirror I saw that I had flawless skin, high cheekbones and large eyes, that my lips were full and prettily pink, and that my hair was curled softly to frame my face. I smiled and my pink lips lifted my cheeks even higher, but when I saw Miss Rani and the group gather behind me with their chins in their hands, my smile trembled at the edges, then fell flat. They were eyeing my green velvet skirt and short black jacket, looking at it through squinting eyes. For several long moments, the only sound was the ticking of the hallway clock until Miss Wickham clapped her hands again and scurried off to her flat, returning with a fringed shawl that she drew out from a wad of white tissue paper. It was of jade silk with a border of delicate pink flowers. "It was my mother's," Miss Wickham said, throwing it over my jacket with a flourish. They all smiled and stepped back to look at me and I twirled like a ballerina in the narrow hallway.

"Come, we'll be late" Miss Rani said. My flatmates rushed to the door and waved as I got into the car.

"Bye, Cinderella."

"Lose a slipper."

"Find your prince."

At the dinner, I sat with a group of young people around a large round table jammed with flowers and crystal goblets and linen napkins folded artistically into the shape of lotus lilies. I chatted with my dinner companions to the left and right of me, the conversation drifting this way and that. I was paying little attention to what I was saying when there was a loud laugh from across the table.

"You've never been to Kew Gardens or the Tower of London?" He had dark brown eyes and wavy hair and he was speaking to me. "And how long have you lived here?"

"My fourth year," I answered, making the words snap.

He laughed again. "And have you ever been out of London? To Paris, to Amsterdam? To Stratford, or Edinburgh, maybe?"

"No." My tone implied that I did not care either, but he did not seem to notice. He moved around the table, bringing his chair with him and wedging it in beside mine and, even before he sat down, he asked, "Would you like to see something of the country, maybe even the Continent? I can arrange it."

And so, it was going to be arranged: trips around the countryside, a tour of the city, flights to Paris and Rome, and Amsterdam blooming with tulips. It was going to happen. He would arrange it, this young man with the waves in his hair and a laugh sitting readily on his lips. He knew I was a girl from back home the moment he saw me, he said. "The face, the hair, the voice: I still remember. I was seven when my parents left for England, but I remember."

His name was Mohammed Dean Yacoob, but he was known as Dean. He was a trainee accountant with the Angus Bank, but one day he was going to be a vice-president and then president. He was going to take all the banking examinations and business management courses needed to get there. "The way the world does business is changing fast and the industry has to change to provide the services needed. I have already designed several strategies to do this for Angus. I have written them up and passed them on to the management already and I expect I'll be ..."

When he paused to ask me about my work, I found I could only stumble around a few ideas before ending abruptly in mid-sentence with a shrug.

He smiled and gave my hand a reassuring pat before picking up the conversation again. He told me about his ideas for developing the bank as an international institution and I looked at him closely as he talked, saw how his face changed – now serious, now laughing – with the turn of the conversation, how all his features were so handsomely assembled, how his broad hands moved through the air to give shape to his words. I knew I would marry him.

The evening flew by and I hardly spoke. I felt no need to. When Dean complimented me on my shawl, and my hair, how it curled onto my cheeks, I smiled graciously and, when dinner was over and we stepped into the cool night air, I looked into his eyes and knew that I was pretty. When he pressed my hand to say goodnight, I nodded and smiled. There would be time enough for talking. It would be arranged.

When I arrived back home, Bea and Vivi ran down the stairs and followed me back up to my room when I swept past them without a word, smiling, floating. Their questions rushed at me from all sides.

"What's his name?"

"Is he tall?"

"Is he handsome?"

"Did you kiss?"

They crowded into my room and I smiled at their eager eyes, then looked in the mirror and when I saw myself and my room and my friends reflected there, I knew then that this was not a dream. I had not said anything to Miss Rani when she had teased me on the drive home. I had hugged my excitement close, wanting to keep it to myself for a moment before I shared it with anyone. But with the girls pressing me with their questions, I gathered them close and told them everything. My words sang and danced about the room and they picked up the rhythms and added to the story.

"When will you marry?"

"Will you wear a gown of lace?"

"Of brocade?"

We laughed. I felt as if I had stepped into a familiar story and all I had to do was follow its path to the happy ending.

We went, Dean and I, and looked at Stonehenge and Stratford-on-Avon, Brighton Beach and the Cotswolds. We travelled by road, Dean at the wheel of a rented car, and lost our way on pretty country byways bright with rape seed, or sped by train past the backs of narrow houses with washing hung out to flap in a cold north wind. In Paris and Madrid and Amsterdam, we stayed at hotels (modest, Dean said, but exciting to me), visited old churches and laughed as we bought souvenirs of gaudy, glass-domed scenes that shook with snow.

He would take my hand when we walked, and hug me warmly and stroke my cheek and I would respond with shy smiles and soft looks, although, with time, my hands felt easeful enough to trace the curve of his cheek and the arch of his brow, and kiss the lids of his eyes so that they would close over their view of the world and see, instead, the dreams that lived in the light of the mind's eye. Then, my head on his shoulder, we would pass sunlit afternoons feeling sure that the world was safe.

His parents were welcoming from the start, from the very first time Dean took me home to Finchley for Sunday dinner just weeks after we met. They asked me about my family and I talked at length of my parents, and my brother and sister. I brought them all, talking and laughing, into the small dining room with its flock wallpaper, its dark, heavy furniture and chiming clocks, its table set with floral china placed ever so precisely on tablemats with reproduction misty Turner landscapes.

"Your grandparents? Are they still alive?" Mr. Yacoob asked.

"Nani, my mother's mother, is," I answered. "The others died years ago," I added quickly, wishing the conversation away from talk about grandparents.

"I'm sorry. My parents are still there, back home. They've visited us a couple of times, but Neisha's parents," Mr. Yacoob said, nodding towards his wife, "are both gone now."

"We must meet your family one day. They must come and visit." This was Dean's mother. She was a pleasant woman, very motherly, with ready smiles that plumped out her round cheeks. Both were retired. Mr. Yacoob had worked for the BBC World Service for over thirty years as a radio engineer, and his wife had been a secretary at the Commonwealth Institute in London. They had left Guyana in the fifties when Britain was open to immigrants from its colonies.

"You're stripped of everything – there's no family, no friends, no known landmarks to help you; it's cleansing in a way, the cleansing of sacrifice. You give up your homeland, everything you know, and surrender yourself to faith. It's you and heaven alone and you've got to make it," Mr. Yacoob said, then fell silent.

He held this reflective mood for several moments, then said, "Looking at our country now, I thank God we left when we did. Suffering racism in your own country; that would be harder to bear." The talk turned to the political troubles at home, fears for family members still there and plans to get them out.

"You won't be going back, Aleyah, will you?" Dean's mother asked.

"Not for a while," Dean said, before I could answer. When I looked at him quizzically, he added, "Well, you've just started your masters programme."

I nodded but explained that the government would expect me to return to work there – that it was part of the agreement for the partial scholarship they had given for my first degree. "But my parents are worried about my return. I would have to toe the line or be unemployed. There's no other choice."

"You could choose to pay off the scholarship, couldn't you?" Dean asked.

I smiled at him. "Yes."

"And stay?" This was his father.

I turned to him. "Yes."

At once, as if everything was settled, Mrs. Yacoob rose to clear the table and I offered to help with the dishes. In the kitchen, she talked about Dean without pause, as if she had stored up a stock of information that she'd been waiting to release once she found the right moment. She told me about his work, his school days, his friends, what he liked to eat, even his former girlfriends.

"English girls with stout ankles and spiky hair. Cha!" she said dismissively. "Not for him, I always knew it."

Dean had already told me about his sister Fazia's marriage. She had married an Englishman, and his parents, even though they doted on their beautiful granddaughter, were stiff and formal around Michael, their son-in-law.

"It's not that they dislike him," Dean had said, "but for all their settling into a new life here, they still long for the way things were back home. It's sentiment, pure and simple."

I knew I fitted these sentiments. With them, I could be the daughter I was to my parents. They didn't wish me to be a sophisticate, a beauty, anything exotic at all. I was known here. I was not required to explain myself and I knew, without even thinking it, that this would please my parents. They would know that I would not put aside all that I was to them and become a stranger.

"Do you like to cook?" Mrs. Yacoob asked as I wiped the plates and drinking glasses and put them away in the tidy cupboards. Without waiting for a reply, she launched into a discussion of the respective merits of the rival food shops in the area. Even if I'd had the chance to reply, I would hardly have told her that I didn't cook much at all, and that whatever I did had to do with opening tins, or packets of stuff that were ready in minutes. She did not ask about my studies or my work. I expected that Dean would have told his parents about these, might even have told them about my thesis, but his mother's steady chatter never paused to change direction from shopping trips and bargain hunting.

"Dean is easy to please, really. He's never one to fuss," Mrs. Yacoob said, smiling, taking a dish from me and placing it carefully on an upper shelf.

"Oh, my boy has great ideas, he'll go far," his father said, after we had settled onto the chintz couch and armchairs in the drawing room.

But the darkness that I know can fall so swiftly is waiting for me one winter's evening when I return home late to find a lone letter in a blue envelope, see the familiar stamps, and rip it open to find Nani screaming.

"We took her to doctors and everything, but no one knew what to do. Your father said she's frightened that what she has dammed up all these years will break loose and trouble the world again. He says she's frightened that the past will get up and walk about on the earth again. I tell him to shush his mouth when he talks like this, but I don't know what to think, daughter. We only know that when we read her your letter she started to tremble and rock herself hard in her chair, then her mouth opened and she started to holler and the screaming pitched itself clear out the windows and doors and made everybody round here shut up their houses. Mansur and Shaireen, big as they are now, got so frightened. She took to her bed for a whole week and more and she was just sinking away like it was her grave, but I think she got so tired that she was waking up every day and finding that she was still breathing, she got up and started to hum again, but all her songs are sad. We don't why your news has upset her so, but we are so happy for you that you and Dean are engaged. He looks like a nice boy and his family sound like nice people."

I put the letter away in a drawer and pick up the photograph of Dean that sits on my dressing table. I look at it carefully to see if I can find traces of anything that could have created the fears that had risen up to haunt my grandmother. His hair is combed back in waves from his smooth, broad forehead, and my eyes follow the straight line of his nose and the gentle curve of his dark eyes. He is smiling up at me, leaning into the camera for a classic studio portrait.

I see nothing that could have raised such alarms, created such unease, so I replace the picture on my dressing table, positioning it so that Dean leans into the light from the window, and I push Ma's letter, push Nani's screams and all her sad prayers, into the very back of a drawer and snap it shut.

CHAPTER SIX

I have different eyes now. They no longer skim the surfaces of things but look deeper, see below the horizon's edge. It can be uncomfortable, making me shift my balance from foot to foot or close my eyes against both light and darkness. I wonder at Nani holding back all that her life has seen behind her eyes. I wonder at her strength and tremble. I have so many disarranged pictures crowded at the back of my eyes and I keep them disordered, apart, pushing against each other and never falling into place. I work hard at this, this disordered pattern, and have come to discern even the slightest change in the quality of light from moment to moment, and try to keep each bit of time neatly contained within itself – as I am doing now, watching Dean, his head bent over a pile of books and haloed by the desk lamp. He is still; his breathing alone turns his stillness into a moving picture. As I watch him, his back hunched over, his lips set in a taut line, other pictures push their way into the night's quiet.

I see him laughing, his cricket bat over his shoulder, swinging off to play a game with Trevor and Raj and a host of friends. When was that? A year ago? It must be longer because he has been sitting at his desk for long ages, poring over books on finance and investment for examinations that come and go, then come again. Yes, it must have been years since Trevor and Raj stopped coming around to take him away for a game and a pint at the pub afterwards. I am sure they are still laughing and slapping each other on the back somewhere – but not here, not in this stillness that is tight with tension, broken only by the slow turning of the leaves of a book.

Was it that, then? Trevor and Raj taking their laughter

elsewhere, no longer calling for him because an examination was always imminent and they were left standing on the front step, shifting about on their feet as he waved away their friendly banter about "all work and no play". In the end, they'd shrugged and given him up. I can only guess at what a loss this was for Dean. I know that he's been at his happiest, most himself, when he was playing cricket or other games. And this happiness he denies himself to study for exams I fear he will never pass. It took me years to admit this truth to myself, and I realize that, without thinking about it, I'd been keeping my own successes from Dean out of consideration for all that he was not achieving.

As I see him bent over his papers, I reflect on how the joy has slowly drained out of his life. I remember his response to Arek's birth that spring morning bright with cherry blossoms. I see Arek so soft and tiny, and remember how his warm, baby scent had taken the edge off the birthing pains. Sweat had poured and pain had rammed its way like a gnawing animal into the world, devouring, spitting, cursing. It had arched my back and fisted my hands and pulled my face into contortions. Dean was there. I remember crushing his hand and looking at him, my teeth clenched, my breaths coming thick and fast. I screamed. I know that I had screamed and he had held onto my hand and wiped my brow and seen Arek push his way into the world, crying his sweet baby cry as soon as he was born. I had lain there, spent, savouring the end of the pain, the miracle of the tiny, breathing baby and watched Dean curl him close to his chest, still bloody, his black hair thick and matted, his eyes closed against the theatre's lights. Dean had smiled at me and kissed me on the forehead. "Look how tiny he is," he had said, tears in his eyes.

This freedom with his emotions has gone. As the years have passed I have come to hope that the clasp of a hand or a move to steady me on my feet expresses some poetry that he could never say. Even with the boys. There used to be rough-and-tumble play with lots of shouting and laughter, especially from Arek, who had his father's strong neck and large square hands and enjoyed games that had to do with running, jumping and throwing balls. He and Dean would make whooping noises in the back yard while Omar would come back indoors to read a book and curl up quietly like a cat in the sun. Dean and Arek would run after him and try to pull him back outside. Dean would tousle Omar's hair before quickly pulling away his hands and laughing and walking back to catch a ball that Arek had thrown. Omar's eyes might follow him for a bit before he turned back to his book or came to me for a hug.

I see the same patterns in Dean and his father. After his parents arrive, laden with toys and sweets for the boys, begging indulgence with laughter and waves of the hands that a little sweet never harmed anyone, Dean and his father settle into conversation, his father's voice booming all around the room. He does most of the talking with Dean nodding, agreeing, and rubbing his hands together. His father draws the familiar grand pictures for him, always sure that the first rung of the ladder of success is just within his son's grasp.

"Just keep at it, my boy. Nothing comes easy. Even the greatest minds had to get through setbacks. You just keep at it."

Dean smiles and shrugs and nods. I watch him and say nothing. I am part of a silent life, and I cannot help but think of Nani and Pa Nazeer. But I push the thought away just as Dean shifts around in his chair and looks at me.

'They would like this one," he says. "There's a big yard. Lots of room to play. Arek is already bowling like a champ." He is looking at a brochure of detached bungalows with bright bay windows and tall chimneys set amidst emerald lawns with neat hedges and beds of sunny flowers. There were drawers full of these brochures. Houses for Dean to pin dreams to, I think, watching his face light up.

"It's just south of the city. I could get the train in and …" I listen and smile. I am not expected to speak and soon he will turn back to his books.

It was Arek's birth that had first hunched him over his studies. With Omar, the piles of books had just grown higher, and Dean's lips more taut, as if he was under intense pressure to prove himself to his sons. Was that it, or was it his father's bright ambitions, or his friend Raj making manager of the Oxford Street branch?

I look out of the darkened window. When did the light go? I'd missed the tiny signs of the darkness moving in. Two babies to

97

take care of, one after the other – like twins almost – growing responsibilities in my work with World Aid: all that had filled the days to bursting for years and left little time to notice any change in the light.

The tick of the hall clock is loud. Pages rustle. They measure time, apportioning the seconds, the minutes, that build and grow into hours, days, weeks, months, years.

We had been so delighted that Arek would have a sibling, a playmate his age. Dean's parents had pampered me, and Ma had written long letters full of advice. I was better prepared the second time, knew at least to expect the knifing pain and the sweetness after. I had been so afraid, before Arek, that I would not know how to hold him, or comfort him when he cried. But Ma had been right all along. "It's all there in your heart," she had written, and when I had felt the soft curve of his cheek on my breast, I knew what she meant. Everything was as it should be and so, when Omar was born I was all prepared, even for the busyness of two boys, growing fast and running about on their little legs. I had never noticed the distance growing nor the light sinking fast. There had been so much light on my wedding day and when the boys were born. On those days it had fizzed and danced. Everything had. Even though Ma and Pa had not managed to get a visa – so much red tape, what with so many people leaving on visitors' visas and never going back home – I knew that the sky was not so big that it would not dip at their horizon and draw them in, make them part of my wedding day.

"All the neighbours will come," Ma had written. "Shaireen will make a cake and I will cook for everyone. Shaireen is seeing this boy, Reaz. He comes from a nice family and he's a car mechanic. They will get married soon. My two daughters, married women. Allah be praised!"

Ma did not need to tell me all the details of Shaireen's wedding when it came. I knew that the house would be busy for weeks with the preparations. They would rub her with dye to brighten her skin for her wedding day, and huge iron pots would squat over fires made in pits in the back yard, and children would be running everywhere getting into everyone's way but everyone would be laughing, competing with the huge speaker

98

boxes blaring out the latest Bollywood hits. And Shaireen would dance, I was sure.

All this came back to me, mixed up in my mind with the time, a couple of weeks ago, when I'd sat in the quiet of my room and looked at my wedding shoes. They had low heels and satin bows. They'd been packed away in tissue in a box high up on a shelf in my wardrobe. Beneath the box, in its plastic bag, was my wedding dress. For some time now I'd been thinking about taking it down to the thrift shop, along with some tired skirts and sweaters and blouses, but that day I'd turned away from the thought and hurried out of the room, shutting the door firmly and running down the stairs.

I think of Ma's last letter bustling on with the news that Shaireen was expecting her first baby, and how Mansur was now at the university studying Chemistry and teaching school to pay his way. "So busy they are, but I will get them to write. When will you come to see us? Arek and Omar must be so big now."

She always asks and I always have a ready excuse. Work, travel, one of Dean's examinations, Arek's chicken pox. There is always something handy to pick up and place in the letter and I wonder whether she knows everything that is not written, knows, like Nani, the words that are held in check in the blank spaces. I think she does because she does not press the question so often now, but reminds me of Allah and His wisdom, tells me that she has me in her prayers.

I want to cry as I sit here watching Dean turning the pages of his books, but I will away all the pictures that might assemble to give reason to my fears.

CHAPTER SEVEN

I shiver in the window full of warm sunlight as I look at the letter in my hand. The words are neatly arranged in brief lines on the buff-coloured stationery of the Angus Bank's Finsbury Square branch. The rest of the papers lie at my feet waiting to be picked up. They fell as I was tidying Dean's desk, spilling out from a large manila envelope, and when I stooped to gather them up, a phrase in the half-open letter drew my eyes to look closer. I pulled away, but even as I did so, my hand reached down to pick up the letter and take it to the window's light.

All around me, the house is quiet. Dean is having a lie-in but will soon be up; he has promised to take the boys to the park for a game of cricket, maybe the last of the season since summer is drawing to a close. Arek and his friends are warming up, taking turns at batting in the garden. I can hear them whooping and hollering. Dean has been teaching Arek how to bowl spinners and I can see him showing off his skills to Jonathan from next door. Omar, though, will soon fall out of the game and drift back indoors to pick up the latest adventure book he has borrowed from the library. It is Arek who is doing most of the shouting.

"Hey, Jonathan, look out for this one!" he yells, and I can see how he places his fingers around the shiny red ball, his thumb, index and middle fingers closing around the stitched crease just as his father has taught him. He strides to the crease, does a hop and jump, brings the ball up and over his head in a graceful arc, then leans into the delivery, spinning the ball with a flick of his wrist. If he gets the wicket, I will hear roars and shouts, but there is only a hollow pock; the ball has probably been sent rolling under the azalea bushes.

Arek wants to be the star bowler when he goes to high school, just as his father was. He has heard so many of his father's stories of triumph. "I took six wickets for twenty-three against Southend Comprehensive once. We whipped them that day!" Dean's face lights up whenever he tells the story and Arek never tires of hearing it. "My team-mates lifted me high on their shoulders and carried me round the field, and the next day the headmaster had the whole school give three cheers for me at assembly."

"Hip, hip, hurray for my dad," Arek shouts and runs around the yard or the drawing room, depending on where Dean is telling the story that day, his hands high in the air.

I can imagine Dean doing the same, throwing his arms high and lifting his face to the sky in moments of victory and happiness. He had so many of those moments on the playing fields at school that he must feel he only has to reach out for the glory to be his again. I can only guess at this, guess at what drives him. Over the years, I have come to recognize the collapsed shoulders, the distracted look, the silence. Books will be put away and the desk lamp will stay unlit for months until another heap of books is assembled and each is opened, one after the other, under the pool of light during long nights of study. I used to listen enthusiastically to Dean talk about his ideas, but over the years, though not knowing enough about banking, I had begun to wonder how much he really understood. Now, I cannot bring myself to ask questions, am unable to connect with what he has to say about his latest course of study.

"Alli, are you listening?" he asked, just a few days ago.

"Yes, yes. I'm sorry."

"That trip to Kenya has tired you out. You should take a break from travelling for a while. I was saying that this new course is just right and when I ..."

I fixed a smile on my face, then let it warm to the chatter and laughter that was drifting in from the sitting room. The boys were playing with the glove puppets I had brought back from the villages I had visited. They delight in the monster faces and make up stories of fierce battles with the puppets in heroic roles – before putting them aside to run after some new interest. Being so close in age, they were almost like twins for a long while, but then Omar overtook Arek in height, shooting up into the sky, while Arek stayed squat and solid, fixed to the earth. He is the tearaway, the talkative one, while Omar is quiet and walks about with his head in the clouds. I wonder if he paints secrets in the sky as I did when I was a child. There was a break in their laughter and I heard Dean say, "… then, you see, the position will be mine. This time. I'm sure of it! It cannot run from me forever."

I remember how I turned away from the shine in his eyes, even now as I look at the neat lines, just six of them, before me. The letter is from the bank's personnel manager. It expresses regret that the post of Assistant Accounts Director has been filled and states that Dean is welcome to reapply for other positions in the future. To this, the manager, Mrs. Barbara Wilson-Piggott, has added the note that he has applied for every senior post that has become vacant, even though he does not have the requisite qualifications nor work experience. She also notes that he has received only pass grades in the banking examinations he has sat and training courses he has attended. She closes by inviting him to meet with her to discuss setting more realistic career goals. He received the letter six months ago.

He must have been devastated, yet at that time I do not remember him coming home showing any distress greater than his usual weariness. I return the letter to the envelope and the envelope to the desk, and wonder whether he met with Mrs. Wilson-Piggott. Had he sat across from her desk and let her redesign his ambitions until they fitted her view of him? Had he let her? Or had he stood before her, his shoulders spread, and told her that he was sure of his abilities, and that if they were no match for the bank's business, then he would use them to better advantage elsewhere? Had he said this then walked out of Mrs. Wilson-Piggott's office, out of the bank, breathed in the fresh air and set off with a quick and purposeful stride to place his talents elsewhere? I knew he had not. He had simply come home to sit quietly before the television, gone to bed, then woken up next morning and gone back to his desk. And still, whenever his father visits and slaps him heartily on the back and asks, laughing, "And how is my big banker son getting on? Sitting in the boardroom yet?" Dean answers brightly, elaborating on his current course of study. If he ever intimates any doubt, his father interjects, "But of course you'll pass, my boy. Top of the class, too!"

I see how I have colluded in his disappointments. I am too close to him to be as blunt as Mrs. Wilson-Piggott, and when he comes home with eyes big with sadness and a body weighted down with yet another defeat – though his words always attempt a different story – I can do little else but give him a comforting embrace. I do not have the heart to confront his distress but skirt around it, careful to find the right time to give him news of my promotions and salary increases over the years. It was months before I told him that I had been made the Financial Director of World Aid. Even though he was full of congratulations, I saw how he sat before his books that night, his back rigid, unbending.

I think of the upbeat articles in glossy magazines that urge one to take risks, go after the dream. The stories, about people who found success after radical career changes, bustle with advice, in ten easy steps, and smiling people who beam from the pages, beacons of hope for the disenchanted. Remembering that I may have one or two of these magazines stowed away in a kitchen drawer, I am about to get up when I see Omar standing beside my chair.

"What's wrong, Mum?" His eyes are large and fringed with long, black lashes. He will be handsome like Pa Nazeer, tall and graceful on his feet.

"Oh, nothing. Why do you ask?"

"Because you look sad."

I smile and tousle his dark hair. "No, I was just thinking."

"About what?"

"Things."

"What things?"

I laugh and get up. This line of questioning can only unravel, so I take his hand and head for the kitchen, "Well, I was thinking that you might like a pop and a biscuit."

He skips along beside me, then runs off with his booty to the sitting room where I will most likely find him hours later, dug deep into the sofa with a book. He will keep me company while Dean takes Arek and his friends off to the park. The noise of their play comes through the open kitchen windows as I search

103

through the drawers for the magazines full of career-change stories. One middle-aged couple now keep an inn in the Orkney Islands and are glad to be away from the grime and crowds of Birmingham. A young woman gave up nursing, travelled through Europe and Asia on her savings, wrote a book on her travels and is setting out to do another. A single mother of two started her own business sewing party frocks at home, after giving up a clerical position in a "big yawn of an office". Her business now operates from a fashionable address off Oxford Street. I read the happy-endings and try to place Dean somewhere other than the bank.

He has never shown interest in any other work, but after thinking about it for a while I place him behind the counter of a shop. He looks at ease there, smiles happily at his customers and is quick with his advice on – on what? What would he sell? I pause then fill in the picture with sporting goods: bats and balls, all kinds of balls, and nets and racquets. He is standing before a rack that displays gloves and helmets as I watch Arek run up to deliver another ball to Jonathan. He bowls him this time and Arek jumps up and down, his hands in the air, just as Dean comes up behind me and gives me a kiss on the cheek.

"Just look at him! He'll be a good bowler. Maybe he'll play for England one day," he says, laughing.

"Do you think that's what he wants to do?"

"If it is, he'll have to learn to bowl fast, like those boys from the West Indies, Courtney Walsh and Curtly Ambrose. That's what gets the wickets these days."

"Things change?"

"Yes."

"And our dreams with them?" I am treading on new ground and my heart tightens.

"I suppose."

"Have yours? I mean, have you ever thought of doing anything other than banking?"

"No. Are you thinking of changing your job, Alli?"

"No, no." I shake my head quickly, laughing, and Dean shrugs and watches the boys play.

When he goes out to join them, they crowd round him and there is a near riot as they try to decide who will bat first, but Dean settles them down and gets them to agree on a batting order. They are all happy as they troop out of the garden, everyone talking at once. Dean waves to me as he latches the gate and I wave back. Only something dramatic and compelling will get him to turn away from the promise he has made to himself and, as I watch him disappear, I know that I shall have to keep watch on the moments, the events of our lives, and wait for the time when I can fetch him in from his despair.

Although I am travelling again, I am never away for more than a week at a time, two weeks at most. I am not just inspecting aid projects any more, but meeting with government officials, and attending conferences around the globe. The ease with which I have grown into my work surprises me. I never expected, when I started, that I would, just twelve years later, be seated so high.

Miss Rani waved this away when I confessed it to her. "You don't know how very able you are, my dear. You could do anything you put your mind to, you know. I'm sure of it. You have the passion and the will, and those, my girl, are what are most needed when you're setting about to change the world."

This idea amuses me, seated as I am at a small desk crowded with reports and financial statements, the dry statistics of the world's pain. There are so many times when, even as I pack my bag to leave at the end of a project, I am made intensely aware – by the large, liquid eyes of small children, by the old men hooped over walking sticks, by the rounded bellies of pregnant women – that I am leaving behind work that is unfinished and may stay unfinished for years, maybe even during the lifetime of children yet to be born, maybe forever. The big picture always cries out for more, and it is easy to become overwhelmed, to lose all hope if I do not focus clearly on the task directly ahead of me: check the reports, the budgets, the personnel and skill requirements, the time frames, and decide yes or no on building this school house or that village health-care centre. Finances are always limited and I try not to weep for the projects that are set aside: the eyeglasses for senior citizens so desperately needed in Guatemala, or the women's business studies centre proposed for Senegal. They have to give way so that we can send basic medical equipment to help save premature babies in a hospital in Gweru, Zimbabwe. Who can turn away from that? Who can live with the nightmare of tiny graves because we did not try?

At the end of the day, I always come home to my family feeling blessed in our circumstances. Even my parents' letters telling of Guyanese woes sometimes fail to move me, and when I pick up their latest letter on my return from a conference in Delhi, I settle back into my chair and unfold it, prepared to gather up the familiar news. But I am startled by the rush of words that come from my father. They are packed tight and close, and race over the pages with excitement. "He's dead! Dead! The Kabaka is dead. There's hope again, life again. He went to the hospital for an operation. He had throat cancer. We were not surprised – all the lies that throat has told! But he died on the operating table. Never woke up. Now his supporters want to embalm him and put him in a glass case. You know, Alli, old people say that there are people so evil that the earth will never take them back into her belly. The earth will refuse him. Whatever they do with him, he will have to lie above the ground, you watch and see.

"There's already talk of new elections. They say that Jimmy Carter might come from the Carter Centre in the States, so his people won't get a chance to rig the votes any more. They were so barefaced the last time. People say that when they opened the ballot boxes to pretend to count, there were whole sets of ballots with rubber bands still round them! But now there is hope. With fair elections, we will win. It's a big fancy funeral they're planning for their Kabaka, but no news of death was more welcome than this. They'll cry long eyewater from eyes that have sunk away into their heads, because he starved them, but he's their boy, their king, and his rich life and big talk made their bellies feel full.

"Your mother started cleaning out the house as soon as we heard. She didn't say a word – just got her broom out and started to brush and sweep every corner of the house and ceiling and steps like she was sweeping out the devil himself."

This is news indeed, and I'm surprised to have missed it in Delhi. Without waiting to read Ma's letter, I find myself in the back yard pulling my cardigan close around me. It is a dark winter evening, starless and cold, and I hug myself, gather in some warmth, breathe the crisp air, close my eyes and imagine myself standing in clear, yellow sunlight. Home is never more than a heartbeat away, but now I long to be there, to be back there, holding everyone close. My work has taken me to so many far-flung countries but I have never gone further south than Jamaica in the Caribbean and that only once for an international aid agencies' conference. Our work in the region is still scant but there has been talk of developing a real presence there by setting up an office in Jamaica or Barbados. I have already provided the board and the trustees with a feasibility study. The region poses particular problems of communication and logistics and the office would have high operational costs. The board is still to make a decision, but if an office is established, I would be able to travel to the region more often, and might even be able to visit my family from time to time. I have been away too long.

Plans made a few times to visit for the summer holidays were cancelled when letters came full of fear or fury. There was a malaria outbreak, a gastroenteritis epidemic, serious political tensions. The last time it was caused by the public killing of a journalist, a Catholic priest, by thugs loyal to the dictator. I remember my father's letter asking, "Does anyone have tears enough for us?" I breathe in the cool night air and can almost feel their relief, now that they can let go of their fear. It will be a good time to visit, to take the boys.

They are old enough now to take the long journey to this world just north of the equator where the sun at its zenith pools your shadow directly beneath your feet, so that you walk through a portion of the day shadowless. They will delight in this, peer closely at the ground and laugh when they find nothing there.

All the people they have come to recognize in photographs will come alive and talk to them, and laugh, and hold them in tight embraces. I smile, seeing already how they will squirm and wipe the kisses from their cheeks. They will play with Shaireen's children – she has two now, a boy and a girl – and Mansur will set up cricket stumps for them in the back yard and bat and bowl with them all day. He is married now, to Leela, a fellow teacher at the school where he works. Ma had written over the years about her worry that Mansur would never find the right girl. "He has a picture in his head and I tell him that this is only dreaming, but he thinks I am just an old lady talking old-lady nonsense." Then suddenly there was Leela and a wedding, in spite of some trouble with her parents. As Ma had written, "Her family are Hindus and they want her to have a husband who believes in their gods, and they want her children to grow up and say all the proper prayers and do all the proper rites for their parents and grandparents and sing all the songs they have sung since long-ago times. Your father and I know how they feel, but when we talked to Mansur we could see that his mind was made up. He never gave up and her parents must have seen how their daughter's eyes followed him about, so after all their vexation they cooled right down and gave them their blessings.

"Your Nani knew of all the worries, knew how Leela's parents were fretting up themselves that this Hindu-Muslim marriage is not going to work out, but she just sat down quiet, smiling to herself all the time like a proper Miss Know-it-all. But she had it right all the time, because now we are busy preparing for the wedding. I don't know how she knew that everything would turn out alright."

When the wedding pictures came, there was Mansur handsome in his wedding suit with Leela on his arm, all sweet and shy in white lace and a billowing veil. Ma, and Shaireen and Reaz and their children, and Pa – they were all smiling. I couldn't help but notice Ma and Pa looking a little older and greyer, but Pa still stood firm and solid on his feet. His cheeks and chin had rounded out and his belt was pulled tightly around his middle. My mother was a little thinner maybe, bonier, but still with such life in her gentle eyes. Great Aunt Shamroon was also there, standing beside Nani in one photograph, looking much younger than when I last saw her. Pa had already told me how since Great Uncle Rayman died, Aunt Shamroon had turned her small kitchen garden into a little business, was selling peppers and tomatoes in the market every day, and "dressing up herself nice and even putting on some weight. She is not a dry stick of a woman any more. She's busting out all over like a barrel! And we don't know where she got her new voice from but it stands up real strong and pitches itself out loud all around her. If you come home, you'll find so much changed, Alli."

I want to tell him that I do not think so. Standing in my back yard, surrounded by bushes and trees whose shapes I have come to know well, I still remember the mango tree's wide spread of shiny leaves and the hammock beneath that would swing high enough to touch the sky. I remember the sky's deep blue that touches the earth at horizons that go on forever. Perhaps a visit would help Dean reconnect to this place. He might find as he walks there a whole new path waiting to be discovered. I pull my cardigan closer still and feel warmer just thinking of the tropical heat and the feel of the earth – hot and baked – beneath my feet. It feels good and, with the dictator dead, it will stir to new life.

Indeed, the coming elections in Guyana become newsworthy when the Carter Centre gets involved, and there is even a feature in the *Observer* about hopes for a return to democracy, and an analysis of how Cold War politics and the unholy alliances these created had thrown Guyana into such turmoil. It's no surprise that when the elections are finally held the party supported by the Indian majority wins easily. Some express surprise that for all the destruction the dictator had presided over, making Guyana almost as poor as Haiti, the African Guyanese voted solidly for the late dictator's party. There are reports that in Georgetown, on the day of the election results, there was looting of Indian shops by black opposition supporters in a bid to avenge their defeat. The rioting and looting is inexcusable, but it doesn't surprise me that the African Guyanese still voted for their own. Why should they expect a better deal when the two main parties, Indian or African supported, both operate in terms of "we 'pon top now"?

The newspaper reports of the violence are brief and sterile. I know that when my father tells it, I'll hear all the noise and fury. He does not disappoint. "All the people that came from abroad to watch the elections were left with their mouths hanging open watching these brutes. They don't know how hard those people worked to build their little businesses, so it's easy for them to break them down and burn them down," he writes, his words running pell-mell across the pages, as if they too were being chased by a mob of rioters. "That's what they went about the streets chanting: 'Bun dem down and bruk dem down' and smashing into people's shops and taking everything. And they laughed all the time. They laughed with their mouths open, big-big like jungle cats ready to eat you alive. These people will not let us breathe, I tell you. The government better have a plan ready to deal with them or else they will always strangle us."

I wince at the racial bitterness in Pa's words, curse what the situation at home has been doing to him. He was always the most open and generous of men, at ease with Guyanese of any race, but now there's this corrosive racism in his language. I understand the bitterness too well, even with the distance of London, but I have seen too much of the consequences of ethnic hatred in my work to think that such responses lead anywhere but to disaster.

Ma seems to have swept away all her interest in politics; her letter bustles with news of her grandchildren. "Yasmin and Zahir spent the whole day here on Sunday and we made ice cream. They helped churn it themselves, packing the ice and salting it down. Your father looks like a child himself when he plays with them. They climb all over him and Zahir sits on top of his head and shouts that he is on a mountain top. If your boys and Dean and all of you could come like you said, it would be so nice. It would please my heart to see you. I stopped counting the years a long time ago because the numbers were getting so big and I got frightened that my eyes will never see your face again. We are getting old now. Your father has high sugar and I get a little pain in my joints sometimes. The doctor says it's arthritis and some days I have to swallow two big-big tablets to get the pain to ease up. It would please my heart to see all of you, daughter."

I want to cut in on Dean's study, sweep him away on plans for a trip home, but his head is bowed over his books, deep in concentration, so I sit and watch him and think of home. When Dean stretches and yawns, ready for bed, I follow him up the stairs and watch him fall asleep.

Thoughts of home follow me to work next day. There are stacks of reports waiting to be assessed, but I stretch lazily and give myself over to my imaginings, watching Arek clamber up the mango tree in the back yard like a little monkey to pick the ripe fruit and eat it perched on a limb, the sweet, yellow juice trickling down his arms. He will throw one down to Omar, swinging in the hammock below, who will bite a small, neat hole at the top of the fruit and suck on its juice.

The English mist turns into rain that hammers like nails at the window. Thunder rolls and lightning forks the sky. It is almost a tropical downpour and when I peer out I see Nazeer tinkering with a car, so engrossed that he pays no attention to the rain pitching down on him. Baby comes out of a doorway with an umbrella and hauls her husband inside, and they laugh as they enter the room, dripping wet. He kisses her and they dance around the room, their clothes clinging, shaping their bodies into sculptures.

"Oh, Nazeer, you said you were going to bring us a car all bright and blue, but it's just a piece of rusty old iron." She is laughing up at him.

"But it's all in the way the eyes see, Baby girl. Look, look." He sweeps her to a stop by the window. "See how she sits low on her wheels. She'll hug the road tight-tight, and squeal round corners. See those bright taillights and the long-long bonnet. She's like a sleek ship and will take us to faraway places."

"You're a dreamer."

"But, my girl, what is life if not dreams?"

"Real things? Real people?"

"Oh, Baby, Baby, why so serious?"

"Because life is." Her mood has changed and Nazeer shifts uncomfortably.

"Come, now, is it really?" he asks, whisking her off in a two-step waltz in an attempt to recover their playfulness, but Baby pushes him away.

"No, Nazeer," she says. "You bought the car with the last of our money and still owe money on it, and we have to get food in the house. We owe money everywhere."

"But I told you – I'll bright up the car with some nice blue paint and I'll get jobs to hire it out for weddings and so on."

"A lot of people getting married all of a sudden?"

"Baby, Baby, have some faith in me, no?"

"That's my life's work? It's my life's work to sit and watch you make sport? No, Nazeer, it's time for you to get serious. I talked to Ram this morning."

"Ram who?"

"Ram Seegobin."

"Car-mechanic Ram?"

"Yes. You go and see him. He's got a job for you."

"No, Baby. I'm my own man. No one will ever throw it in my face that I can't mind my own family, you hear?"

"You'll go! We can't live on your pride."

Nazeer looks hard at her, then turns abruptly and goes back out to the yard. He stands in the mud, shuts his eyes and throws his head back, opening his face to the steady wash of rain. He stretches his arms out wide and I imagine him asking the gods, like a doomed prophet, why he has been forsaken. He stands like this for minutes while, inside the room, Baby raps at the window, calling him back inside. But he cannot hear her. Then she stops suddenly and brings her hand to her mouth, watching in wonderment as her husband lifts one leg high, gracefully bending the knee, imitating the posture of a dancing Hindu god. He draws in his arms and lets the thumb and forefinger of each hand touch ever so slightly, the gesture of wisdom used in classical Kathak dances. There, amidst the thunder and lightning, he begins to dance, slowly, creating one lyrical posture then another, each flowing effortlessly into the next. Whatever music he hears in his head, it is slow at first, then picks up a speed that catches him in a reeling grip. Mud swirls from his feet, and the drenching rain flies off his back and arms. He leaps with legs fully extended, spins, and lets his arms flow about him in movements that are fluid and graceful.

Baby watches and cannot help but smile. The hard edge is gone from her face. I wonder what my grandfather might have been in another place, another time, where his talent might have been shaped into a fine art. He could have been one of the greats. The style, the flourish, the ease of limb and movement are his, naturally. He does not ever struggle to find grace. But he never sought to learn the techniques that would have given purpose to his steps and made his body a lyrical instrument that could have told whole stories. In India, I'd seen classically trained dancers and recognized that there was a depth of reference he had no access to. Maybe he believed that his world was truly defined by

112

the mud dams that marked the edges of his village, and lacked the confidence or will to test the boundaries of his circumscribed life. Whatever it was, it made for easy acceptance, made him content to perform at fairground and wedding-house revelries. There, he was king, dancing with loose abandon, the amateur choreographing his own dance from steps and movements taken from folk, classical dance and from films, and putting them together in his own patchwork. Nevertheless, it is beautiful to watch; his spontaneity and high energy have their own appeal.

In the rain, his postures and steps express a mix of emotions. Sharp movements speak of anger and give way to slower, more sinuous ones that tell of despair. The lack of any music besides the rushing rain makes his movements more evocative, more telling. The dance ends when he kneels and slowly folds his body over, letting the rain drive down hard on his back.

At the window, Baby's face turns hard again and, even though no one is watching, she brushes away the tears as if they are a guilty secret. She sighs and turns away from the window and slowly collapses onto the floor, her face in her hands, her shoulders heaving and shaking. Then I am looking out once more on a mass of grey London buildings and I, too, want to fold myself over and weep, only I do not know whether for the present or the past.

I pick up the newspapers and scan through the employment columns for bureaus that advise on career changes. Dean never bites no matter how many times I leave such information lying around. He simply pushes away the newspaper or magazine and turns to the piles of pictures and details of houses in Surrey and Kent and Berkshire that he keeps in his desk drawer. He sifts through them, weighing up the pros and cons of commuting from this or that town or village, reading about the schools in the area, and deliberating the advantages of the twee thatched cottage over the solid bungalow with bay windows and a tiled roof. Michael and Fazia used to be drawn into these deliberations whenever they visited and were once enthusiastic allies, promising to keep an eye out for a good buy for us. But this was some time ago. Now they shift with embarrassment when Dean talks about either promotions or property. I once caught a glance between them that signified pity – for Dean, for me.

"No shop talk please, Dean," Fazia said cheerily the last time they dropped around for tea after a Saturday's shopping in Regent Street. She looked over at me, wanting help to steer the conversation, but I had already asked Becka to come and help me get the tea things ready.

She is tall like her father, slim, and has her mother's dark, pretty looks. "Mum wants me to be a model," she said. It was a bald statement.

"You have the looks and the height." She was putting out the cups and saucers but stopped when I said this. "But what do you want to do?"

"To be a chef."

"You always liked to cook, even as a little girl. You fed us so many air tarts!"

"The boys used to run away from me, remember? I would force them to sit and eat everything that came out of my pink oven." She laughed. "I want to start culinary school here, then study in France, in Europe, with the best, and have my own restaurant one day. But, well, Mum ..." She let her comment drop away and shrugged.

"Don't worry, your dreams will find you." I went up to her and pushed her hair back behind her ears, and added, "It's what my Nani would say" just as Fazia came into the kitchen, asking, "Who would say what?"

Without waiting for an answer, she picked up a jam tart and said, with her mouth full, "They're talking about cars. Dean is talking about BMWs and Jaguars!" She looked at me and started to say something, but I cut in on her with breezy questions about her shopping trip, then called the boys in from the back yard to join us for tea.

"Haven't you two grown!" Fazia said, tousling their hair when they came tumbling in to the kitchen. "You need some more room or else you'll ..." Even with my back to her, I could tell she was looking at me. She came over and stood directly behind me as I was busying myself with the tea cosy, but finding my fingers fumbly. She reached over and I felt the warmth of her hands on mine.

Just as I am recalling that moment, there's a sharp knock on my office door and Miss Rani comes in, flourishing a set of papers in her hands and saying, "I just got these. Please say yes, my dear, please say yes." She leaves the papers on my desk and sails out of the room, the pallu of her navy blue sari billowing behind her.

I fold away the newspapers – yet again they offer nothing – and pick up the papers Miss Rani has left, turning the pages quickly to get an idea of the project I am about to deal wit, but I can't take in what it's saying so I flip back to the front and read the cover title again: *The Establishment of Caribbean Headquarters for World Aid*. The report gives the details of the office to be set up in Barbados in six months, a budget for the office, the kinds of regional projects expected, and sets out a job description, salary and qualifications for the Caribbean director. To this section, Miss Rani has stuck a note: *You're the first choice. Say yes! You deserve it.*

I am stunned. My heart goes wild. I gasp for air. I had done the feasibility study and discussed the advantages of a Caribbean office, had thought how brilliant such a job would be, but I had never allowed myself to think that I could be chosen for it. All kinds of thoughts run through my mind, jostling for attention. I think of Dean and the boys, of being near to home again, of all the work we could do in the region and I laugh and rush into Miss Rani's room without knocking. She immediately gets up from her desk and embraces me. I smell her soft sandalwood scent and feel the fine silk of her sari on my skin as she hugs me and laughs.

"I knew you would agree; I told the board you would. You must go," she says. "This was made for you, you know."

I collapse into a chair and smile, unable to say anything as she continues to talk brightly. "You're one of our most dedicated staff, you know. And besides all your experience and competence, we think that your first-hand knowledge of the people – the culture, politics and so on – that would help with decision-making. And, well, the trustees and directors all think it would look politically good, too, that a Caribbean person is chosen. A little brown-nosing always helps, you know. They want to offer you the post first. If you turn it down we would have to advertise."

Miss Rani rushes past this possibility quickly and I listen with half an ear as she explains about housing for the family, the setting up of the office, and schooling for the boys. "The education

115

system is good in Barbados, but if you wish to enrol them in a boarding school here, that can be arranged."

I think of Dean. The move would be ideal. The salary they are offering is large enough to keep us all, and give him the space to rethink what he wants to do with his life – and we can decide about the boys and their schooling after a visit there. We would only be a shuttle flight away from both our families. I hold my thoughts close to me, afraid that they will fly off if I am even a little careless.

"Go home and tell your family the good news," Miss Rani says. "You can all fly out there and look around. We want you to find a home for the family and a place to house the office while you're there. We'll start making the arrangements. But, now, go home, my dear, and talk it over. And congratulations."

When I leave the underground station to walk home, I am floating. I am dancing on a cloud. I want to kick up my heels and take a stick and rattle it along the iron fences. A laugh escapes my hands and passers-by crinkle their brows at me. Crazy woman, they think, laughing and skipping around like that. I am early. The boys are not home from school yet so I drop by at Sandra's house next door to tell her to send them home as soon as they get in. Her son, Jonathan, and Arek are in the same class and our boys stay at her place until Dean or I arrive home. She eyes me oddly and asks if I am alright, saying that I look a bit peaky, that there is a nasty flu going around.

"I'm very well, very well," I answer, smiling broadly. She watches me, nevertheless, all the way to my door, and does not go back inside until I turn the key in my lock and wave to her.

The house is quiet and I walk around for a while touching things, running my fingers over chairs and tables as if already saying goodbye. I throw myself into a big armchair and say a prayer of thanks, doing so guiltily. I feel as though a prayer has been answered, though I never knelt or bowed my head or held my hands before me and asked for any help or guidance. But now I place my hands together, prayer-folded in my lap, and hum one of Nani's Arabic chants, hoping it is one of praise and thanks. I drift on a cloud of memories and imaginings until a loud banging on the door brings me out of my chair. The boys rush through the door, breathless with questions.

116

"What's wrong, Mum?"

"Are you ill?"

"No, no, nothing's wrong. Yes, I'm fine, Omar." I laugh, then add, teasing, "I have some big news."

"What, what? Tell us!" Arek shouts.

I get drinks for them from the refrigerator, saying, "When your father gets home."

"Ah, Mum," Omar says. "We won't tell. Promise."

"Tell us just a little bit now." Arek's tone is commanding.

"Well, how would you like to go to a place with white sand beaches and where the sun shines every day?"

"We're going on a holiday, yeah!" Arek shouts and rushes about the kitchen.

"No, no. No holiday," I say.

"We're going to move, live there?" This is Omar's quiet question.

"Let's wait on your father," I reply.

"We're going to live on a beach!" Arek shouts again. "Like Robinson Crusoe. Will it be very hot, Mum?"

I start to get dinner ready and am patient with the boys' questions, trying not to give too much away. They are helping me set the table when Dean pushes open the front door.

Arek runs up to him yelling, "Dad! Dad! Mum says we're going to live on a beach in tents like Robinson Crusoe and we'll go swimming every day."

Dean laughs. "Oh, we're going to a beach this summer?"

Omar says, quietly again, "No, Dad, we're going to live there, Mum says."

"Alli? What's this about?" Dean asks, still laughing.

"Let's eat and I'll tell you all about it."

We are all seated when I take a deep breath and tell them everything in a rush, the words pushing up fast behind each other, chasing each other with excitement. I tell them about the Caribbean headquarters for World Aid, that I have been offered the job of director, that it would mean moving to Barbados, that the boys could go to school there or stay in boarding school if we choose …

The rush of words is knifed abruptly. Before I can finish, Dean asks, "And you've said yes?"

117

He asks the question quietly, in an even voice, and I reply, still excited, "I've said that I'd like to do the job. Oh, Dean, just think: living in sunshine again and so much room for the boys to run about, and you, you could get a job doing something new, something different. It'd be wonderful!"

The boys' eyes are big and shining. They look at their father. He is still for a moment then we watch him fling his napkin onto the table and push his chair back so hard that it crashes to the floor, a sound loud and sharp as a bullet. The front door slams shut with a blunt, heavy thud, and we sit there together, my sons and I, swallowed up in the cavernous silence that follows.

CHAPTER EIGHT

I did not set out to be a sinner, but a sinner's eyes look back from the scrap of mirror above the small dressing table, its frame glued fast to the wall. They are dark rimmed and sunk deep in the skull. They are hollow and empty, peering at horizons that shift further and further towards a place where land and sky meet as one element. I am banished here, a disembodied being in a place without shape, colour, texture. My sin has stripped me of every feature and I am one with this nothingness. But it is comfortable. The monotonous grey rests the eyes; the featurelessness rests the mind. Sometimes the horizon shifts and in the gaps created, memories escape and I grab at them. I see myself laughing. These eyes have laughed. I am almost always younger then, and they shine bright with the belief that the years ahead would be like jewels, each more burnished than the one before.

All through my childhood, each day was picked out by the sun. It shone on home and school and friends and childhood games. Such friends I had – Sita and Indranie and May and Pammie. I doubt that any of them is sitting in a darkened room in a country where the sun is a watery orb that begrudges light. But the truth is that this damp greyness suits me, and if my friends were to visit I would hand around cakes, and our conversation would stretch out like a floating, silken scarf, a billowy cushion against the world. A whole afternoon would go by. Then, I would bustle them out in clouds of coats and scarves and say, "Come again, do," and they would kiss the air around me on parting, and I would find other such afternoons and draw them in to make long days filled with nothing but tea and conversation and brittle laughter.

It would not matter how long the afternoon lasts. Time has unravelled around me. The rhythms of light and shade that enter my white room make no difference. I might sleep in the white light and stay awake in the darkness, or might stay awake for a whole cycle of sun and shade, watching the thin light inch down into darkness and then the blackness turning solid and closing in around me, shrouding itself tight to my contours.

I might hum to myself in the dark and smooth my hair down on my head. It is cut short now, shorter than it has ever been, and easier to manage, I heard someone say from a distant place, her voice echoey and hollow. All sound comes to me as if it has travelled over huge expanses of water and desert, picking up echoes before it rests on my ear. I hear the noise of people speaking, sometimes looking at me with intense eyes, but let the words fall about my feet and never stoop to pick them up.

Sometimes, after the noise, I hear hard footsteps slapping angrily away from me. But soon, they too are swallowed up and stillness returns. Stillness? It is more a cold numbness that rests like a stone over my heart. I stay very still lest the stone shifts and crushes me.

I cannot say how long I've been here or how long I've sat at this window and looked out on this colourless sky.

I peer into the small square of mirror. My nose touches its cold surface and creates a pool of mist. They are there, my friends, at the bottom of the pool. They are laughing. I am the chosen one, they sing. They are happy that I have won, that I will fly away like a bright-plumed bird to a northern country and will return with such honours. I laugh, reaching down into the pool to take their hands so that we can skip and flounce in a ring dance until we collapse in an exhausted heap. But their hands grow smaller and smaller as I reach down, until they disappear altogether.

I turn away from them abruptly and face instead two pairs of eyes staring hard at me. Another pair steps forward and there are three. Then two more pairs. How many now? Five? Six? So many eyes. They are looking at me as if expecting something and I rummage around in my mind trying to find what it is they want, but when I look up at them, my hands are empty and my tongue forms no words. The room is heavy with quiet. It presses hard against my back. I open and close my mouth, gulping air and creating no sound. The eyes watch my fishgulping, then turn away abruptly and leave. Again I hear the angry slapslap of their footsteps fade. I never wish to follow.

I turn instead to my scrap of mirror and see my hollow eyes and draw my lids down over them and hold my breath and feel myself falling into the silver pool of my reflection. I am falling with my arms outstretched and my feet together, pointed towards the centre of the earth. I am laughing as I drift down through the silver light when my head is suddenly yanked back. Mavis has come in and is brushing my hair. She is clever to hold me back like this, by the roots of my scrappy hair.

"Your husband and sons thought you looked fine today," she says, all bright and busy, her white skin and white uniform part of the antiseptic air of my room.

I say nothing, thinking that if I make no sound she will tire and leave and I can again float down into the mirrored pool.

"And your in-laws. They came to see you too. Everyone came today."

I still say nothing.

"We're the silent one today, aren't we?"

Yes. Aren't we always?

"You have pretty hair. One day, it'll grow out again. But you'll have to take care and brush it so it won't get all knotted and tangled."

I let her ramble on like this. My thoughts are scattered everywhere and I try to grab any one of them and hold it fast for a minute or more. Nothing settles though, but a big fear comes as the afternoon sun creeps up to the window, casting long, black, slanting bars over the floor and bed and walls. Once Mavis leaves, I will creep away from their imprisonment into a safe corner and wait for total blackness to swallow up the bars. Darkness is safe. It is wakefulness that presses hard into the room, leaning heavily on my slight form as if to crushpack it into a neat parcel to be labelled and stored safely on a shelf somewhere, god knows where. Sometimes, awake in a lit world, my face finds a smile, dredged up from a memory, and it stays fixed as if determined to ready me for change. I will change, yes, into a pretty, flowered

121

frock, and Dean and the boys will come and I'll be packed and ready to return home. We shall be happy. Everything will be just as before, and we shall be happy because I'll have a nice smile that spreads wide across my face and no one but me will know how it trembles at the corners. Everyone will look at me and smile back and say what a nice change.

"What a nice change," Mavis says.

"What?" I ask, breaking my silence, suspicious that Mavis has got into my head and is walking around there casually, picking up my words and looking at them this way and that, as if trying to make up her mind whether to place them on a trolley and wheel them away forever.

"The weather. It's turned sunny. We can take a walk if you like."

"The weather, the weather, the weather." I laugh, but I feel it could crack at any moment and splinter into screams. Mavis's hands tense around the brush.

"Oh, if only everything could be like the English weather, change and change again. Just think, Mavis, we could do this or do that or the other just as we please, and no one would pay us any more mind than to say, 'She wants jam on her toast today; tomorrow she will shake her hair from her eyes and move the world around, change it around like furniture.' We can play doll's house and all the centuries will wash over us and we'll be drowned things and eat buttery crumpets at the bottom of the sea. And I'll drown so easily, Mavis, because I'm tiny, an atom of life, a whisper, no more."

The words come fast but I am not screaming. They scrape from a dry throat in whispers that barely brush the air. They hang there, suspended by a tension created by their very calmness. But from this still point anything can happen and I hear Mavis scrabbling with trays of instruments and see the small vial of colourless liquid in her hand. My head has split apart and I try desperately to hold its halves together, but my hands are weak and flap about helplessly. That is what the watching eyes say: *You are weak*. Squared shoulders, stocky and strong, eyes that stare at me hard and unblinking, that accuse me of weakness, while they display unflinching strength. Mavis makes shushing noises as she takes my arm and pats a vein until it is fat with blood. The needle pricks my skin, a welcome friend.

Darkness descends. The world has fallen down a hole and I with it. I want to sing one of Nani's prayers as I fall, but I do not remember the words and can only hum the keening tune. I make the slightest rustle of sound and fall into the long-ago music like a leaf borne steadily, lazily downward by a gentle wind.

Stay here a while longer; it's for your own good, they say. They all say that. Three pairs of eyes, doctors in white coats who talk to me from palmed chins. For your own good. Own good. Good. I am good. Yes, I am always good.

I won a scholarship, came here to university and graduated at the top of my class. A creative mind, a promising economist, said the old men in crowblack gowns and white whiskers, looking at me as if I were an exotic and splendid specimen as we drank sweet sherry and made plans for my future. When I told them that I had accepted a position with World Aid, they said it was a start. I would do their tutelage justice by setting the damaged economies of ravaged countries right.

"You could choose anything, my dear girl, the world is waiting," said one.

"A few years of work and then you must return to us," another added.

"Yes. Your PhD, you know."

"Yes. A life of scholarship."

"That's where you belong."

The room was bright with easy laughter. They were proud of their creation and I, appreciative, said my thank-yous and good-byes. I was eager to start my life. I wanted to work at something that made me feel good and made the world a little better than I found it. If I had said that, the professors would have guffawed and pressed me to seek, instead, the ladders runged with power and wealth. To help the world's poor – a waste of talent, dear girl; that's no real ambition.

And my husband agreed. His face was dark with anger when he said, "So, what happens to my years of work? What of my career? And since when do you make the decisions for the family?

I'm the head of this house. You go where I go. It's never the other way round."

I had stepped over his authority. I had overstepped mine. No, we were not partners. Whatever gave me that idea? My highfalutin theories of women's place in the world? Ha-ha-ha. Those lived between book covers. In the real world, men were in charge and their wives followed, so many paces behind.

At this point, even he knew he'd gone too far, was in danger of slipping into absurdity, and his voice softened. "Oh, Alli, come on. I have such plans for us, for the boys. Give me a chance, my dear. You don't really want to uproot us so? Just for a promotion? You are not so selfish a person. I know it, I know you. My dear, look at me. We have so much here, you and I, our family. Don't throw it away for such a little thing."

A little thing! I gasped. A basket of fruit – a couple of pears, some peaches, maybe even a precious mango from Mexico wrapped in tissue – carried home to be sliced and eaten for tea was a little thing. A chiffon scarf wrapped around cool shoulders on a summer's evening, or toenails painted pearly pink with show-off sandals – these were little things. But a career, a life's work, the fulfilment of promise, of self – were these, too, so little?

I was sitting on the edge of our bed and Dean was still talking while my mind darted off, seeking a starting point from which to make sense of all that I was hearing. I had not yet had the chance to explain that no firm decision was taken, but that, yes, I wanted to take the position, that yes, it would make for such a change for him, for the boys, for our life together, and think how nice it would be to live in an island of sunshine.

This was the morning after Dean had slammed out of the house. I had not slept and had heard him come in late and make up a bed on the couch. Our marriage had its share of squabbles, disagreements over disciplining the children and, a few times, over budgeting and finances, but nothing had ever driven him out of the house before, or made him turn away from our bed. I had lain awake all night, listening to the house, the regular on and off of the heater, the light brushing of a birch branch against a window. These familiar sounds were a comfort now the ground had shifted so violently beneath my feet. My thoughts were nightmares, wide-awake ones that did not need sleep to assemble them. I shut my eyes against them but they invaded the dark regions. Deep fissures opened up in the earth; the world was drowned in heavy waters that streamed endlessly from the sky; mountains toppled and crashed, became nothing but grains of sand to be dispersed in the wind. It was the end of the world and I alone knew it, I alone saw it, and I alone had the answer for its salvation.

By morning, I was exhausted and only then briefly slept. I awoke thinking of my family, my blessed family, and knowing what had to be done. When Dean came in, smiling, and ready to talk, I listened. I listened, waiting my turn, but, after a while, I heard nothing but the hum of his voice. I was busy scuttling after the little thing he had let fall, trying to crush down my work, my life, to see how they would fit into a scrap of handkerchief that I could bundle up and toss about like a rag ball. I was still scrambling around when Dean picked up his briefcase and kissed me on the cheek and left for work. The boys had already gone to school. Dean had been all smiles and easy chatter at breakfast and they seemed reassured that the previous night's scene was nothing more than a peculiarity of the grown-up world. They left, all of them, expecting to return to a home that would be as it had always been. Their crisis was over. It had been a storm in a teacup, easily resolved by pats on the back, a peck on the cheek, and a see-you-later smile.

I sat on at the edge of the bed, dressed for work, ready to push my feet into my shoes and set off for the station. But when I got up, I found myself walking about the house in stockinged feet, roaming from room to room as if I were in some strange, unfamiliar place, a country with a different culture and set of values which I must get to know and evaluate if I was to help the people who lived there. The landscape of chairs and tables and lamps and potted plants in a sea of beige carpeting and darker-hued rugs was unknown territory. I was a stranger here and I found myself picking my way carefully, as through wreckage. The telephone rang several times, but even as I stood over it, its urgent jangling sounded distant to my ear. I was too far away to pick it up. If I did, I would hear nothing, nor have anything to say, so I let it ring and ring until it stopped.

After travelling around the house a few times, I realized that each tour took me farther and farther away. Each time, the walls drew away from me, fell back as I advanced, leaving me to grapple with larger and larger spaces that opened up around me. I became smaller, each journey taking longer to complete as the terrain kept stretching itself out to a horizon that was empty and always beyond reach. I dragged myself onward but try as I might, I could get no fix on the place. It was a wasteland, yawning and barren. To survive here, one would have to yield to the sterile order. There was no room for challenge or disobedience. That would mean being cast out forever. The climate turned cold and I shivered. I found a blanket to wrap myself in and, exhausted by my travels, sat down on the floor in a heap with the blanket drawn like wigwam around me. I must have slept, coddled by the warmth, since someone was shaking me awake some time later.

It was my husband. His face was close to mine. It was creased with worry and he was breathing hard. "Alli, Aleyah! What's wrong? Why aren't you at work? They called me, all worried, wondered if you were sick. And I said no, Alli is not sick, she must have got delayed."

I wanted to explain to him about the alien country, the empty horizon, but I only flopped back into my wigwam in silence. I heard him talking into the telephone. His voice sounded urgent, worried. It must have been some time later that I saw feet rushing around me and heard voices – distant voices – and I felt myself being picked up, laid out, covered up, felt the first prick of a long, slender needle, and experienced my first darkness. I was on the edge of a black hole that looked down into myself. I fell into the hole, curled tight as in a womb. I slipped into deeper and deeper blackness. In that blackness, a rope swayed, golden, inviting, its loop shining like a halo. I reached for it but my hands flopped back, overcome by the first rush of sleep.

I slept a sleep deep and blank, brought on by little pills that granted sweet forgetfulness. I awoke only to feed on more pills and to slip back into the comfortable blanket of darkness. Then one day I was brought here to this pale room with its lone window. There had been another rush of feet and voices and I 'd heard my husband saying: "Can't cope. It's too much for the

126

children. Yes, a nursing home is best." And then I was here, looking out of this weeping window.

There was a long drive along narrow country roads with my husband seated beside me. He was distracted and kept looking out of the window. I was a silent bundle of warm clothes beside him. I wanted to reach out and take his hand, feel its warmth and take comfort from it, but I found that my hands were numb, could barely move. His never reached for mine. He just kept looking out at the passing fields. I felt the first stirrings of an unknown terror, a panic that if allowed would stop the heart. I could not identify it nor give it a name but I felt it stir each time I looked and saw Dean's face turned away from me, looking out at the green fields and copses that rushed past the taxi's window. He looked like a man impatient to be done with an errand he would rather not perform. But duty called, and he was obliging.

When the car stopped before a high, ivy-clad white building, gentle hands took me and wheeled me to this room. My husband watched from a place against a sky that threatened rain, watched with a closed face and hands fisted up in his pockets. He was a tight knot – head hunched low into shoulders, arms pressed firm to his sides in soldierly fashion. He too seemed to have travelled to a distant country, but his had strictly delineated borders that could not be crossed. He kept to his side of the line and watched me disappear through a door that closed with a dull thud.

He has come to see me regularly, sometimes bringing the boys and I have tried to put on my best smiles on these occasions. For their sakes, we acted as though I had been prescribed rest and quiet by the doctors after a severe illness. The boys, unsure of how to act around illness, ignored the sterile whiteness of my room and chattered bright as birds about school and friends and their grandmother's cooking. She had been helping Dean keep house and they made faces about her heavy fruit cakes and pungent curries and asked over and over, "When are you coming home, Mum?" and I would laugh and promise, "Soon, as soon as I can."

Dean also wore smiles on these visits. For the boys' sake. I know this because whenever he came alone we sat in silence. At first, silence suited me, even though I know that ours was laden with unspoken thoughts.

These thoughts are there when I open my eyes to the morning light and see the white-coated figure in my room. A young man with ginger hair and a matching complexion. He is much younger than I am but I am expected to open up to him, to his therapy, so that I can come to terms, regain my equilibrium. My life has been knocked askew but there are recovery programmes that can be applied, balm to a wounded soul, to get me on my feet again. And this young man is there to apply the balm. I ignore him. He sits silhouetted against the light, a hunched figure, and I look around him, over him, through him, and hold my silence.

What does he know of the darkness within? It has nothing to do with his neat theories of breakdowns and depressions and withdrawals. It has to do with the spirit being broken, and nothing prepares one for that. Life is built on an optimism that hard knocks can be overcome by grace, love and good friendship. Trials are to be met with fortitude. They are sent to test our strength and since none of us wish to appear weak, they are to be vanquished, to great applause, so that life can resume – the quarrel, the illness, the death in the family – all smoothed over by a life-goes-on sigh, and a sympathetic hand across the troubled brow.

So, what to make of a heart frozen and splintered into a million bits? What to make of the end of the world? Where does one go from there? This young man with the red hair, does he know? He is patient, quiet, pleasant enough, but looks baby-faced still. He is starting out on his career and has been handed a simple case of clinical depression. Each day, he comes and waits for me to open up to him, and each day I look through him and say nothing. After a time, he looks at his watch, scratches busily in his notepad and leaves, closing the door quietly behind him.

I like his silence. I like him for not pressing busy questions into the air. I like his patience. He will make a good mender of broken spirits because he knows that they cannot be rushed by earthly time. So he watches me rest in my quiet cocoon and does not disturb the air. He waits for the troubled heart to surface. When it does he will be there, ready to listen, to counsel, to calm, to catch me as I fall.

Each time I see him there I scratch around inside myself and, some days even take hold of the tail of a thought and try to pull at

128

it, to see where it might lead. Mostly they slip away before I can grasp them and look at them up close. They are elusive because my hands are weak and flap about numbly, the effects of the little pills. But my stillness and calm must have brightened everyone's hope, for the dosage of pills lessens and my hands gain enough strength to grip the end of a thought so that I can pull myself along its trail, like following a string through a maze to reach safety. The trail is confusing, filled with ghosts of the past, veiled women, some crying, some just watching with hooded eyes. A few scream at me, pelt words in a language I never understood. And there are men who smirk and some who laugh openly, pointing at me. I look at myself and see a poor figure of a woman. I'd laugh, too, if I did not know her pain, understand her desolation.

She's on an island, afraid of the sea around her. She stands alone, her arms wrapped about herself. She shivers and makes as if to step onto the water but draws back knowing that she will drown. She has no faith in miracles. She searches about her island and finds that it is empty of all but herself. No one comes to her rescue, to pluck her from her island and plant her into a future time, with solid earth beneath her feet. She is banished here, a sinner, shunned lest she befoul the air and her sinning seeps into the body of the sacred world.

She roams her island, rummaging around, looking sharply at this bit, then that, becoming aware of all its states of being: its intellect, emotions, spirituality; its dreams and ambitions; its fears. So much to contend with. How does one manage? Compromise. It is a mature word. It is used by happy people and unhappy people. You shift your ideas, your beliefs a bit to the left or right to make an accommodation that comforts you and your family, partner, friends, colleagues. You whittle away at your youthful ideals so that they fit into the grown-up requirements of the world. Then you are rewarded. Then you are blessed. Then you know peace.

I think this, sitting on the sunny island of a bench on the green grass of the garden. Spring is here and the air smells fresh and clean. A breeze blows gently. The clouds part to show blue skies and to let the sunshine warm the earth and my face, which is turned up to greet it. My hair has grown longer. I feel it brush

129

around my ears and against my neck. Soon it will swing its comfortable weight against my shoulders again and frame my face. Everything will be different. A new spirit is returning home.

Back in my room, the ginger-haired doctor is waiting. He is called Ross, Dr. Clive Ross. He looks at me and I at him, and I smile. I tell him everything. He makes furious notes and at the end, when the words stop, being completely spent, he squeezes my hands and smiles, giving a reassurance that feels like a priestly blessing.

It is time to return home and Dean comes to fetch me, shaking the hands of the doctors and saying kind words to the nurses, seemingly pleased that I am well again. But on the drive back into London, conversation flags. He only frowns and mumbles some answers to my eager questions about home and the boys. He seems shut away, distracted. Perhaps, he foresees a life confined by the markings of my illness. I want to reach out and take his hands and give them a gentle squeeze of reassurance but his closed face seems to forbid any touch. I tell myself there will be time enough. I sigh and lean back and enjoy the spring landscape of leafy trees that stream past the taxi's windows.

Arek and Omar are there on the doorstep to welcome me. So are my in-laws. They have helped tremendously with the boys and I cannot thank them enough. "You're home now. That's what matters," Mr. Yacoob says, kindly, and I start in immediately on taking over the household duties, fussing over my in-laws as if they were guests just arrived for a visit. I have to gently discourage the boys from rushing about and tugging me everywhere to show me a football Dean has bought for them, new books, and pictures they have drawn at school. Everyone is laughing, except Dean. When I look around for him, I see him looking out of a window, his hands pushed deep into his pockets. He manages a smile when the boys rush up to him, but his eyes never look in my direction. They take in his parents, Arek, Omar, the furniture even, but never look over at me when I say anything. I hurry away to the kitchen and open every cupboard, one after the other, peering inside then closing each door carefully, quietly.

I will need to get groceries, I note, and, after a brief tour of the garden, I see that I have weeks of work ahead of me to weed and trim and prepare the beds for summer annuals. Dean is hopeless at gardening. He mows the grass, but plants and shrubs and the science of tending them – he left all that to me. I enjoy it. It is so different from home, where any tree, any shrub can be planted at any point of the compass and at any time of the year. Here success means taking account of the cycle of seasons, the nature of the soil, the areas of sun and shade. I enjoyed the challenge and had laughed at my earlier mistakes, sometimes moving a tree or shrub several times until I was satisfied that it was comfortable.

I roll up my sleeves and set to work during the first week, beheading dead daffodils, weeding and mulching the flowerbeds, and poring over seed catalogues to decide on the annuals to plant this year. I want a spectacular show of colour. I want everything to be bright. I hope that by then, by the time the marigolds and snapdragons and sunflowers push through the earth, Dean will be less anxious. I am not sure what it is that makes him crease his brows but I hope that my moving through each day so much in charge will calm whatever fears he has. Thinking I can draw him out a little by talking about going back to work, I tell him I am meeting with Miss Rani on Monday.

"There'll be so much catching up to do," I say, laughing, as I prepare dinner one evening.

"My parents will be coming for Sunday dinner." He says this as if in reply to my statement, then leaves the kitchen. I hear the television being switched on in the sitting room and I stand still for a moment, the knife in my hand poised in mid-air. I do not know what to make of the non sequitur. Did he mishear me, or not hear me? I start to move towards the sound of the television but stop. He will probably just repeat the statement, no more, so I wipe my palms on my apron and say to myself, okay, I'll prepare an extra special Sunday dinner. I have three days to plan and get everything ready. It will be nice having the family together, and I'll have a chance to thank his parents properly. Maybe Dean will thaw out and talk to me. I decide on roast beef, with onions, parsnips and crisp, roasted potatoes. I will order from the butcher tomorrow, and see what fresh fruits and vegetables are available in the market. Maybe a peach cobbler for dessert, with ice cream. The boys will like that.

131

I find that I am rushing around the kitchen with a kind of breathlessness, and I stop suddenly and hold onto the kitchen sink trying to keep the lid on a rising panic. I shut my eyes and take deep breaths but hear Dean's silence, see his back turned to me at night, every night, his evasive eyes, his fists pushed down hard into his pockets – I see them all but I see them separately, since to put them together, to see the pattern they create, threatens darkness. So, I make each day full and busy, one task merging into another. Any void, any hollow could become a black hole and I might tumble into it again.

There are times when I want to face him, ask everything, but I am afraid that if I am handed silence, I will ask again and again and my voice will turn shrill and shatter the calm forever.

The dinner is a success. Conversation flows brightly and after the peach cobbler is served the boys are excused and scamper off to the back yard with a frisbee. We relax over the remains of the meal and Dean chats easily with his parents. But he never speaks to me directly. I am sure they notice.

When I get up to clear the table, his mother asks, "Why didn't you tell us, Alli?" Her voice is soft and low but the words have a hard edge.

It takes me a few seconds to fumble around and ask, "Tell you what?" I sit down abruptly.

"About your grandparents." This is Dean and his voice and look are stern, his lips pressed down in a tight line.

Swift on the heel of his answer, his mother speaks again. Her words are a torrent directed at me. "That your grandfather hung himself, that your grandmother is mad – yes, mad! – that there is madness in your family. That your nanny has given herself over to the devil, speaking in tongues all day and screaming down the whole place. You never said anything. You kept it from us all these years. When we wrote to our family back home and told them that you had to be taken away, they asked around about your family and wrote back and told us everything. You've brought all that sickness to us. Now, our boy has to live with this. And our grandsons. God help us!" She pushes back her chair and rears above me, breathing hard. Her husband pats her hand, there-

132

there, and adds in a low voice, "You should have said, Aleyah. You understand that we feel betrayed."

I sit stone still. But I never thought, I never intended, I didn't think – unfinished sentences, broken thoughts are all that come to mind. I want to say that I never intended to hide any of my family's history, that there is nothing to hide, that it never came up. I had told Dean bits, scraps about Nani's life and about Pa Nazeer's, but not the tragedy of it. I had formed the notion that I would tell it all when we visited, when Dean could hold her hands in his and look into her unseeing eyes and know her frailty as I do. But their accusations are so harsh, so sudden that all my words stay unsaid and I make no attempts to brush away my tears. To the eyes looking hard at me this appears as evidence of guilt, of the accused having nothing to say in her defence, but resorting to tears in an attempt to gain sympathy.

Through my tears, I see my grandfather walking with his shoulders borne high like a king's. His head, held aloft, reaches skyward. To live each day with a lessened sensibility of himself was like repeated deaths. He threw the rope and knotted it to save whatever was left of himself. He turns and walks away, his back straight, imperious. It never sags or slumps for even a second into the old man's slouch of his last years. He walks away into the misted distance and I see Nani, seated with her head bowed, humming a gossamer-light whisper that enfolds her like a shawl. Beside her are my mother and father, my brother and sister. They look at me with steady eyes and I catch remembrances of a life that is not without grace, a strength born of a simple belief in the goodness of the world and the men and women who inhabit it. My eyes shift back to Nani's. Her head is no longer bowed and when I look into her eyes, they brighten, come alive, and, for a split second – no more – I am drawn into their brightness.

I sit up sharply. My back straightens. I stand. I stand tall. My movements are decisive. I watch their eyes watching me, registering surprise. Their mouths open as if to speak, but before any words can be uttered, I say, "I have much to do." I smile, pointedly, at each in turn. "I must get started. Do excuse me." I walk away then, like my grandfather had, with the bearing kings and queens are born to.

Upstairs in our bedroom, I lock the door and sit by the window for several hours, trying to construct a new life. I am surprised at how quickly a new life takes hold once the decision to uproot the old is taken. Several times there is knocking at the door but I ignore it: everything has been said. Night drops outside the window and into the darkness I let slip my thoughts. My eyes are dry now. There has been enough weeping for one day. I get up, draw the curtains and switch on the lights, simple acts, but their purposefulness pushes me forward, inch by inch, from one moment to the next.

I start immediately with the closets and sort clothes into heaps: these to throw out, these to go to a charity shop, these to keep. It feels like the sorting out after a burial, like going through the paltry material remains of what was once a full life. Tomorrow, I will see Miss Rani. That is necessary too, another packing away.

She greets me warmly and I cut her off before she starts to talk about my return to work. I say quickly, bluntly, "I'm leaving. I've decided."

Miss Rani sits down abruptly and we look at each other for a long time. I do not have to explain myself. Her eyes seem to know all that I am feeling and we sit in silence for several minutes, as if at a wake.

She sighs. "I thought you would do it, you know, connect the dots, make it work, show us how."

I say nothing.

"I proposed that position thinking you had it together, you know. I'm so sorry, so sorry."

"Don't be. You couldn't know. Even I didn't. It's shocking how swiftly things change."

"Yes. I know." Miss Rani says this then holds me in her gaze and I know, without asking, the story of her divorce. "What will you do now?"

"Go home. Suddenly, I feel such a stranger here. Our dictator is dead and there have been free elections, the first in decades. There's a stirring of new life at home. It'll suit me."

"You go home, back to your country. I left mine, made a life here. That was some fifteen years ago. I felt a stranger in my own country. My children were grown, wanting their own lives. Now, whenever we meet, they marvel at all that I do." She pauses, then adds with a little laugh, "I think they're proud of their mother now."

I want to say that I hope my sons will think well of me one day but, instead, I blurt out, "I feel a failure. I feel wronged and confused. I don't understand any of this, why it's happening. Nothing makes sense any more. I just want to go home."

"When the earth shifts beneath you so violently, you no longer trust the very ground you walk on, you know?"

I find a smile and nod. "My grandmother, she left, stepped out of her life entirely. That was over forty years ago."

"Your grandmother?"

I tell Miss Rani about Nani and her silence, how a life became a death. "Nothing changes," I conclude.

"But it does, my dear. The Indian poet Basavanna wrote, way back in the twelfth century, that things standing shall fall but the moving ever shall stay."

"We keep moving then?"

"Just as the world does. But many are afraid of change. To take a chance on something new, only the brave dare. We all want the future to be better and brighter, no? It's a sweet and simple sentiment, but just as a diamond finds its sparkle only after it's cut and honed, so too the future is shaped."

"And we're its brutal cuts?"

"For those who dare, yes. Nothing worth having comes easily, you know. A platitude, I know, but true."

I turn away from her to look out of the window and she changes the mood abruptly, asking after the boys, and I explain that for the sake of their education, they will remain with their father. "Guyana is broken down. It's no place for them, and this is the only home they know. They will come out on holidays. I'll think of it as if they're at boarding school."

"You *are* brave, my dear."

"I leave in two days' time. It's best I go quickly."

I get up to leave and Miss Rani holds me close for several long moments. I feel her warmth and I am comforted. She holds my face in her hands and says, "I know your family are Muslims, but long, long before they converted to Islam, your ancestors were Hindus and would have known this bit of the *Svetasvatara Upanishad*." She speaks in Hindi, matching the lyrical sounds of the language with movements of her eyes and head. "In English that means that God is found in the soul when sought with truth and self-sacrifice, as fire is found in wood, water in hidden springs, cream in milk, and oil in the oil fruit. I think that the God of your ancestors is with you. Walk without fear, my dear."

I kiss both her cheeks on parting and thank her for all her kindnesses. She has taken me to her heart much like an aunt in the ways of the extended families of old. I promise to write, and leave, walking quickly past the other offices and desks, smiling if I meet anyone's eyes but not stopping to chat. I do not have the heart to talk just now about anything at all. I walk several blocks to the underground, thinking all the way about what I will say to the boys. How do I explain to these sons of mine whose world is painted with crayon-bright colours, who dance to a music of fresh morning notes? How am I to bring the pain of separation into their bright circle of life? Such platitudes as "It's best this way" would cheapen any explanation. I shall have to be direct, truthful. That will be best. There will be tears.

And there are. I tell them that I have to go away because their father and I have grown apart. I struggle to find words to explain the grown-up world of breakdowns and break-ups and all the damage we wreak on each other, in the gentlest terms.

"Whywhywhy, Mum?" Arek asks.

Omar is silent, his head bowed. I stroke his hair and say, "You'll come and spend your holidays with me. You'll like it, I promise. It'll be fun and there are tons of cousins and uncles and aunts for you to meet. And I'll get a phone installed first thing I get home so that I can talk to you every week, every day even." I keep my voice bright, high above its breaking point.

"Is it because you were sick? Is that why you're going away? But you're well now." This is Arek again.

"Not really. But my illness brought some things to light."

They would have picked up scraps of conversation over the past weeks but I am unprepared for Omar's outburst, his sharp accusation. "Grandma says your Nani is mad!"

I hold him and kiss him over and over. "No, my love, no! She had a hard life and she talked so much when she was young that she just decided to plop herself down quietly and not bother anyone with her words. She's strange that way but not mad. Sometimes old people feel they have earned the right to do just as they please and that's what my Nani has done." I laugh and feel Omar relax a little in my arms.

I worry about all they might overhear, but as they grow older they will come to their own conclusions, make their own judgments. They are intelligent boys. I hope they will not now, or in later years, judge me too harshly. I can think of nothing else now but the need to step again on my own patch of earth, walk again in the pool of my noonday shadow, admire the sprinkle of stars in the high night sky, and feel a warm Atlantic breeze finger my cheek. I need to retrace my steps and be welcomed back to a known place before I can turn around and look the future in the eye again. But it is a journey I have to take alone. To uproot my sons would unsettle them, although to leave them behind feels like the most brutal tearing of my own flesh. For me to stay would only open up our home to yet unseen sorrows. Too much lies broken inside me, and inside their father, that is beyond repair.

I hold my beautiful boys close and feel the deepest pain. Later, when they are asleep, I sit and watch them and hum all of Nani's prayers so that the music fills the room and makes a blanket of sound that I hope will keep them safe. When the tears come, I close my eyes and fall into the darkness, down past a girl with her hair flying behind her, down past two boys with similar faces, down past a rope, noosed and golden, falling into a white light that winks just for a moment like the light I saw in Nani's eyes, a bright light that draws me in and washes over me. It feels warm like the sun, like a promise, a blessing and when I open my eyes, my boys are still sleeping, undisturbed. I listen to their soft breathing, then tuck their blankets in closer around them and kiss them on their foreheads. I leave the room quickly, not daring to look back.

I rush down the stairs and find him in the sitting room and tell him my plans. He says nothing, just listens. I cannot get past his stonewalled silence. But he knows everything, I am sure, from my cleaning out of closets, throwing out of scraps of papers and

137

old letters, my furious weeding of the garden beds. He came home that afternoon to a house eerily tidy and put away, and I take his watchful silence as agreement with the decision taken. He may even be relieved that he did not have to broach the subject and find the words that are sensitive but direct, kind but firm. I do not know that I have done much better with my choice of words, but I know that, left to him, he would have put the problem away on a shelf, out of sight, and we would have had to live with the massed unhappiness that has fallen around us.

The hardest part is looking at him and remembering the happy times. Our love was eternal then. We believed that. But I had thought the marriage one thing when it was quite another. I never knew it had room for a fall from grace. I remember my teenage fears, the way my heart would tighten and I wonder at my youthful wisdom. I look away from Dean, cutting short my reverie and I tell him I would not contest a divorce.

"Your share of the house? Will I have to sell the house to …?"

"No, no, no," I answer. "Please, this is the boys' home. Let my share be transferred to them. And I don't need a financial settlement. I have a little put away and I'll find work at home, stay with my parents for a while. The mortgage is nearly paid up, and there's the investment fund to fall back on if necessary." I take a deep breath and continue quickly. "Now is the time, Dean, to get out of the bank and get a job that you can really make a go of. Let it be for our sons' sake. There, it's said, at last."

He looks away from me sharply, his face shut hard. I sigh. All the years together have come to this. He is disappointed that I am not a simple girl from back home after all, someone comfortable with the old ways. He had watched a stranger being wheeled away, had visited a stranger in her white room, and could not find the words needed to address the stranger that was his wife. Silence moved in and grew bigger and bigger until it could no longer be contained. It has overrun our world.

I look at him, his head bowed, his hands worrying each other, clasping and unclasping, the only movement he makes as we sit and survey the wreckage before us.

I say, "About the boys' health, you needn't worry. There is no madness in …"

138

"Alli, Alli…" His hand moves through the air with fingers curved ready to hold me, touch me, and in an involuntary movement, I jerk my body away from him. Dean's hand falls back through empty air. I get up and leave. There is packing to do.

Just then the telephone rings. When I pick it up it is Fazia. "Alli, Alli," she says. Her voice breaks and I have nothing to say. "I wish there's something I could …" she continues.

"I know. It's alright. I'll be fine. Will you help with the …?"

"Of course, I will. Don't worry." She pauses. "There's never a right thing to say at a time like …"

"I know. Don't worry."

"Take care."

"You too. Bye."

"Bye."

I have a new suitcase and the one I arrived with twenty years ago. I have kept it for sentimental reasons. It displays tourist stickers from several European cities – Madrid, Amsterdam, Paris – tokens of summer holidays. But now it is ready to go home again. I long to feel my mother's touch and hear my father's strong voice. Strange, our primal needs. Maybe parents are right: children are always children.

I open my old suitcase and go to work. It is not a matter of flinging a few cotton dresses and sandals into it this time. I need to use every inch of space available. And it is this, putting away toiletries into one of the pockets that causes my fingers to come upon a soft bunch of something. I take it out and there it is: the bunch of pale, golden threads that I had picked up from the floor of Nani's room after my last storm-filled night at home. It has lain here, curled up and forgotten all these years. But now it is found. It will take me home. I am ready.

CHAPTER NINE

There's a crisp, flowered sheet on the bed. Ma likes sheets with gay colours and patterns of flowers and I remember throwing myself onto the bed as a child and thinking I was falling asleep in a beautiful garden. I smile at the memory as I tuck in the mosquito net around the bed. The movements – flinging the net out wide, pulling it taut under the mattress – come back easily. I might have gone away and changed the patterns of my life but here the rhythms have stayed the same. It is satisfying to know that there is such steadfastness in the world. A cool night breeze blows though the open windows as I lay my head on my pillow and let my weariness rest. The quiet of the house feels like an understanding and I fall into a deep sleep.

I sleep without dreaming and wake with the first light and listen to the chirping of the birds outside the window. I'm surprised as at something new, yet I know that I must have heard this dawn music each day I woke in this room. It must have stayed unheard until now when I marvel at the busy, cheerful sound. I get up and draw the curtains aside and lean on the windowsill and see the sun push itself up from the horizon's edge. By midday it will roll about in the sky like a ball of fire but now it is pale gold and radiates a soft light. Under its gentle touch, the hibiscus open their petals, and the morning glory, the vines spread lavishly on a neighbour's fence, unfurl their delicate mauve trumpets. Bougainvillea – pink, purple and white – crotons, palms, mango and tamarind, guava and cherry trees laden with ripe fruit, the never-done periwinkles that sprout in every crack of earth: the sun unveils them all like actors in a tableau, spotlighting each in

140

turn. They too I had taken for granted. Now I recognize the splendour before me. I stretch my arms out to the sun, remembering how as a child at my grandmother's knee, I had gathered its light to my breast in a sky dream. It is only now, basking in the sun's warmth, stretching out like a cat, and watching the sky change from a pale, milky blue to a gemstone brilliance that I feel the tightness around my heart release its hold.

All through the long journey southward, I had such misgivings, wondering whether I should not have stayed and wrestled with all that I was leaving behind, taken the fragments and made some patched creation that might stand for a time. But Dean and I had become strangers to each other, and so quickly. No, the truth was that for many years the strangers had been there, but we had pretended otherwise. So perhaps it was not surprising that the break-up was so abrupt, like the change of direction of a pebble pitched against a rock.

Home. The word holds such magic. Here is where I first thrilled to the wonders outside my window, where I brought my earliest discoveries, my first sorrows. The safest place in the world, this roof, these walls. I want to tell my story here and watch it curl itself up into the corners. They know a similar tale already, a tale of love lost, and may even have been waiting all these years for the past to catch up and spin itself out again.

"You're home. You're home," my mother said to me when I arrived last night. She closed her arms around me like a clasp that keeps a precious jewel safe. "You have not changed at all."

I laughed, knowing that she was looking at my first grey hairs, sagging cheeks, and eyes that were sunken and darkly ringed – traces of my illness. I had not written to them about that. I had claimed busyness for the months of silence.

"You haven't either, Ma," I said, and this was more the truth. Her features were fitted into skin grown older and coarser, her hair was grey, and the raised veins on her hands branched into patterns like intricate filigree, but her eyes still fell on me with the soft look that gave comfort. Whatever changes she saw in me she gathered up in smiles that did not question or criticize. "Get some sleep now. It's late. We'll talk tomorrow," she said, and closed the door quietly behind her.

No one is awake yet and I breathe in deeply and pick up the scent of the river; I let my eyes travel eastward, round the corners of our neighbours' houses. There, just as I remember them, are the glinting, brown-sugar waters of the Demerara. By the time it makes its way past our small township of Victorine it courses by on a slow, snakebelly slither. As children, we had jumped and run along its bank – I and a whole pack of friends. We had played there on Saturday mornings, throwing sticks into the river, watching them bob away. We had waved at passing ships laden with bauxite or sugar or rice. It was a busy river then but I know that if I were to go down to the water's edge now, I would find it still and silent.

The bauxite industry is dead. Our previous government nationalized the mines and between their incompetent management and the fall in world demand for aluminium, ruin came fast. And sugar and rice – our poor crops. That was a World Aid colleague's matter-of-fact comment when, during a conversation one day, I told her what our export products were. Poor crops, she said, in a dismissive tone and turned back to her desk. I remember drawing in my breath and thinking: but that's all we know. We eat, sleep and breathe sugar and rice. Our brief history contains little else. At the end of their indentureship, some of my own foreparents stayed and bought land, or accepted crown land in lieu of a return passage to India. Many stayed close to the sugar estates and became part caneworkers, part small-scale rice growers. The plantation owners needed a reserve labour force near at hand and rented out small plots of land to their labourers. So Indians dug their neat rice beds, shied the paddy and watched the rice grow.

Life has not changed much in a century and successive governments have brought no new vision. They fret over sugar and rice prices on the world market, without having any clout in the global arena. Prices fall, more competitive countries elbow us out, and our poverty sprawls and turns squalid. With little to go around, we scrap with each other, finding ready reasons to do so. I saw it in all the countries I visited. Everyone wants the little for themselves, so the seams of race, religion and culture run red with battles for the spoils. Here, it is race, and our battle does nothing to improve our lot. The global financial institutions do no more than support us in our poverty, because they never insist on bold and creative solutions. Poor people do not threaten, make war, cause trouble. We can safely be ignored. The truth is that we have nothing that the rich world wants, and now that the cold war has ended, even our ideological quarrels have no strategic significance. Maybe the late dictator had a point. His bold plan to feed, clothe and house the nation, to make us independent of shackling aid, had resounded through the Guyanese community even in Britain. But it was a vision that was nothing but empty bravura, grand oratory that fed theatrics to a hungry people, told them of imperialism and neo-colonialism, told them why they were hungry but did nothing to relieve their deepbellied pain. It was the socialist dictator's hallmark: let them eat words, my words.

Pa still talks of him with anger. "He broke the place down with his racism and corruption. All of us were so busy fighting over the scraps we had no time to fight him. Clever! There's so much to do, but this lot just go about crowing like fowl cocks at day-clean about bringing back democracy. People can't eat democracy, no matter how sweet! We need proper plans and fast action to put things right," he said as we rode home in the taxi.

When I first saw him among the crowd at the airport, when he pushed forward and embraced me, all the years fell away and I was a little girl again. His big arms gathered me up and I leaned into his embrace, certain that I would not fall. When he stood back to look at me and said, "You haven't grown a bit. You're still my little Aleyah", we both laughed.

He asked a tumble of questions as we headed for the taxi: how long would I be staying, how were the boys and Dean, why hadn't they come? My telegram had been brief, giving only the date and time of my arrival and the terse message: *Coming home.*

"Your mother's been rushing about preparing the house. We expected the whole family," he continued.

I put my hand over his as the taxi pulled off. "There's so much I have to tell you, Pa. You and Ma."

I smiled to lighten the weight of my words, but tiny wrinkles of worry settled at the corners of his eyes and he said nothing for a while, until the car plunged into a long stretch of deep potholes, pitching and rolling like a ship at sea.

He sucked his teeth. "It's a death trap! They say you have to be a PhD, a pothole dodger, to drive here. They're sitting down in their nice offices and doing nothing, nothing I tell you! We were expecting things to get better but – nothing, nothing!" He continued quarrelling with the government but, as he talked, the words faded into the night, and I heard only his voice, the stout timbre of it, and thought how I had first heard it as a baby, and now heard it as it threaded together all the days of my life, closing up the gap of years as if it had never been.

It's a good time to come home. There's much to do and I plan to take my curriculum vitae to the Ministry of Finance. Many professionals have emigrated and few are returning to work for the poor salaries that a ravaged economy can afford, so I am sure that I will find a position quickly. But all this can wait until next week. Right now, I hear the house stirring. Ma is in the kitchen putting pots on the stove, Pa is opening the shop's doors and windows, and Nani's slippers are making their slow slapslap sound on the polished floor as she moves about her room. I shower and dress quickly.

By the time I am dressed, Nani is already in her rocking chair, humming a faint and familiar prayer. She has not changed at all. I drop silently before her and place my head on her lap. She smells the same: a faint scent of Pond's Cold Cream and baby powder. She places a hand on my head and I close my eyes. I feel no need to say anything and I allow myself to think of Dean and my sons. I settle my head deeper into Nani's lap. I do not know when the tears come and I'm only aware of them when my grandmother's hands begin to stroke my hair and her humming rises higher and higher into the morning air.

I bury my sobs into her lap. Her prayer grows louder and pushes hard against the walls and rafters. It flies through the open windows, bearing its sorrow to the wind. Her hands curve around my cheeks and I hold on to them. I am surprised at their strength. The skin on her hands looks paper-thin and the bones jutting through look frail, as if they might break with the slightest jar, but her hands have the firmness of anchors thrown wide and deep, that will hold fast no matter how turbulent the waters. I only lift my head from Nani's lap when I feel other hands on my shoulders. They are my mother's. They hold me, and my mother shushes me like a baby, then helps me up and leads me to my room. I weep in her arms for all that is lost, all that is hurt, and all that will never be whole again. She rocks me, calling my name softly and promising that all will be well, that everything in the world is always as it should be, that the pain will pass.

"God never gives us more than we can bear, Aleyah." She pauses, still rocking me, then adds, "I'll make some gulab jamun for you today. You used to like that when you were a little girl. You used to let the syrup run down your arms then lick them. You remember? Your face and hands used to be one big sticky mess."

She laughs – a bright sound – then dries my eyes with a corner of her apron. I smile, remembering how many times she had done this when I was a child and had cried over a bruised knee or a cut finger. "Come, have some hot tea, eat some breakfast. I'll make some sweet roti and you can have it hot with butter. Come, Mansur and Shaireen will be here soon."

I follow her to the kitchen and sit at the table, the same wooden table where I had eaten as a child. It is scraped and scrubbed clean. My father joins us, coming in from the shop, bringing with him all the news of the day from the morning newspaper.

"They're trying, they're trying, but there's so much to do," he says, commenting on the government's plans to resurface the roads, fix bridges, refurbish the hospitals, train more teachers. "It all costs money and there's not much of that going around round here. Those damn people stuffed up their pockets with it good and proper, stole the country's money."

"I am thinking of applying for a job with the Finance Ministry," I say.

My parents glance at each other before my father says, "Good, Alli, that's good." My father laughs. "They need the help, god knows." He continues in a more serious tone. "We need some big investors to come in, but the opposition is practising humbug politics, making trouble at every turn for the government, and they're always threatening to put their people on the streets again to loot our shops and beat us up. If this lot doesn't find a way to deal with them, god help us."

"Oh, give them a chance, no? It's a whole lot of things need doing," Ma counters.

"A chance? This is not time for chances. This is time for action, firm action. Am I right, Alli?"

"Yes, but Ma has a point. There's so much to do."

"I know, I know, but they have no plan. They patch-patch here and patch-patch there, when the whole country's come apart. Patch-patch policy won't work."

I wonder if the rest of Victorine's residents have lost their apathy towards politics too. During the dictatorship, everyone had to find ways to survive. Politics forced its way into their homes and, it seems, has stayed there. After breakfast, I follow my father back into the shop, but as I step through the doorway, I stand there, shocked. The shelves are all but empty. Where there had been stacks of boxes and tins, packets and parcels of every imaginable food item, there are now only spaces yawning with emptiness.

"Pa," I say, my voice cramped small and low.

"Alli, what can I tell you?" he says, looking at my mouth hanging open.

I read their letters but never really understood the hardships they had faced. They had eaten into their little savings to survive. I see it all now.

"Pa," I say again, walking slowly into the shop.

A few items – matches, tins of milk, parcels of sugar – are spread thinly on the shelves like fairground targets waiting to be picked off one by one. This shop was one of the businesses that gained Victorine the status of a township. Saeed's Shop was the busy centre from which households for miles around supplied their cupboards. I had helped behind the counter at Christmas time when we sold the salt butter and flour and cherries and raisins for everyone's black cake, ginger for their ginger beer, tinsel and fairy lights and small toys, and the shiny Christmas paper to wrap their gifts in. The shop was a part of everyone's lives, their weddings, their birthdays, even their funerals. Now it was nearly empty. My father sits on his stool, his head in his hands and I put my arms around his shoulders.

"I know what we'll do, Pa, we'll restock the shop."

"Alli, the banks want twenty percent interest on loans."

"No. No loan. I have a little money put away. We'll use some of that."

"No, no, Alli, I couldn't let you…"

"Come on, Pa, I'll be your business partner, a silent partner. You'll run the shop as you've always done. What do you say?"

He is silent. We sit in the gloom of the shop – the electric light bulbs had long since sputtered and died – and look at the achingly bright sunlight that drops outside the wide doorway. It falls like a sheer curtain and makes the shop appear dimmer. We watch people pass up and down, walking past the shop with their heads straight, not even looking in. They know its emptiness.

"We'll need to paint up the place." My father stirs in his seat.

"We'll put up a bright new sign, Saeed's Shop, in big red letters," I add, settling into mine.

"I'll get some new barrels for flour."

"And sugar."

"And rice."

"And new scales."

"And a mountain of potatoes."

"And a seaful of milk."

"And a billion split peas."

We go back and forth trying to outdo each other. We only stop when a shout from the doorway makes us turn around. There is a pretty woman standing there. She has black hair neatly parted in the centre, a face lit up by big, jet-black eyes and a smile that plumps her cheeks out round and pink. It takes me a few seconds to recognize my little sister.

"Shaireen! Look at you, so grown up, a woman!" We embrace, kissing each other. I had watched her grow up in successive photographs, but the frozen images never filled in the details of her woman's voice, her laughter, so the sister who had lit up my memory all these years was still the little girl full of giggling mischief. Now I adjust my eyes to look at her, to look straight into her eyes, and I find them looking back at me, steady and calm, and full of smiles.

She says over and over again, as if the naming made the moment real, "Alli, Alli, we thought you'd never come home. Come and meet your nephew and your little niece. They're dying to meet their auntie from England."

Shaireen pulls me into the kitchen where Yasmin and Zahir

are sitting at the kitchen table. Ma has made more sweet rotis for them. I kiss them each in turn but they are shy before this stranger and rush away to cling to their mother's skirts.

"They'll get to know you soon enough," Shaireen says, laughing. "They like to come here and run about the house, into all the corners, but they never go near Nani's chair."

"Like you and Mansur," I say. "But they'll grow out of that."

"I don't know. They believe she's a jumbie."

"Shaireen!"

"What? All these years and you're still picking up for her!"

"You know nothing of her life."

"I do. People say that she killed…"

"Shush! How can you listen to that kind of talk?"

"Well, why do you think she's so quiet-quiet?"

"You don't know anything and you shouldn't. . ."

"I know what I see and hear and…"

"Stop it, you two!" Ma's voice knifes into our quarrel. "Whatever Ma did she did all by herself and it is between her and God alone. She never threw her troubles around us and she is drawing up all her strength to face His judgment – that is all, so you two just hush up your mouths now. You're frightening the children."

Shaireen tosses her head back, but lets go of her anger and strokes her children's hair, then says to me, "Reaz will come later to meet you. He's busy at the shop this morning."

She does not ask after Dean and my boys; I suppose that Ma has said something to her and I am about to tell her that Arek and Omar will be coming in a few months for the summer holidays when Mansur rushes in and sweeps me off the floor.

"She's got real heavy, Ma," he says, laughing. "Grey hairs, too. It's an old lady that's come back to us."

The kitchen fills up with the noise of everyone talking and laughing at once.

"Bet she can't run after us like before," Shaireen says.

"You just try something and you'll see!" I challenge.

"Ooh, she's still got hot fire in her," Mansur says, then cuts into the banter and brings his wife into the middle of the room. "Alli, Alli, this is Leela."

She's shy and wants to hang back against the walls, but

Mansur takes her hand and holds it. He has grown into a man with a stout neck and large hands. He's all merriment and his hands sweep through the air with bold gestures that turn everything he says into pictures for your eyes. But for all his big talk, he's as shy as a schoolboy when he looks at Leela. My little brother, grown up to be so tender! In all my imaginings of who he would become, I never thought I would see this, see his hands, grown large, light so gently on a wisp of hair. I catch my mother looking at me. She has followed my eyes and smiles.

"Come," she says, "come, help me get lunch started. We'll cook for everybody."

"Do you remember how good I was at peeling potatoes and picking rice?" I ask.

"And when last did you pick rice, eh?" my brother teases. "Bet you've forgotten how."

Our noise grows into a riot again as I take a bowl of rice over to a window and lift handfuls of the pearly grain, letting it fall in a clear shower back into the bowl as the wind picks up the chaff and blows it away. I had done this chore so many times as a child, sometimes pouting, vexed because I'd wanted to be off doing something else, but now as I feel the grains run through my fingers, as I watch the creamy white rice glint like seed pearls in the sun, I can think of nothing else I would rather do.

"She's not forgotten how, Ma," Mansur says, pretending surprise. "Now pick out the bits of black rice and the broken grains. I want to see only whole white grains on my plate, Sis."

Shaireen picks up the teasing. They are still imps ready to throw laughter everywhere and our noise gets so loud that Pa comes in from the shop and says we are scaring away his customers.

"What customers?" Mansur asks softly, under his breath.

But I hear him and announce loudly, "Pa and I are business partners; we're going to repaint and restock the shop."

At once the uproar gets louder. Ma holds her hands over her ears, laughing. Shaireen picks up a corner of her wide skirt and kicks off her shoes and Mansur, as if on cue, starts to drum on the table. We all pick up the rhythm of the drumming, of Shaireen's stamping feet, and we clap and clap as she spins and twirls and moves her hips in a dance of brisk movements and extravagant gestures. Her skirt billows out to every corner of the kitchen. Its scrubbed floor becomes a grand stage on which, like her grandfather before her, my sister places her feet into steps and positions that come naturally. Her hands are clasped together prayerfully then flung out to embrace the world, making her bangles jingle. But where Pa Nazeer leapt and spun with masculine power, Shaireen dances with a willowy grace.

Amidst all the music and laughter and dancing feet around me, I miss my sons. Thoughts of them follow me about like a shadow. What would they make of the way we lived, the open doors and windows, with everyone flowing in and out of the house so casually? People drop in – friends, neighbours, family – and Ma always has a drink and sweetmeats to offer them – metai, cakes, buns, cassava pone, conkie – always on her best plate with its border of delicate pink flowers and dressed with a paper doily. Ma's pots will be busy when my boys come, and I can already see Arek and Omar licking the sugar off the metai, before popping them into their mouths whole.

The music and dancing had fallen away into the background as I thought of my sons, but they rush in on me again when my face is held between strong, plump hands and my cheeks are smacked with kisses over and over by a woman whose features seem familiar, though I cannot place her.

She pulls me onto the floor and, with her hands on her hips or waving about in sinuous movements, she swings and swirls to the drumming and clapping. Everyone is shouting and laughing at once, egging me on to dance. Shaireen pulls her children onto the floor and the uproar in the kitchen cannot be contained by the walls any longer but pitches itself out of the windows, the sound of our clapping and stamping and drumming and laughter spreading itself clear across the town.

"Come on, Aleyah!"

"Dance, girl, dance."

"Look, the children are doing better!"

"It's not every day you come home, you know."

I try to remember steps I had seen Pa Nazeer perform; I try to follow his lead. Place this foot here and that one there, tap twice then spin. I am afraid that I look clumsy but I laugh along with everyone else. In the melee, I hear the name Auntie Shamroon and in the middle of a twirling movement I look closely at the big dancing woman and recognize my great aunt. My father was right – she has grown as big as a barrel! I reach over to hug her as Mansur brings his drumming to an end with a series of quick taps, and Shaireen bows gracefully to our cheering.

"I didn't recognize you, Auntie."

"Because I get so fat, eh? It's because I don't have anybody to suck me dry any more." My great aunt laughs.

"Have some respect for the dead," my mother says huffily.

"I have great respect for the dead – and the buried. Nothing but respect. But I have a big-big happiness for the living – for me!" Great Aunt Shamroon shakes with laughter and all her flesh jiggles. "All my whole life, I squeezed myself up in a small-small corner of this world and was too afraid to say pipsqueak to a mouse. But now I find that I have all this bigness – it's like it's been locked down all these long-long years, and it's only now it's got a chance to spread itself out so. That's wrong, Aleyah? What you say, girl?" She holds onto my hands. Her grip is strong. She is no longer the browbeaten, sorry sight I once knew, someone to whom pity had laid claim and closed over like a grave. She was a whole new woman. "You're a modern woman, educated and so on, you think it's right to let anybody push you down until you turn into a little scrap of nothing? You tell me, girl."

My breath catches in my throat and my eyes shift away from hers as she bubbles with laughter. "Every night I clap my knees on the ground and ask Allah to give the dead peace," she continues. "They lie down in black earth, but my eyes still see light. Every morning I get up and I praise Allah for that. I praise Allah and I go about my day, making a big mark on the world. You don't agree with this old lady, Aleyah?"

I smile at her and nod and allow everyone else pick up the conversation.

"Not even the strongest man in the world could squeeze you down now, Auntie," Mansur says.

"Just let him try!"

"She can more push him down, and with one arm alone." This is my father.

151

At this, my great aunt struts into the middle of the kitchen and takes up a strongman pose, curling up her arms to show her biceps. They are big with fat and the kitchen erupts again into noisy laughter. Mansur whistles and catcalls and the children dance around my great aunt, clapping their hands with delight. Just then, barely skimming the top of our noise, we hear someone calling from the shop.

We all rush in behind the counters, a swarming, noisy group. One of my father's oldest customers, Aunt Gwennie, is standing there. I recognize her immediately. Her head is still tied with a colourful scarf and, except for the folds that run from cheek to chin, she is the same as when I last saw her, skinny as a rake. We are a spectacle, a mini carnival, with the children clambering over the counters like monkeys, and my great aunt still striking poses in answer to Mansur's teasing. Aunt Gwennie puts a hand to her chin in wonder. She says nothing until she sees me.

"Aleyah! My girl, you've come back! No wonder your family is making so much noise. I never heard the like in this house before. I've been calling and calling for hours, I tell you!" She laughs and reaches across the counter to hug me, then out comes a quick-march of questions. "And where is your husband? And your children? Where are you hiding them? Let me see them, no?" Her questions fell our merry noise instantly.

I throw bright words into the silence. "My sons will be here in a few months, in August, for the summer holidays. You'll meet them then."

"Oh," Aunt Gwennie says. "Oh."

She picks up the matches she has bought and with a limp wave of her hand is gone. She walks like she talks – fast. By the time the sun drops from the sky today, my story will be told, retold, filled out and passed along. I sigh. There will be more pity than malice in the handling of the tale, but I sigh that it has come to this, that people will shake their heads whenever they see me and make a tut-tut sound, their tongues clapping against the roofs of their mouths. "Poor thing to lose her husband so. She went away to a foreign place, way up in the north of the world. She met him there and lost him right there, and came back home alone."

Mansur, Leela, Shaireen, Great Aunt Shamroon – they all drift

152

back into the kitchen, avoiding my eyes and taking the children with them. My mother squeezes my arm and returns to her pots, and my father and I take up our positions on our stools and look out once more into the curtain of sunshine that drops outside the door. Pa sits quietly. Then, as if continuing a story whose telling has been interrupted, I tell him everything, the happiness and sadness of it. I tell it without tears or rancour, as if recounting an experience from a book, from someone else's life. My father listens without question or comment, but when I near the end, when I come to the part where we stand accused of madness, I hear him draw in his breath hard and hold it for several seconds before he releases it in a long suck-teeth. "Foolishness!" The word is said in a low tone but it snaps harshly because it is so abrupt. He passes a hand over his eyes. "Your boys?" he asks.

"The schools are better there, Pa. They'll come here for their holidays."

"He has agreed to that?" My father does not speak his name.

"Yes. He's not unkind."

"Hmmm."

"Was I wrong to leave?"

My father is quiet for a while then answers, "Sometimes a clean break is best. Sadness can fester like a sore, eat away at everything. Your boys will grow into men before you know it and understand how things are. This will be their home whenever they're with us." He wraps me in a reassuring hug. "And we're glad to have you back. Your mother and I are getting old, you know, and we need somebody around to take care of us." There is a twinkle in his eyes. "Yes," he continues, "we'll need you to help us with our walking sticks, Alli, so it's a good thing you've come home to be our dutiful daughter."

"Oh, Pa," I say, punching his arm, and laughing with him. "Well, I'll start my duties now and go help Ma with lunch."

"Yes, yes, you go on."

He smoothes my hair from my brow and I think how he must have made this same gesture, moved a wisp of hair gently from my eyes when I was a baby. He smiles. Maybe he remembers such a moment, too. When my sons are grown into big men, grown into their separate lives, I, too, will no doubt still look at them and see

153

the little boys they once were and smile in remembrance of all they had said and done. My father's eyes mist over and I give him a quick hug, then rush through the kitchen and up the stairs to my bedroom, closing the door before the tears come.

I lie on the bed and trace the outline of a red rose with my finger. I laugh through my tears at its hugeness and its redness. As I look at it, the sheet suddenly rises and then the whole garden of flowers – roses, pansies, sunflowers – is laid down gently on the bed and smoothed over by a pair of young hands wearing jingling bracelets. The woman is smiling. It is my mother. She tucks in the corners of the sheets with quick, practised movements. When she straightens up, I see her rounded belly. She is pregnant. The door opens and Nani comes in. Her hair is as black as my mother's.

"Shabhan," she says, "lie down and rest yourself a little."

"Ma, there's so much work to do."

"Come, rest. You have to rest the baby even now, you know, or else she'll be one of those colicky children, crying all the time."

"So, it's going to be a girl, Ma?" My mother is smiling, teasing. "Yes."

"But Saeed wants a boy. He wants a boy and we'll call him Mansur. And I want a girl and I'm going to call her Shaireen."

"It's going to be a girl baby and we're going to call her Aleyah." My grandmother lengthens the first vowel of my name into a musical note.

"That's a pretty name."

"She'll shine like a star, our Aleyah," Nani says, her eyes looking into the window's light.

"You want her to be like you? Put herself up high above everybody on a stage and talk and talk and break up everything around her?" My mother is agitated and her words tremble. "I won't let that happen to her. I won't let her become ..." Her voice drops away suddenly.

"Like me?" Nani moves over and sits by the window. Her head droops onto her chest like a wilted flower, and she shakes her head from side to side, swinging it loosely as if it were broken from the stem of her neck. "Not like me, no, not like me." She repeats this like a mantra, and it turns into a hum, and the hum becomes a prayer that floats into the open air.

154

My mother kneels before her, taking her hands. "I'm sorry, Ma. I didn't mean…"

"Shush, child. You're right to think so. No one wants pain for their children. I have little else to do in this world now, so I'll pray that she will always be safe."

"If my children ever hurt – I don't know, I don't know."

"It would kill you."

"That's why you kept me home, to keep me from…" But my mother's sentence hangs unfinished in the air for just then she sits up and smiles. "Feel her, Ma, she's moving. That's her head," she says, making a stroking movement.

I feel her hands. They are so gentle. My eyes are closed and I am curled up into a ball. I feel warm and safe. The hands are stroking my hair and when I look around, look away from the red, red rose, my mother is there, smiling at me and bearing a pretty china dish full of golden gulab jamuns. She wipes my tears and smiles as I spoon the first gulab jamun, along with some of the rose-essence syrup into my mouth. I close my eyes. The sweetness spreads over my tongue. It is intensely satisfying, this smooth, creamy sweetness and I spoon another golden ball into my mouth.

"Mmm, Ma, this is so good." She must have been working since early that morning to prepare the smooth dough of milk powder and butter and flour, then frying the balls of dough in light oil gently gently until they become golden, ready to be steeped in the sugary syrup that tastes of roses. "You haven't lost your touch."

"You're feeling better now?"

"Yes. If only life could be this sweet all the time, Ma."

My mother sighs and pulls my head onto her breast. Her heart beats against my cheek. It is so steady. It never misses, never wavers. All around us, the house is quiet. Leaves rustle outside the window and a lone bird, a yellow-breasted kiskadee, sits on the electric wire outside and calls out over and over into the empty air. Nani, sitting in her rocking chair, unwinds a humming prayer that grows louder and louder and swirls about us before lifting itself up to the roofed spaces of the house. I listen to the tune, then fit my words to its rhythm. "I met him one night at a dinner party,

Ma. He sat down beside me at a table full of crystal glasses and flowers and fine china and everything sparkled under chandeliers that bloomed above us like flowers spread with a million lights. His face was all lit up. He was so kind, so nice, Ma. He had dark hair, thick hair, and a nice laugh. Everything was beautiful. He was beautiful. And I fell into his eyes, Ma, deep into his eyes. When I looked at him I saw myself there, smiling from the light in his eyes."

The story unfolds. I tell it without tears. But when my world falls apart and I look again into the eyes of my sons the tears come unbidden and I weep again into the rose that blooms on my bed, and my mother strokes my face, my hair.

"You promised your prayers will keep her safe." I hear my mother say, but there is no reply, only a deep silence.

I feel another pair of hands stroking my hair, my shoulders. They are bony. "They have." The answering voice has a thin, rustling sound. It scrapes up from a throat unused to speech.

"What do you mean? Look at how she hurts," my mother accuses.

The answer comes again, raspy and breathy, is given with the finality of an ameen. "But now she is safe, safe, safe." The words fall away into a long sigh and I turn my head slightly and see my mother raise her hands to her mouth and look into the unseeing eyes before her. The eyes are calm but hers are wide with fear and trembling. I look away quickly and curl up tight and feel their arms close in around me.

CHAPTER TEN

They both laugh into the telephone. "And will we really ride donkeys when we come there, Mum?" Omar asks. I can see his eyes light up when I say yes, and how they get even brighter when I tell him that the water coconuts are bunched up on the palms in the back yard, waiting to be picked. "Your Uncle Mansur will chop them down and make a neat hole at the top and then you'll tip the coconut to your head and drink the water straight from the shell." They laugh again. This is so different from when I first called. Then it was hard to get a word out of them. It was painful to listen to their doleful voices, to endure the long spells of silence. I always felt like packing up and returning and trying, somehow, to see what could be mended. I cried each time, but not into the telephone. I would wait until I hung up, when Ma was there to hold me close. She would rock me gently until my tears were spent, then put me to bed like a child.

"I must go back, Ma, I must go back," I would say, and she would smooth my hair from my brow and answer, "A house full of sorrows is no place for children to grow up."

She would recount how she had lived within the weeping walls of this house, lived with its heavy silence each day, passing before the closed door of her father's room with light footsteps that always hesitated, slowed down, hoping the door would open, hurrying away each time that it stayed shut.

"He locked himself away, but Ma, she fluttered about the place like a busy bee, her hands flying around like they had lives of their own, like they had spirits in them. I was afraid of those fidgety hands, even though she never raised them against me. I was

157

always afraid that they might spring about and do whatever they wanted because they were so wayward. So, I would do all my housework and fold myself up in a quiet corner and stay out of their way. Children used to run past the house because everyone called it the jumbie house with Pa jailing up himself, and Ma walking around with hands that flew about like trapped birds. I had no friends. If your father hadn't come along, heavens know what would have happened to me. And to her."

She would talk like this, giving the story the rhythms of a sad song and I would be lulled to sleep. As I drifted off, I would hear her promise that all would be well, Inshallah, but even as my eyes grew heavy I always knew that nothing would be whole again.

"I love you. I love you," I say before I hang up. The words are not large or singular enough to hold all that I feel. It is early. The sun has just cleared the horizon and I look into the pale morning sky and try to think of grander words but I give up after a while.

The house is waking up around me and I replace the telephone neatly in the middle of the small table that my mother found for it. My parents had stood about in amazement when a five-man crew from the Guyana Telephone Co. arrived in two trucks with long ladders, fat rolls of wire, and heavy tool boxes to install the telephone just days after I had returned. I got plain lucky at the company's head office on Brickdam when a burly man behind the counter, sweaty and harried, perked up at a certain clipped English-ness in my accent and smiled at me, asking whereabouts in Britain had I lived. He needed very little encouragement to launch into a story about a sister, Cheryl, who lived in Birmingham, was a nurse there, and about his visit two years before.

"But that place is cold, eh? They said it was summer but I was shivering like hell! And all that boiled food. Not for me, man. I was too glad to get back home and eat some fresh pepper again!" He threw back his head and laughed, then asked what I needed done.

My voice was cool when I told him, and even cooler when I added delicately that I knew there would be an extra charge since I wanted the telephone installed immediately. Selwyn Jacobs – the name on his company badge – laughed again and said, "No problem, man" and disappeared through a doorway behind the counter, returning with a young man in tow. In a quiet corner of the counter I handed over half of the money asked for and as Jacobs pocketed it with practised ease, he nodded at the young man. "This is Andy," he said, "he'll have a crew over there in a couple of hours. Just fill out this application form for me."

He pushed a form and a pen towards me and I dashed in the information needed, shook Jacobs' hand, and hoped he would have better weather the next time he visited his sister. He laughed. "From what I hear that place never gets hot, man. You must be glad to be back."

I returned home just in time to receive Andy and his crew. Through the open windows of one of the trucks a Bob Marley tape blared out the lyrics and drumbeats of Rastafarian revolution and the men whistled along while they worked, breaking off to shout instructions to each other. They outdid themselves and installed an extension in the shop. Pa chuckled when he picked up the receiver and heard the dialling tone, but I avoided all the questions in his eyes about the crew and their prompt and ready service.

When they were through, the men sat at the kitchen table around a big jug of limeade Ma had ready for them, while Andy followed me into the back yard where I handed over the rest of the money. He smiled, showing a mouthful of gold teeth, and told me to call on him or Mr. Jacobs if I had any trouble, any trouble at all with the lines.

Everyone lives on their wits. It is how they survived the dictatorship. Laws, rules, even good manners had been put aside since all that mattered was that you were loyal to the party bosses and did their bidding. No one knows when the society will become whole again. The rot is deep set. I see it every day at my place of work, at the Ministry of Finance where I am an assistant to the minister with the Development Aid portfolio. Everyone moves slowly. Nothing requires urgency. Dog-eared papers are shuffled and returned to the spot from where they were picked up, as if that movement is work enough. Large manual typewriters peck, peck, peck at slow speed and everyone eyes me with suspicion when I move through the corridors with quick footsteps. I am stirring up dust that has lain undisturbed for decades, so there are suckteeths and sullen faces watching me. I ignore the cut-eye looks; there is just too much to do.

159

My desk is crammed with reports and statistical analyses, most shifted from the minister's desk to mine in less than a month. I was swept into the seat behind this wide desk so quickly that I still feel breathless. I had brought my curriculum vitae to the ministry one day, was called for an interview the next and was immediately offered the position. I could not help laughing when the minister asked if I could start the next day. He was a young man, several years younger than me, who had been educated in Moscow by the ruling party. He picked his words one by one when he talked, like a man careful with his steps along a rocky path.

I sat across from him, from a desk piled high with papers and knew he needed all the help he could get. "With your experience," he continued in his plodding style, "you can prepare the submissions and reports needed to apply for overseas aid, and you can do the follow-through on the projects that are approved. You will need to travel, not too often, so maybe you'll need to talk this over with your family and get …"

As he talked, I looked over his shoulders through the plate-glass window that looked onto the street. The mid-morning traffic of buses, trucks, cars, cyclists, horse-drawn carts and pedestrians was pelting down the road and some of the thunder of screeching wheels, honking horns, clopping hooves managed to invade this closed, air-conditioned space. Outside, there was chaos, but within his office, with its lacquered wooden walls, we talked in cool, even tones of stabilizing the country's macroeconomic systems, of fiscal policies and budgetary considerations.

"We have to increase revenues by upping production, but that is going to take some time. The whole infrastructure is badly damaged through the years of neglect and we have to get the massive foreign debt that was racked up – over two billion Guyana dollars – reduced right now. We have to borrow to service that debt and that is unacceptable and …"

At this point, I smiled and jumped in, "Yes, yes, I understand."

The minister, Vijay Jagdesh, stopped and looked at me expectantly, his hands clasped as in prayer on his executive desk.

I nodded and said, "I'll do it. I'll start tomorrow."

He arose, smiling, and shook my hand, giving instructions to his secretary for me to see the personnel director to arrange my contract, salary and other details. I laughed when I realized I had not even asked about the salary. By Guyana's standards it was handsome and when I returned home with the news, my mother hugged me, and my father puffed himself up with pride and said, "Now this country will get moving!"

There is a photograph of me at my desk with a brief story of my appointment in the newspapers a few days later. With the dearth of qualified professionals around, it seems no one will question the speedy appointment.

In the next office there is another official, for local development, a graduate of the University of Guyana, and we became friends from the first, especially after I regaled him with the story of my telephone installation.

"You learn fast," he said, laughing. His name is Peter Gaskin and he's of Portuguese and African parentage. He has reddish brown curly hair, light brown eyes and a European complexion; his African ancestry is there in the curl of his hair, and in the fullness of his lips, which gives him a brooding sensuality. He's handsome. While we were chatting over cups of coffee in his office on my first day at work, his telephone rang several times and from the nuances of the conversations I gathered that they were from various girl-friends. He actually blushed when, after the third call, I smiled and said, "You're busy. I'll get back to my desk."

There is no playfulness about his work, however. We have to consult each other on various projects and I discover quickly that his analysis and grasp of situations is sharp and accurate.

"We go a-begging," he says one day as we look over the proposals for a road-building project for the Essequibo coast. There are questions in my raised eyebrows, so he continues, "I guess that's okay up to a point, but there should be more emphasis, I think, on working with the local banks, or Caribbean ones, to fast-track small loans at reasonable rates to farmers and local manufacturers to get production and revenues up rather than waiting on the large sums to come down from the IMF and World Bank. You know the local saying that goes: one, one dutty build dam? And, of course, there's always the huge interest to be paid on those big loans. We write off the old debts, okay, but then we turn right around and create new ones. Where's the sense in

161

that? Even if the debts are written off eventually – always the hope – the loans come with big strings attached. Like ransom notes."

"The private sector? How involved are they?" I ask.

"No one has talked to them, not seriously."

"Why not? I should think they would be an important partner if we're to get things moving. They must have good practical ideas of what can be done."

"Of course. There's a Private Sector Commission, but remember this government has its roots in communist ideology." Anticipating my question, he continues, "Yes, the Berlin wall fell but the roots go deep and it's not easy for them to change overnight. The old suspicions linger."

"My father says the government has a patch-patch policy."

"He's right. There's no overarching development plan with specific targets so we bumble along blindly."

"And the workers strike, too."

Peter looks at me and laughs. "Cynicism already?"

I shrug. "Four places are on strike – my last count – for more pay. Why not invite the unions to the table when the budget is being decided, get them involved?"

"That would be too much like common sense – and remember, some of the unions are still loyal to the opposition."

We both look out at the mad dash of the traffic outside my office window. Clouds of dust swirl about in the air. The honks of horns and the swish of speeding tyres rise above the hum and whirr of the air conditioner in my office that drips water onto the frayed carpet. I had asked twice whether the drip could be fixed and the maintenance man had eventually obliged by coming and looking at it, listening to me patiently, then shrugging and saying he would see what he could do. As he had shuffled away down the corridor, I knew nothing would be done.

Peter cuts into my thoughts. "Vision. We need vision and leadership. Come to our meeting on Friday."

"What meeting?"

"There's a small group of us, just ten right now, friends, young professionals. We meet to talk things over, exchange ideas. I think you'll be interested in what we're saying. And I'm sure they'll like your ideas. I've told them about you." I look at him quizzically

162

and he laughs. "Nice things," he says as he closes the door and returns to his office.

I am curious about the group as we walk over to the meeting place, the Georgetown Club on Camp Street. The club is just two blocks away, but during the short walk, I am reminded why this once-famous Garden City of the Caribbean is now called the Garbage City. Paper, thrown from passing buses and cars, settles on the roads and pavements only to be picked up again by the rushing air of other speeding vehicles, then drifts down once more to resettle in different patterns. Piles of garbage fester at street corners or in front of homes that were once gracious. Now, they are carcasses of rotting wood and peeling paint that crouch behind falling-down fences and open drains clogged with bottles, paper, tin cans – anything that can be tossed out, discarded, thrown out of doors. By the roadside, a beggar sleeps with his mouth open, an old man with a grey beard, part of the human debris that floats about the city and lies down wherever sleep catches them. And more than once on the short walk I avert my eyes from men who open their flies and urinate openly against fences.

The Georgetown Club is an oasis amidst the rot, a gracious structure built during colonial times. Plantation owners and businessmen once relaxed on its wide verandahs as they sipped tall rum-laced drinks served by liveried, black attendants. The colonizers are gone but their romance with the tropics is still there in the high, cooling ceilings and the jalousied windows designed to catch every breath of wind that sails in from the sea. Now, it is the local business and professional class who are served by liveried, black attendants as they sit up at the mirrored bar on high stools. They eye us, these late-afternoon drinkers, as we step onto the verandah. Peter waves to a few of them. It is a small city and our presence will be noted, may even raise some speculation.

Peter leads me down a short corridor to a small room where a few young men are sitting around a table and drinking Banks beer straight from frosty bottles. As soon as I am introduced, they ask questions about my work with World Aid and I talk of the poverty I have seen, of the tragic waste of human life caused by corruption, poor economics, wars, and the stubbornness of peoples who cling to outdated cultural forms and systems.

"Women in purdah, girls being kept from school or from certain careers – these create poverty, too," I say. I am listened to politely, then a young man, small and slight with a narrow moustache, asks, "What do you make of our situation?"

"In part, it's fixable. It's not nearly as desperate as many of the countries I've been to. The infrastructure – the roads, water, housing, the education and health systems – all that needs money and planning and the will to do it, and I think there might be better ways to fund the recovery effort than we are currently doing – like making more use of the private sector. Peter and I have talked about this many times."

"You don't think there haven't been attempts to raise this issue? From the Chamber of Commerce and in the press – but this isn't a listening government," another young man says. He is black and sports a neat, pointed beard that he strokes from time to time. "But how do you find us Guyanese, coming back as you do after so long away?"

"Well," I say hesitantly, hearing the veiled reproof. "I think that's where the real problem lies. It's how to motivate a people who've been so badly brutalized. Corruption and lawlessness have been the norm for so long that most people believe that it's okay, that's how things are done. And, there are the racial antagonisms. It's a society in real trouble. I think fixing the infrastructure is the easy part."

"You heard about the post-election riots?" one young man asks.

"Yes," I reply. "Exactly my point. I've heard the horror stories. Not just about the burning of buildings and the looting and beatings, but of Indian women being stripped in the streets while the opposition thugs – including women – stood about laughing."

The room becomes quiet. I am one of only a couple of Indians in the room and the only woman. Several of the young men look at their feet and shift about uncomfortably. I think I may have been too blunt, but then one young black man says in a low voice, his head in his hands, "It shames us all."

"They follow their leaders." It is the bearded young man again. "But what's the solution?"

"To start from the position that that kind of behaviour is unacceptable, criminal. That we can't conduct our politics like that. The leaders themselves must be held accountable."

"But after that? Don't we have to go beyond agreeing that such behaviour is unacceptable to understanding why we Guyanese keep on acting in this way. Okay, we have had fair elections and the majority will has been expressed, but how are we better off with what is mainly just an Indian supported Government?"

"Now African Guyanese feel just as excluded as Indians did under Burnham – just as they did after 1957 and 1961."

"Racism is an easy tool to use."

"It was the tool of the colonizers. They taught us well."

"Lazy politics."

"Lazy politicians."

"Lazy followers."

"But don't we have to start with our political system? How can we go forward when whoever loses the elections feels racially excluded?"

"That's true. We don't take account of how insecure people feel. OK, the rhetoric's extreme and the leaders exploit it, but the insecurity, the fear of exclusion, of being left behind is real."

"Isn't the answer to create a constitution where there has to be power-sharing between the races? It's been the way forward in places such as Northern Ireland where there has been hatred between Protestants and Catholics for centuries."

"We've cut across our racial divide with this group. It's a start."

"And women?" I ask.

Someone across the table laughs and the tension eases when he says, "There's no prejudice. It's just that this started out as a group of friends, but now that we're thinking of a more serious commitment, they'll be involved, as you are."

"More serious commitment?" I ask.

Peter clears his throat. "Well, we've been thinking that we ought to take a more public position. It's all very cosy sitting here, but it doesn't change anything. Some of us have been toying with the idea of a political party to fight the next elections, but at the least we ought to form an independent, public pressure group."

"A think tank, and God knows, we need some fresh ideas."

"Why not form your own party?" I ask.

"Well, it's true there are three years to the next elections, but the past twenty years are littered with the debris of new political groups who make a splash, and then are completely trounced when elections come round. People go back and vote race."

"Because none of the parties have been honest about the past, or the current violence either. Appeasing and explaining away violence and brushing aside past atrocities – people aren't stupid."

"They end up going back to the devils they know."

"It's time to exorcise the devils."

"It'll take time. Let's all understand that."

"However we go about this, we've been lacking a good public spokesperson, someone who'd be seen as intelligent, strong, principled."

"Someone who can inspire people."

"And is good looking, too." It is the slight young man – Prem, I think his name is – who says this. Everyone laughs at his comment but I stop short when I realize they are all looking at me.

"No, no, no," I say immediately.

"Why not?" Prem challenges.

"You would be perfect," Peter says. "I've been listening to you for over a month. You have what it takes – the confidence and the ability."

"I've only heard you today and you speak from the heart," someone adds.

"I think this country is ready for women taking leadership roles. Mother to a troubled nation. During the years you were away, the position of women in this country really changed. They were the most energetic traders. They played a big part in the unofficial economy."

They all speak at once but Peter raises his hand and there is silence. "Think about it, Alli. Think it over. Talk it over with your family. It's a big commitment so consider everything carefully."

I breathe in deeply. "This is all happening so fast. I've only been home for a couple of months."

"Exactly why you'll be good," Prem says. "And you would be part of a team of people who've been here all along."

"We need someone untainted with past politics."

"Someone who is not seen as bogged down with the past, the old political bickering, and whilst that's true for most of us, most of us would be seen as too young."

I smile ruefully, and the last speaker hastens to add, "But I don't mean that you're old; you're young, but you have a maturity and experience most of us don't have."

Peter concludes, "And your fresh eyes are just what's needed, Alli. Think about it."

Fear creeps into my mother's eyes. She is seeing my grandmother with her fists raised, surrounded by a crowd of shouting people, then watching as the crowd moves away, leaving her standing alone. My father, unaware of her fear, hops around the kitchen table laughing and whooping, "My daughter, the president! That I would live to see the day! Of course, you must say yes. You can do it, you can do it!"

"We're not even planning to become a political party, Pa," I say.

"Why not dream?" he says. "But there's no reason why you shouldn't get involved."

Then a late customer calls from the shop and he dashes back behind the counter leaving my mother and I to sit across from each other with a deep silence between us. I do not meet her eyes.

My eyes light instead on a small blue envelope lying at the far corner of the table and I pounce on it. It is from Katu and I rip open the envelope and read her brief lines. She is worried about me, and says that I should write and explain everything. My one letter to her since returning home only stated my new address and my move. I could not find the words to explain. She has enclosed a recent photograph and I look into her face, at its new largeness, at the big arms that are spread wide to gather in her children, and I push it away, push it over to Ma.

"My friend, Katu," I say as she picks up the photograph to look at it. "She was so beautiful once. Long ago."

Ma puts down the photograph and smiles at me. "But you, you're still beautiful."

I laugh. "No, Ma, I was never a beauty. Now, you and Nani and Shaireen…"

She waves away my words, then takes my hands. "Be careful," she says. "Just be careful."

I only nod at her and smile, for just then Shaireen and Mansur arrive and Ma gets up to set out two plates for them. They have taken to dropping in most evenings with or without their families and her pots always have enough to go around. "You're like Jesus with his miracle fishes, eh Ma?" Mansur says as he takes a plateful of rice topped with curried mullets, and ochroes, fried with peppers and herbs picked fresh from the garden.

"Has Alli told you yet?" my father asks loudly, bustling in from the shop. Without waiting for an answer, he adds, "They want her to be the leader of a new political group of young people."

"Alli!" Mansur's eyes are shining.

"You might be our president, Alli. Just think, eh?" Shaireen laughs.

I explain again that this is just a pressure group and that I hadn't even made the decision to get involved.

"Why not? Why not?" asks Mansur. "Think what you can do with such a chance. Much better than this lot, that's for sure. Take it, Alli!"

"Yes, yes. We'll help. What fun!" Shaireen adds.

"Tell us about these people. Who are they? What's their thinking, their policies?" Mansur asks.

"What's the name of the group?" Shaireen asks.

"It's early days yet. I don't think anything like that's been decided. What the group wants to do is generate new ideas, look at ways of overcoming our racial divisions, release the energies of all our people. There would be so much to do. I have to think about this very carefully."

Everyone rushes in with ideas of their own, of what should be done and how. As I listen to their busy voices, I think of Nani and, looking up, I catch my mother's eyes on me. She and I are the only ones to hold back our words. Fear still sits in her eyes but I smile at her, pushing away the past, and her face relaxes as with a promise received.

"We'll help, Alli. Do it!" Shaireen gets up to leave. "Must get back, Ma," she says, kissing Ma on her cheek. She gives Pa a hug, then laughs as she heads for the door. "My sister, the President."

Mansur gets up, too. "Think about it," he says to me in all seriousness, but adds, laughing, "then say yes, sis."

While Ma busies herself with the dishes, I slip away upstairs to sit with Nani who is half asleep in her rocking chair. I spend each evening with her like this, sitting across from her, listening to her hum a prayer while I wish my sons sweet dreams. And if I do get involved, what would they think, my sons? Would they be proud, or would they turn on me with accusing eyes? I ask these questions of the night and throw a tumble of others after them about my ability. I consider the dangers. I am working for the government. I suspect that they will not be pleased if I take on a more public role.

"Can I do this, Nani? Can I?"

I turn to her and find that she is wide awake. The darkness is filled with the whistles of tree frogs, of dogs barking in neighbours' yards. The sky is spread with stars and a half moon has risen, golden, from the horizon's dark edge. Nani is sitting up straight and looking steadily into the patch of night framed by the window, her hands laid one on top the other in her lap. Her face is at rest. She is serene, peaceful and quiet, ever so quiet.

I draw in my breath and hold it, scarcely breathing, and when my mother comes up behind me and places her hand on my shoulder, I reach up and take it. We take Nani up, one on each side, to her bed and Ma hums a prayer as we lay her down to sleep, drawing a cool cotton sheet over her, up to her chin.

When we return to the kitchen, we find that Great Aunt Shamroon and Shaireen have arrived.

"I heard the night turn quiet so I came," my great aunt says.

"I heard it too," Shaireen adds.

"I'll make some tea." Ma moves over to the stove.

I get the cups out. "I was telling her about the new group. I was so busy asking her a whole set of questions, I don't even know when the silence came."

The teapot stands hot and full on the table. We feel its warmth.

"It's time," Great Aunt Shamroon says, looking at me.

"Why now?" Shaireen's voice is high, insistent. "I never understand anything."

169

Ma puts a hand out to calm her. "You need faith not under-standing."

Shaireen pulls away. "People say that she …" Her words fall away abruptly when she feels our eyes drop hard on her. She shrugs. "What happened?" she asks. "Tell me."

"Only she knows." Ma sighs. "And Aunt Khadijah, and she's gone."

"And she'll take it with her to her Maker. There'll be her judgment," Great Aunt Shamroon says. "There it'll end."

"It never ends," I say.

"What do you mean?" Shaireen is frightened.

"The past is always here. It shapes us, walks with us," I say.

"But what if she did…? That too?" she asks.

Ma places her hands over Shaireen's again. "Whatever is done is done."

"The past is past," my great aunt says.

"A lesson."

"A warning and a guide."

"And a blessing for all that is still to come," Ma says.

"Ameen," Great Aunt Shamroon says.

Ma pours the tea and as she sets the teapot back on the table, we see Leela standing at the kitchen door, standing against the night darkness, then moving towards us into the kitchen's bright lights. She takes a cup of tea and sips it. It is hot and sweet and milky. She joins us in our silence and looks deep into Ma's eyes, smiling and blushing. Ma takes her hand, throws her a question-ing look and Leela nods.

"A baby!" Ma says and the kitchen bursts into laughter. It draws my father in from the shop where he was working on his accounts.

"A baby!" he says, throwing his arms out wide.

"New life," Ma says and gets up to fuss over Leela.

"Ameen," my great aunt says again, bunching up her fingers, kissing them, then raising them high to the heavens.

I am up before the sun the next day, a Saturday, to talk to my sons before they start to dash about with their weekend play and activities. I catch them just in time. They are going to the shops, then to the zoo with Aunt Fazia and Uncle Michael and Becka, then going on to their grandparents for the rest of the day. They tell me all this quickly, in high, breathy voices, the telephone going back and forth between them.

"And Dad's going to come and meet us at Grandma's after work," Omar says, "and he says he'll take us to a movie tomorrow."

"Work?" I ask. "On a Saturday?"

"Yes." Arek has taken the phone. "Dad has a new job. He's working at Sainsbury's. He's a manager and he's …"

Arek is cut off in mid-sentence and I hear Dean's voice, the first time for weeks. "Hi, Alli."

"Hi. How are you? What's this I hear about a new job?"

"I wanted to tell you myself. I've changed my job. I'm now at Sainsbury's, a purchasing manager. They have a good in-house promotions scheme." As he talks on about his work, I hear the high notes, the flow of words that I knew so well when I first met him.

"I'm so happy for you. You sound well," I say.

"I am," he says, then pauses. "Alli, I want to ask you something." His tone changes. He becomes serious.

"Yes?" I ask. "Is it about the boys coming out for the summer?"

"No, no. I wanted to ask whether you would come home." He says it quickly, then stops, but before I can reply, he continues in a tumble of words, "I'm settled in at this new job and it's really going to work out for me and…"

I continue to listen to him, his words rushing ahead as my own thoughts come to an abrupt stop. Come home? My heart tightens. My breath stops. Come home?

"I don't expect you to answer me right now, but think about it. Please. The boys, our sons. Think about it, will you?" he asks and I nod. Then, realizing he cannot see me, I say, "Yes, yes, I will," and hang up.

I replace the telephone on the embroidered cloth Ma has placed on the table. I study the floral pattern carefully, following the winding trail of pink and red flowers. I start to count the number of shells on the crochet edge but I shake my head clear and look away quickly and see that the sun is starting to clear the clouds. It rained during the night and raindrops sparkle like bits of crystal on the leaves and hang like tiny stalactites along the edges of roofs.

I go out into the back yard and breathe deeply. I close my eyes and take another deep breath, smelling the grass, the trees, the rich earth. I stretch my arms out wide, pushing my fingertips out as far as they will go. My feet feel planted firmly, and my body taut, like the strings of a well-tuned instrument. I stand like this between the mango tree and coconut palms and, even with my eyes closed, I know that as the world spins round and round on its still centre, that this ground beneath my feet will never yield, never give way.

CHAPTER ELEVEN

"Take this to your nanny," Ma says, handing me a big enamel cup of hot, sweet tea. She pours more condensed milk into the teapot to make the tea the way my father likes it, very milky and sweet. As I move towards the stairs, she asks what I was doing out in the yard so early.

"Nothing. Just feeling the ground beneath my feet," I reply, not turning around. But I feel the questions in her eyes as I hurry up the stairs, bearing the cup carefully. There's no sound from Nani's room and I tap softly on the door before I enter. She is in bed with her eyes shut and I stand for a moment, watching her. When I see the faintest rise and fall of her chest, I relax and shut the door noisily and place the cup on the bedside table with a clatter.

"Assalamo-wa-alai-kum, Nani," I say loudly, but she does not stir so I open the curtains to let in the morning light. "It's a sunny day, Nani," I say, continuing my bright chatter. "My boys are going to the zoo today, it's so warm in London."

I stop and listen to the room, to its profound silence. Her breaths are so shallow that they don't stir the air with any sound at all. I sit on her bed and take her hand. Outside the window birds chirp and my father is making loud banging and rattling sounds opening the shop, but within these walls, the world has fallen silent. I want to hum a prayer but I am afraid that it will break away into tears, so I start to talk again in my parrot's chatter.

"They're going to the zoo to see the elephants and tigers and the monkeys. They'll feed them peanuts. My boys, my two sons, Nani. They'll be here soon, in a month's time. You'll hold them in your arms, your great grandsons, Arek and Omar, my two boys."

Nani's hands suddenly grip mine and I am surprised by their strength. She hangs on as I pick up my talk again. "You'll love them, Nani. Two beautiful boys."

"Yes, two boys, twins, twin boys." Nani's voice scrapes from her throat in a hoarse whisper.

"No, no, not twins," I laugh.

"Twins, twin boys. They were twin boys. I remember. She told me." She speaks in a whisper, her eyes still closed.

"What boys, Nani? Who told you?" I ask, recalling scraps of a memory, a floating dream of two boys with similar faces.

"Ma." The single word hangs in the air like a sigh. "Ma," she says again. "My mother. She told me."

I look at her closed eyes and wait. Her grip tightens as she gathers up all her strength, and when she speaks again, her voice puts away its breathiness and bristles with energy and spirit.

"Her mother told her on the day when her first baby was born – when Khadijah, my sister, was born. My grandmother told her about the twin boys, the sons she'd left behind in Bihar, in India. She had run away. They were going to kill her."

Nani's eyes fly open. "Her husband and his mother, they hated her. They kicked her and cursed her, told her that she was nothing but a low chamar woman. She was a slave to them and she was fifteen, a little girl still, when she birthed the boys, the twin boys with heads full of curls. Their smiles, like cherry rosebuds, she said.

"They took them away from her, her sons, and laughed at her and kicked her even more. Like a dog, she said. They had no more use for her, so they kicked her in her belly where she had sheltered the boys all their growing months, where she had felt them move. His mother had given her water to drink when she had the birthing pains on her. She had smoothed her daughter-in-law's hair and held her hands and talked the pains away, but once the boys came, once they were born, they dashed the water from her mouth and the kicks and curses started again. She watched the boys creep and walk and run about on their little legs. They called his mother 'Ma' and thought the chamar woman, Gaitree, who was so kind to them, was nothing but a servant girl who was hired to cook for them and keep them tidy."

Nani's breaths are coming fast and she continues to grip my

174

hands. She breathes in deeply, then continues, "One day when they were playing, she called out to them and was telling them that she was their real Ma when his mother came upon them and raised herself up and looked down on her from a giant height. She saw then that her mother-in-law was Kali, the goddess who wore a necklace of skulls and a skirt of severed hands and had a long bloodthirsty tongue that dripped with blood. Kali cursed her and kicked her so badly that day she could hardly walk, but that night, she said, that night a sign came to her. The moon hid itself away from the world and, under the cover of darkness, she ran away. To go back to her parents' house would bring shame and disgrace to her family, and they would only send her back to live out the fate of her marriage, so she set her face away from her village and dragged herself all night along a dark road – walking, running, tumbling, not knowing where she was going. 'I loved my sons, but I wanted to live, I wanted to live. God, forgive me.' She cried like this to my mother, my mother Lena, named for the ship that brought her mother to this new earth."

Nani pauses and I hand her the cup of sweet tea, now only warm. She sips the tea slowly and I wait to hear the rest of the tale.

"Go on, Nani," I say softly. "What happened to Gaitree? Did she escape? Did they find her and take her back?"

Nani shakes her head and continues, "She walked all night with only the stars for company. She fell over and picked herself up and walked on, until morning brought her to a busy market where she stole a piece of watermelon and it was when she sat down to eat it that a man came up and started to tell her about a ship that sailed across wide oceans and atop waves as high as mountains until it came to a land on the far side of the world where gold and diamonds glittered in the belly of the earth, and where sugar cane grew like golden arrows that reached all the way up to a big blue sky, and that she could go there if she wanted and live on its sweet juice all her life, and wear the rich jewels delivered up from the earth. He gave her milky tea to drink and bought her a hot paratha to eat, and he talked to her in a soft voice, watching how her eyes grew bigger and bigger as the story rolled off his tongue. She was not afraid of the man, so when he got up and took her hand, she followed him.

"He took her along dusty roads. They walked or rode on

bumpy bullock carts, and he fed her sweets all the way until they came to a big city that was sprawled out at the edge of a big set of water. She thought it was the sea but it was only a river, the Hooghly River that turned south and emptied into the Bay of Bengal. The man told her this, told her this was where her journey would begin. He handed her over to other men who looked at her face closely and asked her questions – her name, her age, her caste, her religion – and wrote down her answers in a big book. She answered their questions quickly – making up what she didn't know – because she wanted to get away from the compound and run to the water and dip her toes in it and chase the froth that lapped onto the brown sand. She was going to sail away on it in a big ship with white sails and live on the sweet juice of sugar cane. She laughed and laughed and wished her sons were there to see this wide, brown river that flowed out to a sea that joined up with another and another and took you way to the other side of the world.

"She thought that when she went to the new land and was grown rich and fat on the sweet sugar cane she would return in bright clothes and chinking bangles and golden necklaces and take them away with her. When she returned, dressed up in her riches, neither her sons' father nor grandmother would dare stand in her way. That's what she thought as she raced up and down the sands."

When I hear Nani's words, I remember my dream clearly and see the young girl with her hair streaming behind her, running across the sands. "I saw it, Nani. I saw her and her boys, her sons. I remember it all now." I take the empty cup from her and she eases back onto her pillow. I look away out of the window and my dream, all its fragments, comes together in the dancing sunlight.

"She is running, Nani," I continue, "but she stops suddenly because she feels that someone is looking at her and when she turns around, she sees a young man, tall and fair-skinned with a narrow moustache standing a way off, watching her. He is skinny just like her, Nani, all long thin bones, and his kurta and dhoti flap about him like sails. His face is serious. He looks as if he is trying to be older, like someone who is bearing grave responsibilities on his small shoulders. He comes up to her and asks her what she is doing running about like that, only she doesn't understand him because he uses different words. So he speaks to her with his hands and she replies like that, too, shaping her words with her hands. They try to outdo each other's shapes and after a while they lay themselves out on the sand and throw loud, long laughter up to the sky. It is only when the river washes up to their feet that they run up back to the big bungalow where a whole hundred and more people are waiting for the ship, just like them."

There my dream ends, falls away again into fragments. "That's all I saw, Nani. I saw her long, flying hair and how they laughed and shaped their worlds with their hands. Why did they visit my dreams? Who are they? What happened to them?"

Nani waves a hand to slow my questions down, then continues the story her mother had told, in a calm, even voice. "He was called Janki, Janki Khan, and he came from a big-big family who were packed into four rooms in the bottom of an old building in Calcutta, just a little walk from the river's edge. He just upped and left one day and he didn't think his family would miss him; there were so many people in the house, and more coming every day, family from the country coming to make their fortune in the city. He wanted to find new ground to stand on, he told her, his own patch of earth. He drew his shoulders up straight when he said this, shaping the words for her with his slim, tapered hands. She started to understand some of his words, and he, some of hers, and when they sat by the river on the days that followed, he told her about his future. He had already built it, knew every part of it like he knew his own palms and all that the lines foretold, and one day he took her hand and told her that she was to become part of his future. She said she looked away from him, blushing when he said this, and that the very next day he found a moulvi, a man with a bushy black beard, to do the nikka that made her his wife. They stood in the yard of the bungalow and she repeated all the Arabic words after the moulvi, accepting the guidance and mercy of Allah through all their married life.

"When word went out about the marriage, all the people, so bored with the empty days of waiting on the ship, picked up themselves to celebrate. The women fetched Gaitree away from her husband and found a red sari to dress her in, and decorated her

177

palms and feet with henna paste, making markings of flowers and suns and graceful arches all the way up her wrists and ankles. They lent her their bangles and earrings and necklaces, since all she had of her own were her foot rings, a nose ring and a couple of bangles. Her mother-in-law had stripped everything else from her. Her bridal dress was complete when the women placed a silver mangtika on her head, and painted a large henna dot between her eyes. They danced around her as they took her out into the yard to present her to her husband. When Janki looked upon her, he saw a rich Hindu bride. The men had wound a turban around his head and garlanded him with flowers.

"Everyone gathered around a fire in the yard and Janki led his bride round and round it, letting the flames purify them as they began their new life together. They threw offerings of rice into the heart of the fire to pay homage to the gods, and when someone took up a tabla and another a flute, everyone spun around them in such a dance, such a dance. The men leapt so high in the air they looked like the ancient gods flying about the sky. The women spun round and round so that their gangari skirts, so wide and long and full, flowed out around them in rich circles of colour. And so they were married, Janki and Gaitree, in the eyes of both their gods, before Allah and before Bhagwan. No one questioned this. It was as if they had already taken up new ways as they sat at the water's edge and waited on their passage to a new world.

"She told my mother how on that night, with the soft fragrance of the henna on her hands and feet, they stood on the sands by the river, and she told her how when he unwound her sari and saw, by the light of the moon, the slivers of stretched skin that scarred her belly, saw the silver streaks on her honey skin, he asked no questions, just kissed each one tenderly. When she made as if to talk, he put a finger to her lips and shushed her. All their whole married life together he never asked, and she told no one until she told my mother, when she held her first-born, my sister, in her arms. She told her then about her twin brothers who lived on the other side of the seas."

Nani lets the story rest awhile and I place my head next to hers on the pillow. We lie there quietly facing the window, watching the beam of light cast on the polished floor by the sun.

Nani raises her hands into the light and it shines through them. They are translucent, spectral, as they wave and dance about. "They sailed for days, for weeks, for months," Nani says, her hands shaping waves in the light above us. They slice through the air as the prow of the ship cuts deep into the heavy waters. They belly out when the sails pick up a fair wind to speed them on, and flatten as the wind dies and the ship lies becalmed on the still seas. When a storm breaks, her hands tumble about. They rock and roll, tip to one side, then the other, clapping together loudly when it thunders, and breaking apart when lightning electrifies the sky. There is a sickness and many die and Nani's hands close together to pray for the dead who are slipped over the side into the dark waters. Her voice follows the whole story, raging when it storms, softening when the gentle winds blow, and becoming heavy with sorrow with prayers for the dead.

All this they survived, her grandparents, my great-great grandparents. Nani reaches high into the beam of light and says, "And so they crossed the big water, the kala pani, and brought us here to this new earth. They brought us all, and Lena first, their daughter named for the ship that bore her like a seed on the wind across the oceans. Janki and Gaitree came here to this earth, each with their own gods.

"Such a hard life they had. It was no sweet, sugared life. They woke before the sun, he, like a warrior, bearing on his shoulder a cutlass sharp enough to slice iron. With this he cut the tall arrows of cane. She was a weeder, helping to clear the fields. It was a poor life. They came to Plantation Versailles, just up the road, and lived in the old slave quarters, clearing land, planting cane, burning cane, cutting cane, loading cane. Ma said they made much of what their new life gave them and thanked their gods for their child, a pretty girl, their jewel. Gaitree had another child, a boy, who died when he was just days old of a big fever, and another son was born to her early when she was still working in the fields. She was there, crouching low with her cutlass, when the pains came, and when the baby came, he came into the world dead. None of the sons born in this land quickened to life, and so Lena was everything to them. When she was fifteen they married her to a nice boy from good parents. He was called Ahmad Bacchus. Janki and his father were friends and the match was made. They too worked on the plantation – my parents. Her parents had done their duty, saw their precious daughter married. And so they lived, and so they died, and the old world went with them."

Nani closes her eyes and falls silent. I let her rest, but after a few minutes, I ask, "What were their names?"

"Ma never said. We never asked. She told us about our uncles in Bihar on the night before our weddings. Khadijah and I, we were both yellow from the turmeric dye rubbed on our skin to make it clear and bright. We were getting ready for bed when she told us the story of her mother and her journey across the seas. I remember saying how brave she was and Khadijah said, 'What a sacrifice.' She cried for the twin boys lost to us, and Ma held us close that night, the night before I became Nazeer's wife."

I hold my breath expecting my grandmother to fall into the telling of the sorrows that overtook her, but I hear her laughing instead. She appears younger. Her eyes are bright and her hands pick themselves off the bed and swoop through the air making giant arcs and circles. "We were so happy, so happy. My gentle father with his sweet face – we got anything we wanted from him. He would do anything to make us smile. And Ma. She made every copper penny stretch so far that we always had the prettiest dresses in the world, Khadijah and I. We went to school for a couple of years and Teacher Mary taught us to sing the alphabet and count numbers on our fingers and toes, and one day Khadijah swallowed a tamarind seed and her friend, Janey, told her that a tamarind tree will grow from her belly. She cried so much and all Janey did was laugh and promised to pick all the tamarinds from her mouth. But I, too, used to look closely at Khadijah every morning to see whether the tree was growing from her belly, to see if shiny leaves were peeping from her mouth."

Nani stops and giggles into her hands like a little girl. "But we forgot about that after a while. We must have started running after something else, wondering about something else. I remember seeing a chrysalis hanging from the bottom of a leaf one day and Pa telling me that the world was making a brand new butterfly. I didn't believe him but I watched the leaf every day and, one morning, the chrysalis was gone and I ran to my father, crying. But he just looked out of the window and pointed to a pretty, orange butterfly zigzagging between the trees and bushes. 'There it is. See!' and that was my first miracle. I jumped up and down, I was so excited. From then on I believed that the world was just packed full of wonders – I just had to keep my eyes open to see them."

The story stops for a few seconds to take a different path, for when she picks up the thread again, Nani's voice has grown serious and she is remembering a conversation she overheard between her parents: her father was saying that he did not like Baby spending so much time with Pandit Seecharran, that the man was filling her head with all sorts of ideas about the plantation masters and slavery and indentureship and so on.

"My father said it could lead to no good because these were big men's affairs, not the kind of things the pandit should be putting into a little girl's head. But Ma just waved this away and said that it was all fairy stories to me anyway, and that the pandit was teaching me to read big books. 'There's no harm in that, Ahmad,' she told him. But Pa was still worried and said that all that reading could fill me up with all kinds of ideas, and when my mother said, 'They might be good ones', my father shrugged and walked away. I stood there outside the kitchen door and wondered whether the questions I asked the pandit were bad things. I couldn't see how. I talked to him every day. He lived next door. He had shelves full of books and he would let me pull down whichever one I wanted and we would read it together. I followed his words until I could read them for myself. He had books and books of poems so I knew Byron and Shakespeare and Tagore even as a little girl. There were days when he would draw himself up and become Mark Anthony standing over Caesar's poor body, or stoop over from his waist and be the Jew asking for his pound of flesh. Or he would recite passages from his favourite book, the *Bhagavad Gita*, on quiet Sunday afternoons:

The Atman is the light:
The light is covered by darkness:
This darkness is delusion:
That is why we dream.

"So many pretty words. They sing in my ears even now. He was an old man. He had a round belly that shook when he laughed. He died when I was still small and I don't know what they did with all his books. I think Pa was relieved. He must have felt that I would now become content like Khadijah who helped Ma with the housework and the kitchen garden and learned to sew and cook. I did learn some – to sew and cook and clean – but I found all kinds of things to read too. I read the newspapers every day. I read the words and filled in the blank spaces with all that Pandit Seecharran had told me. I knew the truth of things. Once you see that, how can you turn your back on it?"

Nani closes her eyes and continues her story in a voice that drifts away like a dream. "Everything was good for a while. We got this bit of land from the estate – Nazeer's sweet-talk with the manager made it happen – and our parents gave us some money to make a start. So we built a little house and planted a garden and Nazeer hustled his hand at everything and did well, and your mother was born, our baby, Shabhan. The world was smiling on us. Then there was the strike. A big strike. I forget now what it was about – better pay, something. But they shot people with long guns. Shot people in the back. Some died. And I could not stand by and be silent. I spoke and these two hands rose high up in the air and closed like this."

Nani's fists shake and tremble above her before she uncurls her fingers and brings her arms down to lie quietly at her side. "It's true, you know, that the end of everything lies in the beginnings we make. I did not see how my Nazeer became a quiet man with hands turning up empty at everything he tried. And I did not see how he started to walk around on slow footsteps, dragging his shadow behind him. And poor Shabhan. Poor, poor child with only the walls to weep with her."

Nani lets out a long, weary sigh and I fear she has stopped breathing. But then her eyes spring open and she puts a hand to her mouth to cut off a scream. She grips me with her other hand and holds on for dear life. "Do you see? Do you see?" she asks, her eyes searching the room wildly.

"See what, Nani?"

"See her. See him."

"Who, Nani, who?"

"Look, look, don't you see?"

I follow her pointing finger and the walls of the bedroom give way and open up to the kitchen where a woman stands dark as a shadow in the doorway. She is small. She wears a Madras kerchief on her head, and a nose ring, and small, hooped earrings all along the edges of her ears. My grandmother, Baby, is there and invites her in, and the woman seats herself on a small bench and clasps her hands in her lap. Baby stands before her, her hands in her apron pockets, and the woman speaks.

"My husband is dead, God rest his soul. He dropped dead on the punt-trench dam one day. He was walking on the dam, going to the rum shop and he dropped dead – braddam! – just like that. And he was only thirty-five years old, that's all the life he lived. And he worked since he was a lil boy cutting cane and loading cane, breaking up his back, and it's only the rum, he used to say, only the rum gave him a lil ease. I have four children to mind now, the big boy is only six and the baby is seven months, and the overseer tells me that I have nothing to get, that Ramnaresh – that is my husband – that Ram didn't die on the job so I have nothing to get."

The woman weeps and rocks herself. "How I will feed my children, eh? And me? My bubbies are dry, sister. There's no milk for the baby. I've been everywhere, asking everybody for help. But people just walk away from me, stewpsing their teeth, even laughing. To tell the truth, my husband was a hot-mouth man, always picking trouble with everybody, and when he drank his head full of rum, he used to come home and turn the house upside down with curses, and frighten the children. But what I must do now, Sister Baby? Is it true that after all the years he worked, his family can get nothing? That he can drop dead and it's nothing more than like a dog dying on the road-top?

"I've been thinking about you, Sister Baby, for some days now, and this morning my feet just picked themselves up and brought me here. I know that you and Pa Nazeer living quiet-quiet now, and it's years and years since anybody heard you talking, your voice coming out so big-big through the loudspeaker, but I didn't know where else to turn, Sister Baby. You're my only hope now. I was wondering if you could talk to the manjah for me. He's called Massah Jessop and I hear he's a reasonable man, so I was wondering, Sister Baby, if you could go and see the manjah and talk to him for me. I am not a beggar woman. I only want a lil something to get me on my feet and once the baby is bigger, I will work a full day and make a living and look after my children. It's just a lil something I'm asking for now, Sister Baby."

Baby puts her hand on the woman's shoulder. "Come back tomorrow."

"I knew you would help me out, Sister Baby. You're a good woman. God bless you. I'll be here tomorrow, bright and early, Sister Baby. I have a big-big pumpkin on the vine. I will bring it for you tomorrow, Sister."

The woman smiles and leaves through the backyard, and out of the gate that leads onto the dam and into the market square. Baby watches her until she disappears from view. When she turns around, Pa Nazeer is standing in the middle of the kitchen.

"So it starts again?" he says.

"What?" Baby asks. Her voice cuts his off, sharp and abrupt.

"The whole business. You know what I mean."

"No, I don't."

"So, what she coming back for tomorrow? What you will give her? A drink of water and send her home to her hungry children? I know you better than that."

"Good. Then you don't need to ask any more questions."

"Yes, I know what you'll do and I'm not going to stand by and watch. Not this time."

"So what you will do, eh? What you will do? Tell me." Baby's tone is taunting.

"I'll kill myself, I tell you. I'll hang myself first." Pa Nazeer's voice is hot with anger.

"Then why don't you? Here!" I see Baby reach over to the table. I see her lean forward, her own face tight and angry, and I see her pick up something lying there in loops and coils, but before I can get a clear view of her hands, the air is split with a scream pitched high to the heavens. Nani is screaming and holding out her hands, presenting the streaks of sunlight that lie golden on her palms to the empty air. "Here," she screams. "Here. Take it!"

184

I take her hands and hold her until her trembling stops. I shush her like a baby and wonder at my own calm. Now that I have heard the words that I have wondered about so long, they hold no surprise for me. It is as if I have known them all along, known that they were there under her tongue since I was a child when she watched me catch dreams that ran free above the treetops.

"Sssh, Nani, ssh," I say.

I release her, let her head rest again on her pillow and when she speaks again her voice is low and whispery, so I put my ear close to her lips. "Now that you are home, daughter, the rope will never again throw itself over…"

I sit up and pull myself away from her, shaking my head. I cut into her words, "No, no! No, Nani, not that! Never! I could never have done…"

She waves a hand to shush me, and makes as if to speak again, but sighs instead, then says, "Safe. We are all safe, safe, safe." Her words fall away, fade slowly, slowly into silence.

A play of light and shadow makes a loop over the beam that crosses the room. The light dances then races away and, in that moment, when the room darkens, Nani sighs again and is gone with the rushing light. I gather her up and hold her close, feeling the last of her warmth before I lay her back gently on to her pillow. Her eyes are closed and I place her hands, one on top of the other, on her breast.

When I call to my parents from the top of the stairs they look up at me, then Pa turns back to close up the shop and Ma goes and turns off the stove before they enter the room where we stand at the foot of her bed. It seems like just minutes before the room fills up. Shaireen and Reaz, and their children, and Mansur and Leela, and Great Aunt Shamroon, and the children of Great Aunt Khadijah, and all of their children – they all arrive. The news travels and the house fills up and the yard fills up with friends and neighbours and distant relatives.

By mid afternoon Nani is laid out, swaddled in white cotton, in a simple coffin, measured and planed and hammered together in a few hours from silverballi wood. The men form three lines and we, the women of the family, stand behind them, and, with the coffin laid out before him, the moulvi leads us in the recitation of the prayers for the dead. The men then bear the coffin away to lay it beside the grave of her husband, and when the house and yard are empty and the afternoon becomes quiet, my mother and sister and sister-in-law and great aunt and I, we take all the flowers, brought as parting tributes, and lay them out like a blanket over her grave. There are hibiscus, oleanders, roses, ixora, bougainvillea, ginger lilies, birds of paradise, anthuriums, poinciana, orchids, periwinkles, frangipani, zinnias, marigolds and sunflowers. We pour them from our laden arms onto the earth under which she lies, as my mother sings one of Nani's favourite prayers. "Allah-o-Akbar, Allah-o-Akbar," she begins and we pick up the refrain.

They leave and the song trails away in the afternoon air but I stay and kneel by the grave, patting the flowers into the fresh earth. A soft breeze blows and curls a wisp of cloud high against the sky, and I watch as the cloud unfurls and drifts away, disappearing into the heavens.

Jan Lowe Shinebourne
The Godmother and Other Stories
ISBN: 1 900715 87 2; price: £7.99

Covering more than four decades in the lives of Guyanese at home or in Britain and Canada, these stories has an intensive and rewarding inner focus on a character at a point of crisis. Harold is celebrating the victory of the political party he supports whilst confronting a sense of his own powerlessness; Jacob has been sent back to Guyana from Britain after suffering a mental breakdown; Chuni, a worker at the university, is confused by the climate of revolutionary sloganizing which masks the true situation: the rise of a new middle class, elevated by their loyalty to the ruling party. This class, as the maid, Vera, recognises, are simply the old masters with new Black faces.

The stories in the second half of the collection echo the experience of many thousands who fled from the political repression, corruption and social collapse of the 70s and 80s. The awareness of the characters is shot through with Guyanese images, voices and unanswered questions. It is through these that their new experiences of Britain and North America are filtered. One character lies in a hospital in London fighting for her life, but hears the voices of her childhood in Guyana – her mother, African Miss K, the East Indian pandit and the English Anglican priest. Once again, they 'war for the role of guide in her life'. In 'The Godmother' and 'Hopscotch', childhood friends reunite in London. Two have stayed in Guyana, while one has settled in London. The warmth of shared memories and cold feelings of betrayal, difference and loss vie for dominance in their interactions.

These stories crystallize the shifts in Guyana's uncomfortable fortunes in the post-colonial period, and while they are exact and unsparing in their truth-telling, there are always layers of complexity that work through their realistic surfaces: a sensitivity to psychological undertones, the evocative power of memory and a poetic sense of the Guyanese physical space.

Denise Harris
In Remembrance of Her
ISBN: 1 900715 99 6; price: £9.99

Why does the Judge, powerful, wealthy and Black, bring his world crashing down by murdering his son, Baby-Boy? And why was Baby-Boy wearing a dress of feathers, his face painted white? These are the mysteries the Judge's old friend, a private eye, sets out to uncover, though it is not until the very last chapter that the whole story emerges. Until then, the reader is engaged in a journey of twists and turns as complex and surprising as life itself.

A work of gothic splendour, *In Remembrance of Her* has all the complexity, poetry and moral depth of a dark, late, Shakespearean comedy – the wronging and death of a first wife, a lost daughter, and a disturbed and rebellious son – in a world out of joint and crying out for compassion and restorative justice.

Set in Guyana, where colour and class still count for much, it is the Judge's servant, Blanche Steadman, who, though confined to her one-room shack behind the Judge's splendid mansion, is witness to the pain locked deep in the household's secrets. She becomes the warmly sympathetic guide to the novel's unfolding mysteries, along with her friend, the formidable market woman, Irene Gittings, whose role in the novel is one of its surprises.

At the heart of the narrative is the ghostly presence of the Caul Girl who, through the survival of her diaries, becomes the prophetic conscience of both the present and the past.

Denise Harris's first novel, *The Web of Secrets*, was welcomed as "a brilliant cautionary tale… a most complex and aesthetically satisfying web" (Sharon Joseph, *Mango Season*), as a "startling and mesmeric novel" (Chris Searle, *The Morning Star*). More ambitious and daring in its scope, *In Remembrance of Her* is quite simply one of the most remarkably imaginative novels to burst from the Caribbean in recent years.

Mark McWatt
Suspended Sentences: Fictions of Atonement
ISBN 1 84523 001 9; price £8.99

Back in 1966, each of a group of Guyanese sixth formers is 'sentenced' to write a short story that reflects their newly inde- pendent country. Years later, Mark McWatt, one of the group, is handed the papers of his old school friend, Victor Nunes, who has disappeared, feared drowned, in the interior. The papers contain some of the stories written before the project collapsed. As a tribute to Victor, McWatt decides to collect the rest of his stories from his friends.

Whether written by their youthful or adult selves, the stories reveal not only their tellers and the Guyana most of them have left, but offer an affectionately satirical take on Guyanese fiction making. Amongst the stories, we read about the sexual awakening of a respectable spinster by a naked bakoo in a jar; an expedition into the Guyanese interior that turns into a painful homoerotic encounter; a schoolboy who is projected into an alarming science fiction future; and about an academic (in a brilliantly tragicomic story) who confesses the betrayal of his friend. There is Victor Nunes' visionary story that blurs the frontiers between past and present and, in the concluding story, Mark McWatt reveals how the group came to be handed down their suspended sentences.

In this tour-de-force of invention, by ranging across Guyanese ethnicities, gender and time in the purported authorship of these stories, Mark McWatt creates a richly dialogic work of fiction.

Mark McWatt was born in Guyana in 1947. He has published widely on aspects of Caribbean literature and is joint editor of the *Oxford Book of Caribbean Verse* (2004). He has also published two collections of poetry: *Interiors* (1989) and *The Language of Eldorado* (1994).

OTHER GUYANESE FICTION

Harischandra Khemraj
Cosmic Dance
ISBN: 0-948833-45-9, Price: £7.99
Khemraj writes acutely about race and gender, intention and chance in an authoritarian, post-colonial Caribbean state where a young doctor is brought the stories of a young girl's rape by a state official, and of a seemingly altruistic gift of blood.

Cyril Dabydeen
Dark Swirl
ISBN: 0-948833-20-3, Price: £5.99
When a European naturalist arrives in a remote rural village, folk belief confronts rationalistic science in this poetic fable which explores the Guyanese legend of the monstrous Massacouraman.

Denise Harris
Web of Secrets
ISBN: 0-948833-87-4, Price: £6.95
Set in Guyana during the 1960s racial disturbances, this novel, told by an overhearing child, embroiders a dazzling fabric of whispered family conversations, fantasy and folklore to make connections between divisions in the family and the nation.

Peter Lauchmonen Kempadoo
Guyana Boy
ISBN: 1-900715-56-2, Price: £7.99
A classic novel, first published in 1960, of a boy growing up in a Madrassi Indian community on a sugar estate in Guyana in the 1940s, whose access to education leads him inexorably away from the world of his parents.

Moses Nagamootoo
Hendree's Cure
ISBN: 1-900715-45-7, Price: £7.99
Blending fiction and documentary, Nagamootoo reanimates the world of the Madrassi fishermen, market-traders, rice farmers, Kali worshippers, cricketers, turfites and see-far practitioners who inhabited the Corentyne in Guyana in 1950s and 60s.

Rooplall Motilal Monar
Janjhat
ISBN: 0-948833-30-0, Price: £6.99
A frank and moving portrayal of the beginnings of a marriage of a young sugar worker and his bride under the eagle eye of his domineering mother in a novel which reveals the Indo-Guyanese community in the grip of cultural crisis.

Sasenarine Persaud
The Ghost of Bellow's Man
ISBN: 0-948833-31-9, Price: £6.99
When Raj, reluctant schoolteacher with a weakness for schoolgirls, Hindu activist and would-be novelist, protests against a breach of tradition at his temple, he uncovers a trail of corruption which leads to the heart of the post-colonial Guyanese state.

Jan Lowe Shinebourne
The Last English Plantation
ISBN: 1-900715-33-3, Price: £6.99
As colonial rule comes to an end, the struggle for a new order is witnessed by an eleven year old girl of a mixed Indian-Chinese background involved in her own battles with her mother over the nature of her education and her cultural identity.

Narmala Shewcharan
Tomorrow is Another Day
ISBN: 0-948833-47-5, Price: £7.99
In portraying the social fragmentation in Guyana during the later Burnham years, this novel shows the temptations to individual solutions whilst asserting the moral basis of community through the impact each individual choice has on the lives of others.

All Peepal Tree titles are available from our website:
www.peepaltreepress.com

Explore our list of over 160 titles, read sample poems and reviews, discover new authors, established names and access a wealth of information about books, authors and Caribbean writing. Secure credit card ordering, fast delivery throughout the world at cost or less.

You can contact us at:
Peepal Tree Press, 17 King's Avenue, Leeds LS6 1QS, United Kingdom
Tel: +44 (0) 113 2451703 E-mail: hannah@peepaltreepress.com